Parktilden Village

Born in Indiana, George P. Elliott received his M.A. from the University of California at Berkeley. After a variety of jobs—as ship-fitter, surveyor's assistant, taxi-driver, real estate broker, and reporter for a labor newspaper—he settled down to the work he enjoys most, teaching English. He has taught at St. Mary's College (California), Cornell University, and is now at Barnard College. Mr. Elliott has had many poems and short stories published in literary magazines, including several stories in Martha Foley's *Best American Short Stories* and the *O. Henry Prize Award Stories*. He also edited the anthology *Fifteen Modern American Poets*. On a fellowship from the Fund for the Advancement of Education in 1953-54, he studied modern staging of poetic drama and wrote the first draft of *Parktilden Village*. Under a Hudson Review fellowship in fiction he has begun work on another novel, to be published by the Beacon Press.

Parktilden Village

GEORGE P. ELLIOTT

Beacon Press   Beacon Hill   Boston

To My Parents

One

Hazen, having studied sociology for a long time, was inclined to think of places people lived as "housing," to look with a real estate agent's eye for square feet of floor space, exposure to sun, convenience of the kitchen—in a word, what do you get for your money? Partly this attitude came from his having lived, during the thirteen years since he had left his parents' home, in boarding houses, in Army barracks, and in a New York apartment with three fellow-students. In any event, if a man wasn't underprivileged, had so many cubic feet of air to himself and a toilet to flush, Hazen was not likely to look for any connection between the state of his soul and the place in which he lived. But the first morning Hazen woke up in his brand-new apartment in Parktilden Village, he lay in bed looking about him with untoward pleasure; everything he saw, from the handles on the closet doors to the sound-absorbent ceiling, was of that smooth simplicity proper in things which, like flattering compliments, serve efficiently the uses of comfort; even, obliquely, from where he lay, the prospect of eucalyptus and pine on a distant slope was a sort of essence of "view." Indeed, as he stretched out on the foam-rubber mattress, with his left foot poked out from under the covers into the sunlight and his hands clasped behind his head, he fell to making amiable resolutions: to get up early every morning, to cut down on his smoking, to keep his quarters always neat and clean, to eat a balanced diet. They were far from the harried and squeezed-out vows of doubt; they all seemed easy of accomplishment to him, only a matter of habits whose strength would yield before conscious determination; and besides, as his confidence knew, none of them were very important.
It was an expansive sort of start to the day, but his own delight

in generalizing contracted him presently. He had begun to compose, in mild, alliterative fantasy, an essay called "Problems of Place Adjustment," when he offended himself with the jargon he used. That was a resolve he had taken with his doctor's degree, to abjure jargon; yet now, even in his daydream, "thing-orientation," "in terms of," "primarily in view of the fact that," "enlightened self-interest as goal," kept rolling out like marbles in front of a prancing horse to send him sprawling. He was sobered, and he cursed these bad, extraneous habits he had acquired from reading too many social scientists. Yet, from uneasiness, he sat up in bed, for he was not quite sure that jargon was a habit like coffee merely to be dropped as you wish. He had known a poet at Columbia University who had taunted him: "Anything worth saying has to be said well," and the crueler converse, "Nothing said badly is worth saying at all." He jumped out of bed rejecting the whole trouble.

On the back of the door was a full-length, very clear mirror. He adjusted his pajamas and looked himself up and down perplexed. There was absolutely nothing objectionable about his appearance: he was well built, lean, firm for an intellectual, over six feet tall, and handsome enough in a bland way. It was the blandness that was perplexing, an open-eyed, unfurrowed, masculine, American blandness of a sort which some Europeans take for innocence, experience of evil with the sin taken out. Now as he scrutinized his affable, healthy face, it occurred to him that no man at the age of thirty-one had the right to look as untouched as he. Usually when he looked at himself seriously in the mirror, embarrassment made him laugh and turn away; today he felt too grave to turn. He felt in need of change; he felt worthy of change.

"I must take women more seriously." His mother had been pressing him to produce grandchildren for her; on his way out from Columbia the week before, she had dropped oblique, Nebraska hints about gay ladies in New York. His mother had been, as often, crudely right; in any event, Berkeley, where he came as a stranger, was a good place now to look around for a wife. It was time. "I must prepare all my lectures carefully. I must do my research conscientiously. I must never cover up with mumbo-jumbo when I don't know what I'm talking about. In other words, I've got to quit making things easy on myself." That was the accusation he could never deny, that he made things easy on himself; he was enough the great-grandchild of covered-wagon rigor to be ashamed of settling for a minor success plucked because it's easy. The sort of success he was after never came easy; by most, perhaps by him, it was not to be had at all. He suddenly grinned at his clenched-fist earnestness, and opened the door to the bathroom. But even while he was running the hot water to shave, as a last resolve he reminded himself of his chronic task, to be obliged to which was his secret shame (in this he was his own accuser): "I must always give credit where credit is due."

He thought he heard music. He turned off the water and listened. Chimes in a mellow chord announced someone at the door. He hoped it was a man delivering his books, and went to the door in his pajamas. But there, smiling and saying "Peter!" in a happy voice, ready to embrace him friendlily if he wished and only to shake hands if he'd rather, eager, advancing, was the first woman he had fallen in love with, whom he had not seen for twelve years. In his confusion of strong feelings he said, "Mrs. Devereux!" as though he were still a sophomore baby-sitting for the young professor's wife, and yet he embraced her warmly and kissed her quite as though he, whom honor and despair had then left mute, had now an old lover's rights of salutation. She held him in surprise at arm's length, surveying him, a woman proud of a man. "You *have* changed," she said. "I want to hear all about you. Now get dressed and come right on over, there, and I'll make you some waffles and we'll talk."

The Devereux' apartment had two bedrooms instead of one, their walls and rugs were pinkish grey rather than bluish grey, their furniture was blond ash modern instead of steel tube modern, and instead of a copper-wire spiraling mobile over the dining table they had on the wall a black wrought-iron outline of a fish with an iridescent eye. Otherwise the apartments were identical—and identical with the 1120 other apartments in Parktilden Towers, except for the furnishings, in which there were these two or three other choices, and the colors, of which there were eight hues of grey.

As he ate the waffle Eleanor had made, she practically yet gaily doubled the shopping list he had made the night before and offered

3

to go with him; but he wouldn't hear of it, so she insisted he come to dinner the very next evening and see Jefferson again ("He has turned grey") and Jacqueline ("She is still a tomboy though she is a freshman in college now") and Mama.

"Mama?" he said.

"You never met Mama?" Eleanor cried. "I forgot. She wasn't with us in Nebraska. Come along."

She took him by the arm and marched him down the beige corridor to the apartment next to his, where Mama lived in an off-white, modern-antique, one-bedroom apartment. Mama was hard of hearing and hadn't many teeth, and she wore old slippers because her feet were bad. It was hard for her to understand where Hazen fitted in, but finally she seemed to decide that he was a friend of Jacqueline's. Mama smiled. "Ah," she said in her thin old voice, "any friend of Jackie's is a friend of mine." Her total ingenuousness gave the careless, baggy words a strange look: she meant what they said. "I hope you come to see us often, Mr. Hazen. It's so nice."

"But Mama," said Eleanor, "he lives right next door to you."

"Next door?" she exclaimed in a sort of tiny alarm. "There?"

"No no, Mama. The Erskines live there, remember? Between you and us."

"He does?" She threw her hands back with a new amazement. "Forgive me, I keep forgetting things."

"But Mama, you couldn't forget, he just moved in."

"I know it, Ellie," the old woman said fretfully. Then she beamed at Hazen. "Mr. Hazen, you are a blessing to us. You will be good for Jackie. She's a little bit wild now, the way girls get nowadays, nothing serious, no no nothing bad at all. She stays here with me, you know. You're a blessing, a blessing."

They left her sitting by the window, her dress pulled up to her knees, her face tilted up, eyes closed. "The sunshine is like an ointment," she said. "It's like an ointment from God all over me."

He came back from errands humming, made his bed and set his kitchen in order. At 3:30 he was standing at the window gazing, slantwise as he had to, out at the view, when he noticed that to the left he could see into the Devereux' living room. Eleanor was washing the window; she waved and beckoned him over.

4

"Peter," she said at the door.

"Would you mind," he said grinning, "calling me Hazen?"

"By your last name? But I always called you Peter."

"Everyone calls me Hazen now. If you don't mind."

"As you like.—Look."

She approached with a changed air a letter spread out on the glass-top dining table. It was dated July 5 and addressed to Professor Jefferson L. Devereux; it invited him to deliver a series of six lectures on a subject of his own choosing at Cambridge University, and to receive from that University an honorary LL.D.

"It came just at noon," she said.

"Has he seen it?" Hazen asked.

"I read it to him over the phone."

"Wasn't he excited?"

"He was already given one by Columbia."

"Well, even so." Hazen was strangely intense, and stared at her demandingly.

"Jefferson is not very excitable," she said. "He told me not to tell everybody about this, but I had to tell someone so I thought I would tell just you. Isn't it wonderful?"

He could see how serious, how deeply, she felt. "But how could he help being proud?"

"Well," she said, "he is not at all vain. He doesn't like to be congratulated."

"I won't mention it to anyone." Suddenly he felt filled with a sort of elation. He took her hands and looked at her again like a former lover. "I am glad for you, Eleanor. I am so glad I don't know what to say. You don't know how lucky I feel to know you, your whole family."

Tears came to her eyes. He half reached out to take her in his arms as though she needed consoling; the expression on her face before she hid it in her hands moved him towards her. But lord, he thought, these were no more than the tears of too much happiness. How should a wife feel sadness for the just recognition granted her husband, whose work she admired, who was one of the best? Yet, his powerful impulse had been to console her; just that, to soften her sadness as he might. Shaking his head, he turned and left.

"So now I have neighbors," he sang in the shower before dinner. "Hello," he sang at the top of his voice, "hello, hello, hello." Nothing made him feel better than a proof of luck. "I'll lend you my bread and borrow your butter." Surely the Devereux were his good luck. "I'm fine, how are you? Do you think the weather will change tomorrow? Hello, hello, hello."

Two

As Eleanor lay hour after hour beside Jefferson asleep, she tried to understand why she was staying awake. Her body was well, the bed was a perfection of comfort, the apartment was so still she could not even hear the refrigerator whir off and on, no radios were blaring nearby; all she knew of the city, which stretched back beyond the crest of a ridge, was a tinge of light on the cloud she could see; once in a while she heard airplanes, once a screech of tires and wafting of laughter, occasionally, alien and intrusive like a ghost from its altogether other realm, the hoot of an owl. But she could not pretend that these bland evidences of the world were keeping her awake. She needed a jackhammer to curse as a rejected lover needs a chair to kick. She had not even the consolation of Jefferson's snores. She let him sleep, not just because he was tired but rather because they had never enjoyed that intimacy of pillow-talk which her friends sometimes mentioned, that talking for the caress of the sound of a voice, that snuggling in bed with no end in view; she thought her friends silly, a little self-indulgent for this, but tonight she envied them.

Her thoughts revolved around Jacqueline. Hazen's presence had somehow made her feel the threats to Jacqueline more acutely than before. Not, of course, that Hazen was any threat. She re-

6

membered with pleasant indulgence how moony he had been over her when he'd used to baby-sit for them. He had been touching to watch; his infatuation had given her a sort of sentimental confidence in her attractions, at a time when Jefferson's indifference was making her doubt herself. Well, if she had attracted Hazen then without having done a thing to stimulate his interest, surely she would have the power now, if she put her mind to it, to divert him from Jacqueline should he show any signs of becoming interested in her. She was glad she had never been unfaithful to Jefferson, but sometimes, as now, she was a little regretful that there were few years left in which she was at all likely to be invited again to be unfaithful. She flopped over in bed, annoyed at her own silliness. It was Jacqueline that mattered. She did not know what Hazen had to do with it, but one way or another his presence made her conscious of a serious threat connected with Jacqueline. Jackie was such a dear child, such a tomboy yet on the verge of womanhood; she must learn to settle on a steady course; she was a little wild; she must accept her responsibilities. Eleanor sighed to think of the easier days when Jacqueline's gravest troubles had been chicken pox or, once, a broken leg. Those had been, no doubt of it, happier days for them all. Not that she loved Jackie any the less now; not a bit of it; it was just that things had become so much harder.

She reached a moment when she had circumscribed the cause of her trouble, and she shook Jefferson by the shoulder.

"Jefferson, I want to talk to you."

"What?"

"It's important."

Like an oiled bather, with one shake he emerged dry from sleep. "Have you been lying awake here, my dear?"

"I've been thinking about Jacqueline."

"Is there something I don't know about?"

She did not know exactly how to answer his question. She tried always to emulate him in conversation, that is, speak to mean; but now if she said, "Yes, something you don't understand," he would, quite reasonably, want to know what and want to know it in meaning words. Therefore she said no.

"No, you know about it, but I think you don't attribute

7

enough importance to it. I mean the Ford." She did not mean the Ford; she didn't give a snap of her fingers for the Ford; she meant all the circumstances and danger of Jacqueline's owning it.

But Ford signifies a thing. "To be sure," he answered. "The brake cylinder and feed lines have to be checked, and I won't let her drive it without new linings. Why don't you leave all that sort of thing to me?"

"I do, Jefferson, I know you will take care of it." With the habit of twenty years she assured him that she trusted him. "You know I don't understand things like that."

"Then what is on your mind, my dear?" He spoke reasonably, without annoyance, his head turned so that he could be watching the daybreak.

"It's dangerous." That's all there was to it; she had provided herself with a barrage of articulate reasons when she had awakened him, but that's what they came to. "Darling, it's so dangerous." Her reasoning would sound weaker, coming afterwards; she couldn't help it. "So dangerous."

In the same reasonable voice he answered, "Of course."

"How can you just lie there and agree with me? We must do something."

"She is old enough to marry without our consent. She is old enough to earn her own living. We can't stop her from risking her neck if she wants to."

"You have thought about this already?"

"Of course."

"Well, why didn't you tell me before, so we could be talking it over?" Her voice was scaling the slopes of indignation.

"Because I thought it would upset you. It did."

On the peak she shouted, "But she's my daughter as much as yours!"

"Of course."

She grabbed his beard and pulled his head around. "You've got to let me in on things." But she knew she was losing, by the look of patience in his eyes, the weary patience of a man whose wife is obliging him for the thousandth time to defend obvious truth. She knew his arguing would be immaculate as an onion layer upon layer perfect and that her reward for peeling it would be tears; yet she started to go on.

"Wait," he said sharply. "Since you seem determined to quarrel so early in the day, at least decide on what we are going to quarrel about, the Ford or the way you are neglected."

She was confused; his clarity only confused her the more; his controlling clarity was a given, one of the things beyond challenge with them just as the impossibility of their separating was another; she felt in the wrong. But that feeling only intensified her anger, for in a furious sort of way she knew she had the right to quarrel on two fronts at once whatever clear logic might say about it, and she knew that she had the right to be alarmed about Jacqueline even though she could not act on her alarm. "Jefferson," she pleaded, "all I care about is Jackie's welfare." This was another given, their daughter, one about which neither of them so much as thought of challenging the other.

Therefore she listened without rejoinder to him drive his arguments in like taps into a maple tree; she felt them draining her dry. It was true that Jacqueline was old enough to take charge of herself if she had to; true that she had a driver's license and drove well; true that she had been given the car outright, and by Eleanor's own nephew. But it was just as true that Floyd *should* not have given it to her, that life presented a thousand dangers which her parents *should* help her past. It was her should's that weakened Eleanor's case, for against his statements of fact her statements of duty always wasted themselves. She did not give voice to her should's. He was not being summary in his argument but was exploring every reason why they must not interfere. He pointed to Floyd for example: Floyd had come to the university a track star from a country high school, lonely and they had befriended him; he had two passions, throwing javelins and driving his car expertly; Jacqueline and he had been no more than horsey good friends and necking companions, and when he had left a week ago for his two years' conscription, he had simply given her the car. The friendship had been simple and strong, unchallenged, and this gift was the token of it, too late to be challenged. If they opposed her now, they would succeed only in forcing her away from them-

9

selves and possibly towards Floyd. She was of an age when a girl is tempted to run off and marry a soldier she could not possibly live with successfully, just to be rid of her parents, to spite them. All true, all true, all desiccating true. She wept.

At the quaking of the bed he stopped talking. She felt his hand brush her shoulder, not tentatively, but lightly recognizing her unhappiness; still, he did not hold her firmly and comfort her. "Jacqueline is nearly grown up now," he said, "and we must not try to restrain her." But even when he said this he was declaring a fact, and facts to him were like stones, lying around to be ignored or studied as you wished and some even to be shaped into gems to be admired, but none, certainly, to be reproached or thanked or regretted. She listened dully as he got up and dressed. He made a breakfast, but when he offered her a cup of coffee she did not respond and left it on the bed table to cool off. She wondered, vaguely, what he was going to do so early in the morning, but then she heard him crank the window closed in the workroom and heard the sound of the shuttle; before long she could detect the faint susurration of his whistling between his teeth as he worked, evidence of the fact (as he had often told her) that he was feeling nothing and thinking nothing but only, like a schizophrene therapeutically, weaving well. Whenever he thought that he was as probably right as a man is likely to get, even on a matter as near to him as Jacqueline's welfare, he refused to worry, and he was, she knew, now again probably right. All the same, she wept, for sometimes it's a pity to be right.

As he did every weekday morning at 7:30, he took out his oboe, opened the window, and played a fragment of tune to the morning. She had felt it to be a sign of his grace, that by doing exactly what he felt like doing, even in the trivial matter of awakening his daughter, he should manage to please everyone. She never took him for granted, he could always surprise her, as she felt she could not surprise him. It was a sparkling morning; children were chirping in the play-yard below. Jacqueline was already awake, for he had scarcely begun playing "Greensleeves" before she answered with her clarinet; between them they played a twining duet on the theme that drew neighbors to their living room windows to cock their heads listening for a moment. But at a window in the top floor opposite, Eleanor could make out behind the reflection of the sky a heavy man in his undershirt scowling down. She hated him. She had seen him once in the lobby, his forefinger wrapping a cigar, guffawing with a frump; she had not liked him then and she hated him now. It was an antic sort of hatred, separated thus as they were by 150 feet and two thicknesses of glass, but she grimaced and shook her fist at him, and though he could hardly have seen her behind her Venetian blind, she felt much the better for her silliness.

Three

The finger which Hazen stretched out to press their button trembled. All his undergraduate timidity of Jefferson had been reawakened by the thought of the letter from Cambridge; he was not comfortable about what tone to take with Jacqueline, whom he had bathed and kissed good-night the last time he had seen her; with Eleanor he felt a special intimacy, but one so uncircumstanced he didn't know what to make of it more than a quality of voice and a broken impulse. In all he was afraid he would bumble and grin awkwardly and make them regret he had ever appeared.

Eleanor, smoothing out her apron, opened the door. "Peter!" she said cheerily. "You must just rap twice, like this, and come on in. When we don't want visitors we lock the door."

He knew where he was with her at least. "Here," he said holding out a bottle of red wine, "I hope it goes with whatever you're cooking."

"Perfectly," she said and pulled him into the kitchen, which was next the hall door. "See!" In the oven was a leg of lamb. "And here." On the refrigerator cooling was a lemon meringue pie. "We want you to like being here with us." Before he could say yes, he liked it, she popped an olive into his mouth. "I think it's nice having you here." Then, in a voice suddenly flat-footed, she called out, "Jefferson." It was slow, and closer to a question than to a mere call. Hazen stepped out into the hallway. "Jefferson," she said again and came out of the kitchen smoothing her apron. "He's probably in weaving."

"Weaving?"

She nodded as she went.

Hazen was not delighted to learn that the great man had an unusual hobby, but was confused and made more uneasy yet. It seemed to him unfitting that a virile and busy man should pass his idle time at an archaic and womanly pursuit, that a mathematician the quality of whose work had twice been rewarded with the highest honors learning can bestow should find his play in a sort of parody of usefulness. Then the phrase "aristocrat of the mind" occurred to Hazen and arrested him in the middle of the room. With that phrase, the idea of aristocrat was taken out of a museum for him and given life without being absurd: here was no milord the Duke of Burgundy in a ruff, no Rumanian count drooling over Texas oil heiresses; here was a university professor living on the tenth floor of a brand-new apartment house, Parktilden Tower Number 6, whose wife did the housework and whose colleagues called him Jeff, but who was yet noble. He was indifferent about whether his work was useful—Hazen, years before, had heard him say so but had thought he was joking—and he didn't even care about fame: as for his work, intellect could do nothing higher nor finer than study and chart the ways of probability, and that telephone companies or makers of atom bombs should find these charts convenient was good for them; as for honor, he wanted only the deference of his peers, and had it; as for all the rest, he amused himself, courteously. Hazen was so taken with painting this picture that he quite forgot to be uneasy.

Jefferson entered, not stately and slow, not saying hello down from an eminence; he came in like an actor who wants to give the impression he has been hurrying to get here for the last block, and said "Hello, Peter" like a cousin-in-law at Christmas. The only thing aristocratic about him was his beard: his chin bore the scar of an old burn and he had grown, since Hazen had last seen him, a Vandyke to cover it. Hazen thought that the beard, which was motley, made his face seem smaller. Suddenly this stringy little noble mathematician who never put on the dog was very dear to him.

"I'd love a highball," he said, instead of "Yes thanks." "Lots of soda and two cubes of ice."

"Good," said Jefferson, pleased at his warmth. "It's nice having you near us, Peter."

"Oh," cried Eleanor coming in, "he wants to be called Hazen, dear. I'm sorry, I keep forgetting." Jefferson shrugged, amused, and went to mix drinks. "Hazen," she tried it out; he blushed. "It makes you feel more grown-up, doesn't it?" She spoke matter-of-factly. "Well, a college instructor has a right to feel grown-up. I remember when I lost my wedding ring. It was as though I had lost my certificate of adulthood. Jefferson had to get me another the next day. I haven't taken it off since, fifteen years."

"Your fame," said Jefferson returning, "has come before you."

"You mean Stoodley?"

"Of course. It is not often that a man makes a good living out of his Ph.D. thesis."

The title of Hazen's thesis had been "Superman and Law Since 1911: The Changing Conception of Social Responsibility as Reflected in 416 Representative Comics." He had never been particularly fond of comics, but they provided exactly the sort of subject his sponsoring professor liked, so he had studied them. All that had relieved for him the special aridity of analyzing pleasure, other people's pleasure at that, was proving he knew what makes comics popular by doodling one of his own, Stoodley. Stoodley had sold immediately and had created a minor notoriety in Academia by demonstrating the soundness of Hazen's thesis and grossing him $10,000 a year at once. He'd had his picture in magazines for it; he was the object of foolish scorn and of yet more foolish praise. But he felt embarrassed at so low, so vulgar, a triumph, and for Jefferson to congratulate him on his fame seemed to him at the moment almost like a dig.

"Well, I'm dropping Stoodley."

"You are?" said Eleanor. "I got to like him."

He heard the sound of a door opening.

"There's just enough backlog to keep Stoodley going till September, and that's all. I can't say I'm sorry."

"What?" It was a girl's voice behind him. "How do you know?"

"Jacqueline," said Eleanor, going to her. "You're all dirty."

"I was just under the Ford, Mom. I'll wash up. But how does he know about Stoodley? I like Stoodley."

"You are being rude," said Eleanor. "Go prepare yourself for dinner."

"Well," came a piercing undertone, "who is he?"

"Peter Hazen."

There followed an absolute silence. Hazen had not thought it polite to watch them during this little altercation, but at the silence he glanced behind him. Eleanor was closing the hall door, and not even the shuffle of Jacqueline's footsteps came from the hallway. It was as though the sound of his name had made her, unprotesting, vanish.

And Jefferson, as though she had not even been there at all, continued, "I hope you're not ashamed of Stoodley. Speaking for myself, I would rather have made up one comic strip than written a thesis about a thousand. I rather enjoyed Stoodley, and no one ever enjoyed a Ph.D. thesis." How delicately had Jefferson, samurai at the delicate arts of imbalance, tossed him under the table.

"As though it were just a matter of enjoyment!" said Eleanor. She leaned over Hazen. "You've offended him, Jefferson."

He flipped Hazen a "sorry" as though it had been a nickel. "Tell us about your trip out."

But Hazen was in confusion.

"No," said Eleanor. "You show him your work while I fix dinner."

"Very well," said Jefferson.

"He's making an altar cloth," said Eleanor; she was a matter-of-fact woman.

"Altar cloth!" cried Hazen. He felt like a folk-lorist exploring the dark of the Congo and finding sleighs and reindeer in tales by the way.

"Yes, for the chapel at St. Anselm's College."

The door he followed Jefferson through presented on the other side a regulation Parktilden room, but with a harpsichord, a sewing machine, and a fair-sized loom in it; the linen was worthy of admiration, and the operations of weaving had a certain interest for him. This was only a hobby, a sensible hobby for a man who lives in an apartment; no doubt the altar cloth could be explained. He could hear the electric egg-beater going. Mama came in and clucked happily over every pot. Jefferson opened the wine. Eleanor leaned out the hall door and called to Jacqueline to hurry. Hazen began warily to feel normal again, Congo normal. He asked Jefferson for another highball.

Then Jacqueline came, in sweater and skirt and bobbysox, her feminine voice harsher than it needed to be, flatter. She presented herself to Hazen and said, "What do you teach?" and went back out to the kitchen. Her shoulders were angular for a girl's, and she swung her shoulders and hips when she walked as though she were imitating a cowboy with his thumbs in his pockets. Her hair was straw-colored, but her brows and lashes were so dark around her green eyes that her gaze seemed always intense and sharp. All such change Hazen was prepared for; what astonished him was her breasts. They were as heavy as though she had been suckling twins, and when she walked they swung not provocatively but irrelevantly, irrelevant demonstrations of sex that she carried as though they had been added onto her without her consent. When she returned, after a whispered conversation with her mother in the kitchen, it was all Hazen could do to keep from staring at her breasts like an old lecher. "I'm being absurd," he thought; "I'm still trying to think of her as six years old." He could not help noticing that she kept seeking the left corner of her mouth with the tip of her tongue, automatically and easily like a child with a little cut, not at all self-consciously like a girl filled to the elbows with desire to attract male notice; but he could also not help noticing that Jacqueline's lips were full and beautifully curved, and that she had carefully rouged them a bright red.

She sprawled opposite him on a contour chair and spoke abruptly. "How did you ever think up Stoodley?"

"Well, I was studying comic strips."

"In courses? For credit?"

"Not exactly. I was studying them sociologically. You know, not artistically but for their social significance."

She looked at him steadily, as though she neither knew what he meant nor believed that he did. "Go on."

"Don't be rude," said Jefferson.

"Excuse me," she said promptly, but the apology was all a memorized trick of the voice.

"Well, I tried to find out what gives comics their appeal, as you might say. Then I thought I'd test my theory."

"You mean, if you just study what makes something successful, you can *deduce* how to make another success like it?"

"In a way."

"I don't believe it."

"Jacqueline!" said her father.

"Well, I don't," she said sullenly, not looking at her father but at the knot of Hazen's tie.

"Neither do I, but there are more polite ways to let him know it."

"OK, Mr. Hazen." (She used to call him Petie and trade him kisses for nursery rhymes.) "How did you deduce you should make Stoodley have a big nose like that?"

"Well," he said, "I didn't exactly. It's just the way I like to draw faces. Do you remember the little gnomes I used to draw to illustrate stories for you?"

Jacqueline answered, as though in reply to his question, "Stoodley's nose is the best thing about him, and that was just your own idea. See? What's the matter, don't you get paid enough to make it worth your while?"

So he began expounding his views on the serious nature of his researches, and the frivolity of $10,000 a year when you have all your debts paid and a good steady job, and the importance of the social sciences in the modern world. At a clatter in the kitchen she rose and left, remembering at the last minute to say in explanation over her shoulder that she ought to go help her mother. Jefferson, gazing at him ironically and gently stroking his beard with the backs of the fingers of his right hand, said the cabernet was excellent.

Hazen drank too much wine with dinner. But the food was

delicious and the atmosphere increasingly congenial and easy—if only because of the beneficence of Mama, whose worrying chirped like a cricket but whose happiness glowed like a hearth. "Ellie," she would say, "did you remember to get the coffee today? I'm nearly out. I don't know what I'd do, Mr. Hazen, without my pot of coffee in the mornings." "Jackie, love, just look under my chair for my handkerchief, that's a dear. I don't know where it's gone. Lordie, I can't keep anything about me." Then she would ask for just a small little third slice of lamb, clasp her hands before her in admiration of it, and smile at them all.

By the end of the meal he was immoderate in what he was saying, so that when Eleanor asked him what project he was working on, he asserted rather expansively, "I'm going to study hot rods," and did not bother to notice that Jefferson dropped his eyes, Eleanor half opened her mouth as though to speak, and Jacqueline put her chin on the heel of her hand and stared at him. "Hot rods and motorcycles. Of course there will be a lot of stuff to do about geographical concentrations and age distribution and mechanical equipment, but the main thing, really, is what this phenomenon is a symptom of. In other words . . ." But he noticed at last the extraordinary squint with which Eleanor was looking at him, and he realized that everyone had quit eating, quit chewing even, so he coasted to a stop.

Just for a second he was angry, and said rather explosively at Jefferson, "What are *you* working on?" He knew perfectly well he wouldn't be able to understand an honest answer to this question and that Jefferson scorned, or at least formerly had scorned, vulgarizations of abstruse theory.

But "*e*" Jefferson said in a cheerful, almost grateful, voice, "*e* and its ways. Do you know about *e*? I'm getting very fond of it again. I have an acquaintance at St. Anselm's, Brother Quintillian, who says *e* is like efficacious grace. You can't understand it, there are important things you can't explain without it, and you're apt to come across it in astonishing places strangely disguised."

Hazen knew just enough about what *e* stood for and its powers, and just enough about grace, to be able to smile not quite blankly. But he felt like a beer-loving burgher to whom the duke

17

is recommending for dessert wine Château Yquem of '29—amazed and somewhat flattered. "Myself," he said, "I have never gotten used to the square root of minus one." He could not remember the mathematical symbol for it.

"Really?" (You prefer Tokay perhaps?) "Functionally *i* has some astonishing qualities." (Premier cru of course.)

Everyone relaxed, and in half an hour Hazen went back to his apartment to finish putting his belongings in order.

Before beginning to work, he sat smoking a cigarette and thought about the evening at the Devereux'. He remembered with some astonishment the decisiveness with which he had announced his intention to study hot rodders and motorcyclists, for this had been only one of the research projects he had been mulling over in his mind; it had been his favorite one, to be sure, but that had been an odd way to discover his decision. And he remembered with some perplexity their strong reaction to his mention of the subject. It was true that, when Jacqueline had first come in, she had said she was dirty because she had been under a Ford; but he could hardly believe that this daughter of intellectual and scrupulous parents, who was studying music at the University of California, could be a hot rodder.

There was a rapping on his door, a hard rap followed by four softer ones, all in a rhythm requiring two hard raps for completion. He went to the door and opened it; no one was there; in this sound-absorbent building, on these grey wall-to-wall carpets, one could scarcely hear footfalls. He poked his head out. There was Jacqueline looking back, not smiling, from the next doorway down, her grandmother's with whom she stayed.

"Hey," he said, not loudly because of the hall. "Come here."

She sidled along the wall till she was about a yard from his door.

"What did that Tum-ta ta Ta ta mean?"

"Friend or ofay."

"*Whose* friend or ofay?"

She shrugged. "Some guys I know."

"What's the answer?"

18

"If you were an ofay, you'd do the obvious." She rapped out the obvious, the two beats that completed the rhythm.

"But what should *I* do?"

"Maybe someday I'll tell you."

Her voice was so noncommittal that he could take neither hope nor offense from what she said. She left.

"Maybe she's shy," he said to himself, striding about the apartment. "But she's a good kid, and I bet I can get her to accept me." He began humming the catalogue of his good fortune that day. Most of all, he liked Jefferson now, his gracious superior. He dilated upon Jefferson's graciousness and ease, magnified them, told himself how warm Jefferson had been, even how he had taken him into his confidence; they were drinking companions, Jefferson had treated him as an old friend out of sheer generosity; Jefferson was an excellent husband and fine father.

And Eleanor, he thought, as he was arranging his books on the built-in shelves, was warm as she had always been. Her handclasp when he had arrived had been warmer than a neighbor's, and she had pulled him into the kitchen without relinquishing his hand. There had always been a touch of special intimacy between them, from the third or fourth time he'd gone to their house as a babysitter. Jacqueline had loved him, and he her, so much that Eleanor had warmed to him very quickly. She had sewed a button on for him and told him that his tie should match his socks; she'd volunteered to teach him the Charleston when there was a revival of that dance on the campus one winter; and, even still, to remember how she had helped him once with a stuck zipper on his fly made him blush with embarrassment. *She* had been oblivious to his shame but had ordered him into the bathroom to take off his pants, had fixed the zipper, and had handed them to him with a snort of laughter at his clumsiness. She was full of common sense, she had a one-track mind, she did not bother to imagine the foolish agonies of an adolescent—and he was glad she had been the one he had first loved. He liked the little danger now of living next door to her.

His excitement precluded sleep. It was a mild, overcast evening, fine for driving. He would cruise around town for an hour or two, getting acquainted.

19

As he emerged from the garage, he saw a fenderless coupé go by in the direction of the main Parktilden entrance. He gunned his Buick in pursuit. In the middle of the second block the stripped car suddenly, apropos of nothing he could see, stopped dead. He crept alongside, looking at the driver hopefully. It was Jacqueline. He stopped.

"Your rod?"

"Sort of."

"Why did you stop?"

"I've been working on the brakes. They're OK." She got out and leaned on the door of his car admiring the upholstery. "Let's hear the horns." He glanced at the two towers nearby. "That's all right," she said scornfully. "Nobody lives in them anyway."

He played the Tum-ta ta Ta ta, and she laughed.

"Give me a ride, Jackie?"

"Not tonight." Her voice became elusive as quicksilver.

"I'll trade you cars for half an hour."

"Why don't you get a rod of your own?"

"I will, maybe, but I'd like to try yours out. You got straight pipes on it?"

She looked at him speculatively. "No."

"Take me around with you and I'll buy you some pipes. A deal?" She squinted for the trap. "Think it over," he said. "How's about us having a little race now?"

"Where to?"

"Oh, just down toward Berkeley."

"OK," she said, "see you day after tomorrow."

He started the instant she did; but when he reached Grizzly Peak Boulevard, she was rounding the first curve, and by the time he came to the first cross streets leading down into Berkeley, there was no sign of her.

He drove all around Berkeley and Oakland, not exactly expecting to find her but still keeping an eye out in case. He liked the feel of the city, he liked the houses and trees and stores. He hummed as he went: doors were opening to him, he was already halfway in, what good luck all around, what luck, what luck.

Four

The violinist played with the San Francisco Symphony; he came every Friday he could get away, always saying, "Good evening, Mrs. Devereux," like a teller to an old customer and then preparing his equipment deftly like a teller counting change; his violin was his mistress, music their bed. The cellist was an acquaintance, the wife of a botany professor; yet no more than Eleanor was she a true member of that subspecies of woman, the faculty wife; she made her own light. The boy who came to play the harpsichord Eleanor had never been introduced to; his first name was Ted, but Jefferson thought his last name was Jones and Jacqueline thought it was Stern; in any case it was known of him only that he tuned pianos for a living and played so passionately well that he put the rest of them on their mettle. He was last to arrive, for which his embarrassment made his stutter agonizing; but he had the harpsichord tuned before the others had left off the chattering of sociability. There were the usual three or four sitters-by whom she knew, and as many whom she didn't.

"My dear," said Jefferson, "where is Jackie?"

"I'll fetch her," said Eleanor. "She said she was going to practice the Scarlatti because you," she smiled abruptly at the harpsichordist, "were going to be here." He writhed, grinning.

Jacqueline was practicing softly while Mama was lying down watching her.

"Look at her, Ellie," crowed the old woman. "She's playing so nice, and she's got a ribbon in her hair."

"So I see, Mama," said Eleanor. "They're waiting for you, dear."

"And her nails, Ellie, she even put red on her nails. Now isn't she pretty as a picture?"

Jacqueline seemingly paid no attention to them; only a little stiffness around the lips betrayed to Eleanor her annoyed pleasure at their attentions. But she was wearing her prettiest summer dress, and she had put whiting on her shoes, and her eyes sparkled.

On their way to the larger apartment, Eleanor rapped on Hazen's door.

"What are you doing that for, Mom?"

"I thought he might enjoy listening."

"Oh, he'll be along about nine. I told him about it last night."

"I thought you went to a movie last night."

"Hazie was there."

Eleanor knew by Jacqueline's tone of off-hand indifference that she shouldn't press further; the truth told in that tone of voice is a shield stouter than any parent's sword can pierce, and Eleanor knew it; yet at the door she said, "I thought you went with the gang."

"Oh sure," said Jacqueline. "It was an old war movie." Eleanor followed her in.

She ought to have been used to these Friday evenings, after so many of them. Yet the music seldom failed to stir her—she was gluttonous of music—and this evening, perturbed as she was about Jacqueline, thinking of her intently, she felt a stirring of her old awe at the joining of these five players. To her now, there was a wonder in their admirable, inarticulate, thoughtless playing together: somewhat as though, walking in a valley, she should see a couple of larks, an owl, a heron, a crow, all suddenly join into graceful formation and fly in a great curve out of sight, presently to reappear. They were slightly absurd, these five, so wholly intent on what they were doing that they waggled their heads or stomped time or squinted or chewed their tongues, oblivious; it was a sort of absurdity dear to her, committed by those who have forgotten themselves, and perceived by those who have not, one which she knew she fell into often enough herself, one which any but the vain delight in. They confessed without excuses their mistakes in performance, and forgave one another bounteously. When the harpsichordist, who was in the far corner with his back to most of them, whacked himself over the head and howled without a trace of stutter, "Repeat, you cat, repeat," everyone laughed, for he had made

22

the same mistake twice; he looked over his shoulder at them a second, then he threw back his head and roared. In the freedom of laughter, she thought, he grew larger. She resolved to make friends with him if he would.

She heard two quiet knocks outside, and Hazen coming through the next room. The performers didn't glance up. He took a seat in a chair in the doorway.

She noticed that his eyes rested on Jacqueline longer than anywhere else. But Jacqueline was not glancing at him or even disposing herself artfully to his attention. She had, Eleanor thought, dressed more carefully than usual, but after all no better than many girls do every day, and now she was quite content to puff with devoted absurdity on her clarinet, lost in Scarlatti. The next time Eleanor glanced at Hazen he was staring out the window, music-rapt, and she admired his long legs stretched out before him. Catching herself, she smiled vanishingly about, and concentrated on the music.

The moment Jefferson said, "Well, people, let's have a break for coffee," Jacqueline put down her clarinet and seemed to be heading back toward her own apartment; even when Hazen addressed her directly she kept on going, but he caught her by the arm and pulled her over beside the large window in the living room. There they launched into a fierce argument in undertones: Hazen pleading and shrugging and pounding the air, Jacqueline shaking her head or looking up at him resentfully or saying "Of course" with elaborate irritation. Twice Eleanor called to her to help serve; without rudeness, neither of them heard her. When she brought them coffee cakes, they acknowledged her presence by ceasing to talk while they served themselves and starting up again as soon as she was out of earshot. They would not have upset her so much if they had both unjustly attacked her; for like a house-cat she found the night never so cold as when she was left out—she would rather take her chances on kicks by the fire. If they had been mooning or giggling or whatever else she had expected them to be doing, she would not have felt so disturbed, for she could have enjoyed her daughter's love-silliness freely, and in any case she would have been able to put herself into it if she wished by saying "No" or "Thus" or "If" or even "Go ahead"; even a lover's quarrel would not necessarily have left her out: "Now now my sweet don't forget." But this was a quarrel of which the only words she caught were pipes and Richmond, and it did not seem to be loving. In her preoccupation she became mechanically polite with the others, and in a moment made better friends with the shy harpsichordist than anyone else had been able to do. Noticing him hunched dumbly in his corner, she beckoned him over, told him to speak his name out loud so she could hear it (it turned out to be Burns), and gave him the cream and sugar to pass around; his gratitude drew her notice, so that she smiled at him himself for a second. The next time she glanced at the two by the window she saw Jacqueline, still scowling, hold out her hand and the two of them shake like men; but she noticed too that Hazen held her hand long after the bargain was decently sealed and that Jacqueline did not seem to be minding.

"I'm glad to see," she said approaching them, "that you have settled your differences."

Jacqueline started to withdraw her hand, but Hazen was smooth.

"With two such charming hostesses," he said, taking Eleanor's hand in his left, "I am speechless." And he joined their hands, bowed, smiled, and walked off.

"What was the big argument over?" Eleanor asked.

"He was making me keep a bargain in a way I didn't want to keep it," Jacqueline said and joined the musicians.

Eleanor straightened up the kitchen as silently as she could, her anger disintegrating back into the confusion that had caused it. When she returned to her chair and began listening to the music, she couldn't get in. She tried hard, but Eleanor's trying to give herself over to music was like her trying to be patient: she could do everything about it except fool herself. So she watched the players and marveled, as she often did.

It seemed to her inscrutable that these five should collect from miles around and become totally a part of something else for a time. It was as though some great, selective magnet should have attracted certain electrons of all electrons into its field for awhile and made them indeterminately a part of one whole, so that when they flew out again they were themselves again; yet that was not accurate for it was by their own wish that these five came together. It was as though they were catalysts precipitating lovely crystals, themselves unchanged; yet that was wrong for the notes written down two and a half centuries before were, if anything was, the unchanging catalysts, and what happened to these people no one could guess, even though they seemed to do nothing more than puff and scrape and pound. It had something to do with eternity, though each of them counted time from beginning to end of every piece; and it had something to do with giving up all their freedom to the rules of the music, though they had freely to will to do this; and it had something to do with mastering themselves in a unity, body mind and heart all working together in one action, though in order to accomplish this they had to subordinate themselves to a larger whole. It was like becoming one another, though she didn't know what that meant; yet it was exactly, she felt, that they became one another for a time, even though they did not know it and even though those words did not say what she meant. They were perfectly indifferent to everyone else as they played, yet their glances to each other were as direct as children's: at the end of a movement, when they were relaxing back each separately into himself, their eyes became shy, and she had noticed that Jacqueline had a way of seeking her eye at such a time, asking for a little smile. Eleanor was breathing as hard as though she had just been excited by learning some potent secret, for, while she was not in any way a part of them or part of that whole they were making, she felt proud of her husband and daughter so unaccountably there. Her chest felt pressed outward by pride and joy.

When the movement ended she looked up for Jacqueline's glance, and saw that it was being offered to Hazen and that it was he who was smiling in return. Eleanor rose instantly, translating impulse directly into act, as it were short-circuiting thought or emotion; she hurried over to Hazen and pulled him out with her into the kitchen. A whole plan had just taken shape in her head, which she felt impelled to ask him about immediately.

"Peter," she whispered, "what do you know about Juilliard?"

"Juilliard?" he answered with astonishment.

"The school of music."

"I don't know."

"Oh, you do too." She thought he was being false-naive; his face was a model of agreeable concern, but surely he knew what she was getting at. "It's in New York, right close to Columbia."

"Sure," he said, "I know where it is. I've been to concerts there."

"It's good, isn't it?"

"That's what everybody says."

"Didn't you know any of the students there?"

"Well, I met a few. They seemed nice enough."

There was nothing she liked less than to have a man talk patiently with her. She was afraid she was being unreasonable, as everyone assured her she often was, but this time she didn't see how. She was quite sure, however, that she wanted to enlist him on her side, but that he wanted to get back in to the music.

"But did they play well?"

"Sure," he answered. "I'm no musician, but they sounded very good to me. We really shouldn't be making so much noise."

"Well, wouldn't it be good for her?"

"Jackie?"

"Yes."

"You mean, would it be good for her to go live in New York and study at Juilliard?"

"Yes. Wouldn't it?"

"Good lord. Come along." He led her out into the hallway, in which, because of the muffled quality of noises and of the shadowless, underwater light, he appeared to her somehow remote, hard to get at, not someone she would want to touch. "How in the world would I know anything about how good you have to be before they'll admit you?"

"You might have known."

"Does she want to go?"

"She did a year and a half ago. But wouldn't it be good for her?"

"I don't know whether it's good for anybody to live in New York for very long. Besides, she loves cars and it's hard to keep a car there."

"Oh, Peter." She might have cried a little had she not caught sight of Mr. and Mrs. Erskine down the hall returning from their

Friday night movie. "That's the whole thing.—Good evening, Mrs. Erskine, Mr. Erskine. How was the picture?"

"Fine, Mrs. Devereux," said Mr. Erskine, raising his hat. He was portly and old-fashioned and very timid; he liked nothing so much as to putt courtesies across a rolling green. "I hear the Friday nightingales are warbling as usual."

"They'll be through by eleven as usual," she said. "I do hope they won't disturb you."

"Not a bit of it, my dear. We consider ourselves fortunate in having neighbors at once charming and aesthetic." He raised his hat and took his wife's arm.

"You must meet our new neighbor in number 1005 before you go in," Eleanor said. "Mrs. Erskine, this is Peter Hazen. And Mr. Erskine."

Mrs. Erskine murmured and smiled.

"You are connected with the University, young man?" Mr. Erskine asked him.

"Yes, I'm new here. Sociology. And you?"

"I severed my connections with that institution 43 years ago, and I haven't regretted it for a second. Not a second. No, I am in stocks and bonds, a bondsman I sometimes say." Mrs. Erskine looked as though she might titter.

"Wouldn't you like to come in and listen for a while?" Eleanor asked them.

Mr. Erskine squinted at her for a moment, challenged by this difficult putt over a strip of earth and down a double-sloping green. "Thank you, my dear, but we are selfish. All we need do is open the window in our bedroom and we can enjoy the music as we lie abed." He turned toward Hazen. "I'm a three-pillow man with a bad heart, neighbor, and lazier than sin. Now you're one up on me; you know more about me than I know about you. Balance the scales, Mrs. Devereux, balance them for us. But another time." Again he raised his hat; he took his wife's arm. "Come, my love, Orpheus calls."

"He means Morpheus," she said in a small voice.

"Not at all." And he swept his arm grandly in the direction of the music. "Orpheus." Mrs. Erskine laughed.

"Good night, good night, nice to have met you, good night."

Hazen moved towards the door. "Pleasant people," he said.

"Oh, they're all you could ask for neighbors. We must have looked odd, standing out here like this."

"But they didn't act as though there was anything in the least out of the ordinary about it."

"They wouldn't." She put her hand on the door knob and opened the door only an inch or two. Talking here was laborious, like swimming under water, slow, full of the unexpected, but she did it. "Wouldn't it be best for her, Peter?"

He looked too blank. "To go to Juilliard?"

She nodded. "This fall."

"Really, I hardly even know her yet."

He was being disingenuous. What she wanted to say was, "You've gotten to know her well enough in the two weeks you've been here so that you don't want her to go away," but what she actually said was, "You have changed a great deal in these twelve years."

"What?" he said. "I suppose so."

"You used to be so shy; I could just read everything you felt on your face. Your face was so expressive."

He grinned, boyishly, expressively. "You really knew how I felt about things?"

"Oh yes."

"Even about people, say?"

For answer she smiled and put her hands on his forearms. Then, simultaneously, both their smiles faded, and they looked for a moment into each other's eyes, touching, for touch in the undifferentiated nowhere of this hallway was actual, warm-blooded, immediate; and they returned to the music room.

As though it made no difference at all that they had gone out, had reached a sort of understanding, no one looked up at them when they came back in, not even, Eleanor realized in a spurt of resentment, not even Jacqueline. The nowhere into which those five others had gone together was differentiated by the most scrupulous rules; she did not comprehend these rules in the least; she was altogether left out.

Five

Hazen's investigation of hot rods and motorcycles would be adequately substantial (relevant, aware, a significant contribution to the literature in the field) once he had let its blood, broken its bones, flayed it, and published it in one of the learned journals; publish he would have to or lose his job. Meanwhile he was happy, like a tinkering sort of boy who is supposed to mow the lawn but discovers that before he bends to drudgery he can spend all day taking the lawn mower apart, sharpening it, oiling it, adjusting it, cleaning it. Hazen liked automobiles with a deep, American liking. He liked driving hard, he liked taking chances once in awhile when he was in a hurry, on a beautiful afternoon he liked driving in the country, he liked driving precipitous one-way roads in the mountains or eight-lane freeways or cobblestone alleys in Boston, he very much liked a stretch of good highway in the desert where he could keep the throttle wide open till the car vibrated like a taut wire and loped, when it went over a little bump, in hundred-foot-long luxurious bounds. He liked the raising of mountains, circling of cities, high progress over swamps; he liked the whine of the tires when the asphalt was soft and the hum when he crossed one of the metal gridiron stretches of a bridge and the singing on wet concrete pavement. He even liked long hard trips, such as the one he had just made across country. He had driven his old sedan from New York pleasantly to Detroit, where he had bought a brand-new, gleaming-red Buick convertible with all the trimmings: fog lights, curb finders, necker's knob, heater, radio, white sidewall tires, genuine leather seats, an extension-cord light that plugged into the cigarette lighter, two spotlights, three ashtrays, and five clarion horns; he could raise or lower the top with the turn of a knob, he could make the front seat go forward or back by pressing a lever, he could adjust the height of any window with buttons on the door by his left hand. The car was fat and sleek as a beetle, there were eleven gauges and dials on the panelboard and nine buttons, the aerial rose from a flexible mount on the rear bumper support like a wand ten feet in the air, and the chrome of the front bumper and grill grinned like the bared teeth of a politician a week before election day; inside the car he could hardly hear the motor, but if he stood out in back when the engine was idling he would hear coming out through the stainless steel tailpipe a sumptuous sound as of velvet jugglers tossing silver bells; it rode so smoothly and picked up so fast and steered so easily and stopped so sharply and leaned around the curves so elegantly that there was scarcely any work to driving it at all, only skill and vigilance. To exercise and test this vigilance and skill he had driven from Detroit straight through to his parents' farmhouse in Nebraska without stopping, though he told them it had been his desire to get home that had urged him; and every day he was home he had wiped off his red car, which had cost him more dollars than the whole farm had originally cost his father, and ridden around visiting relatives and old friends, whose cars rattled. He liked as much of national parks and monuments as one sees from the roads and he would rather drive above a gorge than climb down in it to fish for Dolly Varden trout; he liked motels, he liked giving short lifts to hitchhikers, and whenever he had broken down he had found that somebody friendly came along to lend him a hand; and while he did not exactly like that irritable fatigue that came from driving too long, he far preferred it to the trials of the ways he had traveled before, to the tedium of riding in busses or trains, or that blue elixir of boredom, traveling in a plane third-class. What he liked about cars over those others was the control which driving gave him: he became the brain of a powerful organism; he was being active, not passive; and according to the sociological canon of good and bad (though under such aliases as "other-orientation" or "decreased societal atomization") it is better to do than be done unto, that is, it's better to drive than ride.

By the time he had reached California he could feel, through feet, ears, muscles, organs he did not even know he had, every slur and tic and hiccup in the car's working; yet he knew of how it operated about as much, and as little, as he knew of the working of his own body.

"Come on, Jackie, let's get going."

"I want a root beer float."

"My gosh, you just had a sundae."

"You mean you're too cheap to buy me a float, Hazie?"

"Oh, lord, I'm just tired of these neons. I want to get going."

Jacqueline stuck the little finger and forefinger of her left hand into her mouth and whistled shrilly for service. An answering whistle came from the street behind them and the first seven notes of "Yankee Doodle" played on horns.

"Look at Sharon," said Jacqueline. "Hasn't she got a neat figure?"

"Wasn't that one of the people?"

"What?"

"That rod that was passing and played 'Yankee Doodle' when you whistled?"

"Wasn't listening."

"You couldn't help hearing," he protested.

"Hey, Sharon!" she yelled. "She looks like a starlet, doesn't she?"

The carhop was dressed in green sateen bell-bottomed trousers sleek about the hips, a white blouse with full sleeves, and a cocky little red overseas cap; her hair was platinum blonde and her eyebrows were penciled on.

"Exactly," said Hazen coldly.

"What's eating you?" Jacqueline said belligerently.

"Nothing."

"Everybody else thinks Sharon's a knockout."

"She's perfect. Nobody with any character is perfect."

"How true, O Socrates."

"Which would you rather have, a perfect body or some character?"

"You are right, O Socrates."

"Well, which?"

"Both."

"You want your bill, folks?" asked Sharon in a neutrally friendly voice.

"Not yet," said Hazen, "a root beer float first."

"Submarine?" Sharon asked, meaning "Do you want two scoops of ice cream such that one holds the other under the root beer."

"No, a rowboat," said Jackie, meaning "I want only one scoop so that it floats." "And make it pink," she added, meaning "I want strawberry ice cream."

Hazen was admiring the nonchalance with which Sharon cleared their tray, tossed a menu onto the windshield of a car that drove in next to them, and sidestepped the lewd banter of the boys in that car.

"Well, so she hasn't got any character."

Hazen was stuck with his theory. "Nobody who's that perfect could have any character. It would show on her face."

"She's got a two-year-old kid and her husband deserted her."

"OK. You know her better than I do."

"You don't know her at all," she said, looking straight at him.

He was not used to swallowing so many reproofs as Jacqueline had been giving him. "OK, OK. Look, it's 10:30 already. You promised to take me around tonight and all we're doing is slurping in a drive-in."

"What's Mom got against Pearl?"

"Don't change the subject."

"What does she?"

"Will you let me drive when we get out of here?"

"Never said I wouldn't."

"And never said you would."

"OK. *If* you won't drag too much. I'm saving Henry."

"I'll be careful," he said.

"*And* double-clutch. Henry is Floyd's baby."

"I don't want to cause any trouble. Let's trade seats."

"Later. What about Pearl?"

"What's she to you?"

"Great aunt or so. So?"

"Just wondered. She got me my apartment here."

"At a reduced rent?"

"No, but she said she'd get me one of the best locations. And *I* like it." Jackie did not respond to his gallantry. "Why did you ask about her?"

"The way Mom goes on you'd think she's a fiend."

"She did *me* a favor for which I am grateful—putting me next to you all."

"True." Jacqueline sounded reflective, not skeptical. "Anyway it's not worth whacking me about, is it?"

He thought he would try her own tactics on her, and did not respond to her vagueness.

"Is it?" Her voice was flat and mannish, her quality of hostility.

"How can I say? You're not telling me the whole truth and nothing but the truth."

"Who are you I should tell nothing but the truth to? And even if I'm not, she doesn't have the right to whack me."

"Who, Pearl?"

"No, Mom."

"Certainly she does. She's your mother."

"I'm too old to be whacked any more."

"The heck you are. I feel like whacking you myself sometimes."

"That's different. Besides, Daddy never hits me."

"Well, hit her back."

"Hazen!"

"What did she hit you with?"

"A wooden spoon, on the hip, hard."

"Look, quit bellyaching, you've got a good mother."

"I've got a better father." He didn't answer. "So you don't like my father?"

"Oh for the love of mike. Comparisons are odious."

"No more odious than sociologists. Why can't old fogeys like you leave me alone?" She whistled again for Sharon.

Sharon minced up to them, and while she was making change said to Jacqueline, "What's the matter, sweetie, he being mean to you?"

"Men," said Jacqueline.

"Which is better, a man or a gopher?" said Sharon.

"I don't know. Which?"

"A man—he's a gopher plus." She balanced the tray lightly on three fingers, winked at Hazen, and smiled so that little dimples appeared in her cheeks. "Don't do anything I wouldn't do, kids."

"Huh," said Hazen grumpily as they backed out; he hadn't got the point of the riddle and was ashamed to admit it. "Is there anything she wouldn't do?"

"Listen," said Jacqueline furiously and pulled over to the curb, though they had barely left the drive-in, "I'm sick and tired of the way you run everything and everybody down."

"What do you mean?" he said aggrieved. "I was only kidding."

"You jeer too much."

"I do not," he said. "I just didn't like the way Sharon kept butting in."

"She's a friend of mine."

"OK."

"I've got lots of friends and I don't like them laughed at."

"OK, OK." Suddenly he was angry too. "Now for the love of mike, will you let me drive?"

Without a word she slipped out from behind the wheel and walked around the car. He took the driver's seat, and when she had got in he asked her where he should go. "Up San Pablo," she answered and leaned against the door.

For five miles they did not speak. Hazen forgot his anger in the pleasure of driving, for he had never driven a car which would accelerate or decelerate half as well as this one, and the wheels responded as intimately to his steering as though they were a part of himself. He had noticed that Jacqueline, when she was driving, sat a little forward and to the left; he tried doing it too, but he felt awkward and went back to the usual position. He dove between a bus and a car at an intersection when the light turned green; he felt daredevilish, but when he glanced at Jacqueline he saw she hadn't turned a hair. He found a loop of wire sticking above the floorboard in the center, back near the seat, and pulled it; instantly there was a roaring from the exhaust. "Cut it!" cried Jacqueline, and he did. She pricked up like a deer who has just crashed

34

through brush, and looked all about. "The cops don't like it," she said. "That's strictly for the sticks." Everything about this car amazed him by working so well—not comfortably or splendidly like his Buick, but fast, efficiently, like a greyhound.

"You know what I'm going to do, Hazie?" Her voice was a girl's again. "If you keep causing me a lot of grief, that is."

"What?"

"I'm going to enroll in one of your sociology classes."

"Wonderful," he said, trying to fool himself that he liked the idea. "It pleases me to have somebody I know in the class."

But he didn't fool her; he saw her smile. All the same, threat or no threat, she seemed to be saying to him, "You're worth my trouble."

They were rolling through the outskirts of Richmond. "Where shall I head for?" he asked.

"Oh, you might as well turn left at the next signal."

Her voice was light and off-hand; he had heard her use it thus maddeningly on Eleanor when she was being evasive.

"Then where?"

"Around."

So fast that the tires screeched he darted left across the highway into a dark side street and stopped with a jerk alongside an abandoned tenement. She looked at him, startled.

"Look," he said fiercely, "quit giving me the run-around. A bargain's a bargain, and I don't give a darn *why* you don't want to take me to where the hot rods hang out. You're going to take me there anyhow."

"OK," she said, and to his amazement took his hand off the steering wheel, which he was still gripping, and held it in hers.

"Well, how do we get there?" he asked. His heart was beating hard and he wanted to kiss her, but he felt that if he did he would be doing, for the fiftieth time in a row, exactly what she wanted him to do.

"I'll show you."

Her wiles were simple after the erotic sophistication he was used to: she moved her lips a little, looked up from under her curling lashes, and pulled gently at his hand. But he scarcely found strength to resist her.

35

"Well, where?"

She leaned forward a little and gave a tiny tug at his hand. "Well," he thought, "I don't want to offend her." "Let's be friends again," she said.

So he decided to give her a kiss of friendship—he had firmly resolved, days before, not to allow her to fall in love with him, not to allow his experience to take advantage of her innocence—and saying "Darn it all," he kissed her. It was not a kiss of friendship; it prolonged itself and was wholly sensual. When their lips separated she slid across the seat beside him friendlily and said in a voice that betrayed nothing of the perturbation he was feeling, "Let's go, Hazie." "Darn it," he said again, and kissed her again. She was willing; she seemed to view kisses like root beer floats, delights in themselves to be gorged till you can't stand another, inconsequent delicacies, goodies. He sat back behind the wheel. She laid her head on the seatback and lolled over facing him. "Ready to go now?" she said. She wasn't mocking him or urging him, merely asking. Her voice was drowsy. "Damn it," he said, "damn it, damn it, damn it." And he nearly assaulted her with embraces and kisses. She returned them in good measure.

Presently he drew back and, scowling, started the car. "Wait a sec," she said, and wiped the lipstick off his mouth. As he started up, she skewed the rearview mirror around and restored her make-up. Hazen had never seen her without lipstick on, even dishevelled, in jeans, in shorts, even one morning in the hallway in pajamas. She turned the mirror back and settled down against him; her right foot sought for and found something to hook onto behind the dashboard and her left hand rested on his leg as though it belonged there. "You're just about Floyd's size," she said, and he thought her tactless, "and I like it," but he decided she was just being honest and frank. All the same he searched her tone of voice and the way she snuggled against him for signs of the smugness of a woman who has won; but what he heard was the inflection of contentment and his glance showed him nothing but pleasantness in her eyes and her snuggling was neutrally familiar, the way a girl rides with a fellow she likes. He decided there was nothing better to be done than follow her example—enjoy it while it lasted. Solely because he thought she would expect him to, he tried kissing her

36

while they were going along; but she sternly forbade it—driving is serious business. Reproof like this he didn't mind, particularly when it was followed by a squeeze on the leg. Surely he was beginning to learn how to manage her.

His foot slipped off the brake pedal so that the car bucked when he stopped. Three boys slouched elaborately over from a parked car.

"Floyd?" one of them called doubtfully, the one with green glasses and cowboy boots.

"You out on leave already?" said the one with black skin.

"Jackie?" said the one with a feather-edge haircut and acne.

"I'm not Floyd," said Hazen.

"Hi, fellows," said Jackie, leaning across him.

"This is Floyd's car," said green glasses.

"Sure," said Jackie. "He gave it to me."

"That's Floyd's way of stopping."

"His foot slipped on the brake," she said. "It was an accident."

"Who're you?" said the acned one to Hazen.

"My name's Hazen," he said, sticking his hand out; no one took it. "I'm a friend."

"He's a sociologist," said Jackie. "He studies things."

"A what?" said the Negro.

"A sociologist."

"What's he doing around here?"

"He lives next door to me."

Without a word, the three walked to the middle of the road and one of them whistled between his fingers a long, a short, and a long. Hazen had not noticed a car in the field across the paved street in front of him, but at the whistle the car started up with a roar and two shafts of flame shot out behind it.

"Lord!" said Hazen.

"He's mounted plugs on the exhausts. The fumes ignite."

"Who is he?"

"John Henry."

"John Henry," Hazen repeated, but he saw she would answer no more questions. He saw furthermore that he was undergoing an initiation which one could fail without appeal.

John Henry manoeuvred his car as though it was a spirited horse, over the curb, dancingly across to the three in the dirt road.

"Why did you have to tell them I'm a sociologist?" Hazen asked her; both of them were looking at the flames from John Henry's car.

"Because you are one."

"I just wanted to be one of the gang." She did not respond. "Well, couldn't I?"

"They'd take you for some sort of a stool pigeon."

"What?" he cried aggrieved, and looked at her.

"Look, let me give you a piece of advice." Her voice, he noticed, was flat but excited. "Around here the more you ask the less you find out, and I'm not kidding."

John Henry's car had no fenders, its windshield was not more than six inches high and was colored light blue, the roof was continuous with the turtleback, the car was painted an intense violet, and on the hub caps glowed phosphorescent eyes. He backed it a little—it shuddered like a race horse approaching the starting line —and brought it over by Hazen so that the drivers were face to face. He had a Hollywood haircut, there were toy boxing gloves dangling from his rearview mirror, his baby face scowled.

"What's the pitch?" he said. His voice like Jackie's strained to be tougher than it was.

"Nothing," said Hazen, succeeding in speaking steadily. "I'm new in town and I just wanted to come around with Jackie."

"What did you say you were?"

"A sociologist. All I want to know is, find out how people do things."

"I don't like it."

"You mean," came the silly voice of a girl in the dark the other side of John Henry, "like the Kinsey Report?" She giggled shrilly.

"Shut up," said John Henry over his shoulder.

"Who're you telling to shut up, you big bastard?" she screamed.

Before he turned to deal with her, he smoothed down his long dark hair along the sides and patted it on the back of his neck, gazing speculatively at Hazen. Then flashing fingers came from behind to grab his nose and jerk his head around. For a few minutes there came not quite articulate sounds of abuse from the low car.

"Who's she?" Hazen said.

"Fern. His wife."

"Nice couple."

"They're my friends."

John Henry squinted back out at them; his head touched the roof; Fern was not making any more noise.

"Who holds the pink slip on this heap?"

"I do," Jackie answered.

"Let's see it, J.D." He snapped on his spotlight; it was very bright.

She found the paper in her purse and passed it to him.

Three motorcycles roared down the cross street exactly abreast. Presently there came a flock of shrill whistles from somewhere up the street.

He handed it back to her. "You drive the course if it's driven. Owner drives." He revved his motor deafeningly, but before he left he switched his spotlight to full power, the brightest Hazen had ever seen, and shone it full in Hazen's face. "If there's one thing I don't like, Crew-cut, it's too much light." He made a U-turn slowly, like a jet plane taxiing, but by the time he rounded the corner fifty feet away he was going so fast the tires screeched. The three guards slouched to their car.

Hazen and Jacqueline sat in silence for a short time.

"Very interesting," Hazen said musingly.

"Let's get the hell out of here."

"What?"

"When a guy gives you the works you get out."

"He didn't say I couldn't stick around."

"Haven't you got any pride?"

"Pride? Because he tried to bully me? No, I find it very interesting. Why should he be so aggressive? This is the way I learn things."

"Boy, have you got a neat system."

"What do you mean?"

"If you get what you want you have a good time, and if you

get jumped on you learn something. You've really got it sewed up going and coming."

"You talk as though there were something wrong with it."

"Oh no, *I* think it's great. Only thing is, if I didn't know you so well I'd think you were scared of him."

It occurred uneasily to him that she did not in fact know him that well. She was staring at him expressionlessly.

He spoke in a dry, pedantic voice. "I was in the Army Engineers. We used to go over fields sown with mines and take them out alive." He was not bragging; what he had told her was the truth, a shell-case for the truth at least, as "I love you" is another sort of shell-case, an exoskeleton that can endure for a time after the life inside has gone.

"That's what I said," she answered, but her voice was entirely altered, "if I didn't know you so well." She snuggled over beside him again. "Let's go, Hazie."

A car poked up the road from behind them; the guards stopped it with flashlights and headed it back the way it had come.

"Do they have the right to do that?" he asked her.

"They do it."

"Don't the police care?"

"You wouldn't want an innocent passer-by to get hurt, would you? Let's get going."

"What're they going to do now?"

"Oh, they'll probably run a chicken or two. You'd better hang around Iggy's Igloo a while and get acquainted before you try to muscle in."

"What do you mean, run a chicken?"

"Chicken," she answered, "is a game. You'll see."

"Just tell me this one thing and I'll quit pestering."

"You get two hot rods a couple of blocks apart and draw a line halfway between them. Then they race for it with their left wheels on the white line down the middle of the road. The loser's chicken."

"Suppose they both get there at the same time?"

"Yep."

"You ever run a chicken?"

"Once with Floyd. John Henry tries to make you. He wins."

"He's got lots of drag?"

"*And* he's never turned. There's a guy in L.A. never turned either, I hear." He could feel her excitement.

"I'll be damned." He turned around slowly. "Would they let me run one?"

"Not in my car, you can't, and your Buick hasn't got the drag."

There was the sound of explosion, perhaps a great backfire, up the cross road; they turned to watch. Five cars zoomed past, the cut-down violet flame-shooter in the lead. Jacqueline leaned forward, eyes gleaming.

"A drag-race," she said.

"How far?"

"A measured mile." She dug him in the ribs with her elbow. "Let's get the lead out. I don't like to hang around when I'm not in on it."

"OK." He started up. "Where to?" They cruised down the street.

"Haven't you got any imagination?" she said.

"Sure, but I'm a stranger in these parts."

"Well, it depends on what you had on your mind, where we go," she said neutrally.

The truth was he had hot rods on his mind; but when he came to consider what they might do next this evening, he discovered that her lips were on his mind. He pulled up at a stop sign and looked into her eyes. She returned his look a little quizzically.

"Your eyes are very beautiful," he said.

"Can the corn," she said. They kissed. "There's a nice place out on Point Richmond. It won't take ten minutes to get there. Let's get going."

He thought it unseemly of her to be so openly practical and eager about necking, perhaps even coarse of her. Yet in the past he had inveighed against coy women who pretend to be up to something else when what they really want is to make love. Only, he had been around them for so long.

"I like a view for when you're resting between smooches," she said.

For the twentieth time he decided she was pure and honest. He stepped on the gas.

Six

Pearl Vinograd, Eleanor's aunt by marriage on her father's side, was one of the chief stockholders in Parktilden Village Investment Corporation and a member of the board of directors. She lived in one of the Parktilden Manors, #14C, and the extra bedroom in her manor was usually occupied; Pearl was avarice itself in getting her money, but a member of the family, or anyone she took a fancy to, she would indulge herself in glutting with good things, like apartments for half rent, as she glutted herself on buttermilk creams and Brazil nuts. She was stout; that is, by grace of a stiff and bounteous corset her fat did not jiggle much when she walked, and by good fortune her arms were full but handsome. She wore a housecoat in the mornings till she was obliged to go out on business; from that time on she would wear a tight-fitting dress with short sleeves or no sleeves, and a hat, indoors or out a wide-brimmed black hat. She had a suggestion of dark mustache; she smiled; she watched with lubricious intentness the lips of whomever she was talking to; she liked to talk about nothing so much as her constipation, and anyone who had a good case of piles could live off her in style for a week talking them over. She knitted.

The manor in which she lived was precisely what had been master-planned: because it was in unit 14, it had only two bedrooms, for there were no children in manor units above #11; because it was C, it was furnished in what was called Parktilden Swedish Modern; because 14 is not divisible by 3, it was on the south, sunny side of the towers. Yet she did not much like the place; she lived in it only because the rent was free and because she liked to be near her investment. What she preferred was some old-fashioned house she could fix up to suit her own tastes; however, she had let herself be persuaded that a great many people in the East Bay were willing to pay dearly for ready-made luxury, persuaded to the extent of a $250,000 investment, for which she had received in two years not a cent in return. Eleanor and she did not like each other; they had nothing in common but family; family was enough.

Eleanor went to the end of the hall where the glassed-in fire escape zigzagged down the tower, and leaned over the rail to see if she could tell whether Pearl was home. The ground-floor windows of the manor were open to the warm morning.

"Eleanor!" Pearl said, embracing her, kissing her. She was in her housecoat and her knitting was by her chair. "Come in, sweetheart, I'm just drinking some tea."

"Tea, Pearl? I thought you were a great coffee woman."

"Leaves, precious, leaves." She put a cigarette into a long gold holder and lit it with a silver lighter. "I haven't seen you since Easter. It's too long. Where've you been keeping yourself?" She poured Eleanor tea in a glass cup and put some buttery scones on a plate for her. "You got to come see me, sweetheart, I hate those elevators like poison. Say, how's my boy friend getting along?"

"Hazen?"

"Sure Hazen. How do you like having him next door? I wouldn't mind having him in the next room myself, but he told me he wanted an apartment to himself. How did the little surprise work on him?"

"Fine, Pearl. We all enjoy being so near together."

"You bet you do, sweetheart. If we don't enjoy one another while we can, what's it all about anyway?" She took up a nail file and worked on a jagged fingernail. "I'm getting far-sighted," she said calmly. "Would you give me my glass eyes, Ellie? They're under the fish bowl." The fish bowl was a large glass doughnut with one flat side against the wall, in which three large goldfish lounged. She took the spectacles in her left hand and paused a moment, looking at Eleanor a little humorously. "I like that Hazen," she said, and with her right hand, the nail file indifferently in it, she made an odd gesture as though she were guessing the weight of an orange, hand cupped a little and moving up and down judgingly. "He's solid, but he's not too hard." She fell to work on her nails. "Now what brought you over here, honey, just to see me?"

"Well," said Eleanor hesitantly, though she knew Pearl too well to be thrown by such directness. She began with intensity to pick little pieces of lint off her skirt. "I've got Jackie on my mind."

"That little greaseball, that little suckling pig, my God how I love that girl. She reminds me of myself when I was that age. What a bottom, Jesus what a bottom. It's a sin and a shame to hide a bottom like that in a pair of jeans. *That* I never did." She smacked her lips in a sort of caricature of lewdness. "Ellie, if I was a man you'd be having trouble. I'm surprised you let her out at night." And she snorted and stamped like a stallion.

Eleanor rather enjoyed the spectacle of a vice so gross and pure. "Do you ever see her in those frightful hot rods?"

"Lord, yes. She came to see me this morning in one."

"She did!" Eleanor knew that Jacqueline had never liked Pearl. "Did she want to borrow some money?"

"No." Pearl's tone of voice on that no rang true. "She just came by to pass the time of day." But on these words it did not. "What's the matter with her, sweetheart?"

"I'm in a quandary. I'm thinking about sending her to Juilliard School of Music."

"So?" Pearl was assuming the voice of one who calculates the costs.

"I just wanted to ask you whether you could help at all."

"Money?" The Devereux had never asked her for money or favors, and they took their reduced rent as a gift to Mama. All the same.

"Of course not."

Pearl began filing again. "Then what?"

"Friends. Do you have any friends in New York?"

"You mean you're worried about sending your little lamb to the sacrifice? You'd better be. That place is full of wolves."

"I'm afraid she would get so lonesome."

"Friends? Ellie, I've got friends everywhere. I love 'em. Look, I'm sick of this hole and besides I'm losing money hand over fist here. We don't even have half the apartments rented after two years. You know what that means to my investment?" She made a noise like a deflating balloon. "I'll pick up and go to New York myself and keep an eye on her. There's nobody there I'd trust with her. She's special. I'm disgusted with Berkeley, San Francisco, California, the whole damned West. All I've been needing is an excuse to pick up and go have myself a good time." She peered at Eleanor, who was dismayed. "Don't you look that way, sweetheart. I've been thinking of New York already. This just triggers it. Well, let's set your mind at rest. Let's find out what's right in this deal. Countess!" she bellowed suddenly. "Hey, Countess!"

"Oui, chérie?" came a heavily coy voice from upstairs.

"You got a couple of minutes, Lisa? I want you to meet my niece."

"Oh, how lovely," she called back down in silvery chimes.

But when the Countess appeared, her eyes were in no way full of the loveliness of the occasion. She was little, painted, and hunched; she walked lightly but carefully like a sick bird; her elegant black shoes were stained and scuffed.

"This is Countess Lisa von Placken, Eleanor Devereux. Lisa," she said to Eleanor impressively, as one speaks of a good juggler or of a child with absolute pitch, "speaks six languages."

"Really!" said Eleanor, and looked, as one foolishly does, for symptoms of prodigy. She did not like the sharpness with which the Countess was sizing her up; it was not the eye-flicking of vanity to which she was accustomed, judging clothes and hair and nails and figure as though every woman were entered in some beauty contest, but the quick and expert survey of a sapper who wants to know where his small mine ought most accurately to be placed to topple you over.

"You're a Libra!" the Countess cried suddenly and pointed straight at Eleanor. "When is your birthday?"

"September 28."

"On the cusp, cara mia, she's on the cusp of Virgo. You did it again!" said Pearl and embraced Lisa.

"You're a Libra with the qualities of Virgo," said the Countess to Eleanor. "You are conscientious and well-meaning but you often make mistakes. Have more confidence in yourself; you are not as weak as you think you are. Assert yourself."

"But," said Pearl uncertainly, "are you sure that's right, dearheart? If I remember . . ." She started toward a huge astrological reference book in which dozens of markers had been placed.

"Chérie," said the Countess, and her smile flickered on like a

45

slightly defective neon light, "what the books say is no concern of mine." She turned her back on them and started toward the kitchen. "I am interested only in the truth of these matters."

Pearl pulled a wry face; she stuck out her middle finger at the Countess, just as that one glanced back over her shoulders. The Countess' laughter at catching Pearl out was as melodious as though it had been played on a xylophone, but it made Eleanor more uneasy than anything else about her; after all, one should not be able to tap out laughter with a mallet just as one chooses. Eleanor got up and began making the sounds of a departing guest; Pearl simply pushed her back into her chair and shushed her.

"Lisa," she called, "Eleanor is wondering what she ought to do with Jackie." Then sotto voce, "If she's in the mood she can say a lot."

"I don't *like* all this stuff," said Eleanor.

But Pearl only smiled and patted her arm.

"Jackie?" asked the Countess. She was eating cherries, the juice staining the corners of her mouth.

"Jacqueline, baby."

"Ah, Jacqueline." Her accent when she said the name became pure, caressing French. "She was here this morning, non?" The Countess gazed speculatively at Eleanor. "Your daughter, non?" She ran her hands ruefully down over her chest as one might smooth out a shirt on an ironing board; her blouse streaked with cherry stains. "What élan. She will have no common destiny." She glanced at Eleanor. "Her birthday, it is near yours, no?"

"Yes; as a matter of fact, we have the same birthday."

"Ah ha," said the Countess.

"You talked to her?" said Eleanor, eager in spite of herself to know what this shrewd creature thought of her.

"No," said the Countess shrugging. "I learned English. I am not at ease in Jacqueline's dialect. I listened. I watched her walk." Suddenly this little face looked very stern; she described a vague shape, palms outward and fingers crooked, a shifting ominous shape; her eyes oddly altered. "That is the way one walks who knows dark things. Brave."

"Knows dark things?" cried Eleanor. "Jackie?"

"Yes."

"What does that mean?"

Without answering, the Countess darted like a bird and seized Eleanor's hands. She studied them rigidly for a minute or two. Then, as a priest might glance at the sky for auspicious flights of birds after he had read the guts of a sheep, she glanced at the leaves in Eleanor's empty teacup. She went back, in the silence she had created, to her cup and concentrated on stirring her tea.

"You are not entirely fortunate," she said. "Your trouble is complex. I do not perceive it clearly. It has something to do with one who is not so young as you think. But your life-line is very strong."

"What about Jacqueline?" said Pearl. The Countess seemed not to have heard. Eleanor was looking at her intently. "Lisa baby, what about what she's got to do about Jacqueline?"

"Suddenly the Countess shrugged, the neon flickered on, and there was a short trill on the xylophone.

"Pearl darling," she said, "this tea begs for a little strawberry jam. Do you mind?"

"Go ahead, go ahead. There's white bread in the bin."

"No," said the Countess sharply, "not with bread. In the tea itself."

"My God," said Pearl, "this I want to see."

"You've seen me do it before."

"I can't get used to you, Lisa." And she bellowed with laughter.

While they both went off into the kitchen, Eleanor contracted into herself. She had absolutely no use for astrological mumbo-jumbo; all the same, she could not ignore the Countess's feeling of something ominous surrounding Jacqueline. She had felt it herself, something like it at any rate, nothing so strong as the Countess had suggested but threatening all the same. These people sometimes had valuable intuitions, despite their charlatanry. It was the hot rod gang, of course. Just at an age of great difficulty, when a girl is about to make the most important decision of her life, whom to marry, Jackie had to get involved with irresponsible hoodlums. She was not as mature as her body would make one think. She needed protecting. Eleanor shivered once, herself in dread because of Jacqueline. What had the Countess meant, that

Eleanor's own trouble had to do with one who was not so young as she thought? Peter Hazen? She thought he was as old as he was, around thirty, and besides, what real threat was he to anyone? Jefferson? Absurd. Jacqueline? She knew exactly how old she was. Who should know better than a child's own mother? "But your life-line is strong." How did that come into it?

When they reentered the room, Eleanor leaped up from her chair, thanked them almost in a panic of politeness, and ran out the door.

Hazen was on the walk coming in.

"Hi, Eleanor," he said. He seemed so boyish.

"Peter," she said. She was confused by the complexity of things. "How long have you known Pearl?"

"Oh, six or seven years. Why?"

"It seems so extraordinary."

"Is that so?" he said, and she thought he looked slightly uneasy. "Well, I'll be seeing you around."

She saw him poke his head in the door and call out "Pearl?" She heard her cry, "Lover boy! Come on in." "Hi, Countess," he said familiarly, and the Countess cried, "Pierre!" Just before the door closed Eleanor heard the smack of one of Pearl's voluminous kisses. She did not know which of their laughs rang most falsely.

She was embarrassed that her eyes were streaming with the tears of confusion. She knew from long experience that when oppressed by a mood like this it would be better for her to tire herself physically; therefore she began climbing the fire escape the ten flights up to her floor, oppressed, but not feeling much. There was nothing but looking out the windows to relieve the tedium of the climb, and she was inured to this view by now. These were wholly efficient steps, handrail, walls, glass, doors. Nothing in the making of this building had been put there because it was delightful but only, as in a honeycomb, because it served its purpose well. Suddenly she heard footsteps. Behind her came, springing two steps at a time, easily and regularly, in shorts and tennis shoes, a tanned young man who lived on the thirteenth floor and ran up the building at least once a day; she had once seen him plodding up with a fifty-pound sack of wheat germ on his shoulder; he worshipped health, not himself healthy, but Health. She loathed his idolatry, but all the same, after he had smoothly gone by without even glancing at her, she was ruefully aware of her puffing and her tired leg muscles. Then, on the ninth floor landing, his wife joined her, saying apologetically, "I got to stop every third floor and count fifty. The pulse isn't so steady since the baby." This did it: *the pulse* isn't so steady. In a fury Eleanor raced up to her floor, ran down the wholly efficient, wholly oppressive hallway, into her empty apartment, and threw herself across the bed. She was ashamed of herself for having listened to that atrocious little Countess, she was accomplishing nothing in her life, she did not know what connection Hazen had with Pearl, but she doubted that it was honorable, she was getting old, she hated her abusers, there was no health in her. She bit the covers, for the regions of her fantasy were wholly governed for the time being by that proconsul of confusion, wrath.

Seven

The semester Hazen had been deepest and most hopelessly in love with Eleanor, he had gone with his roommate to a party to raise money for Spanish refugees, drunk whiskey for the first time, and found himself on the back porch kissed by and kissing the girl who sat next to him in History 20 A. Next day in class he had felt honor-bound to ask her, who kept smiling at him, to go to a movie with him that night; she was a plump, good-humored girl who was as ready to fall in love as not; they necked and necked. But he was thrown into a great turmoil, for though he was dismayed that he could betray so agreeably his pure, austere love for Eleanor, yet he necked avidly with this jolly girl whom he did not love. For two weeks the turmoil endured, and then, the night before they had to go to their separate homes for the summer's work, the two of them gave each other, very clumsily, their virginities in the back seat of a borrowed car; and next morning at the bus station he told her that he loved her. (Yet when she did not return to school next fall he never went hunting her.) One result of this was that he threw God out the window, as perpetrator not only of sermons, Sunday schools, and Presbyterian hymns, but also of lies about the sweet putting off of clothes. Another result was that, while he remained shy about making overtures to a woman, yet once he had kissed her and she had accepted his kiss—as well be hanged for a sheep as a lamb—he was all for getting right into bed, for he could never be sure that he was in love.

Sociology had not helped him, science had not helped him. Not that he had ever asked them to; rather he had avoided things like the Kinsey Report or manuals of sexual instruction; yet his faith was in science. What he believed of all this, in arguments at least, depended on which side his opponent was on, for like a drunken Irishman he was likely to take the other side. His faith was that analysis and correct description is the only secure way to see the world and furthermore that everything could be analyzed and correctly described if we only knew how; but his experience was that love is beyond analysis, so far beyond it that he scarcely approved of analyzing even the physics of love. It was only occasionally, of course, that this faith and this contrary experience interfered with each other; believing in them both is like believing in God's omnipotent goodness and also in Adam's fall, perfectly easy till they're put together. He was no theologian to wiggle off the horns of dilemma; he refused to deny the importance of his faith and he refused to deny the truth of his experience; he had become a practising cynic, a sentimental idealist, and one who asks other people questions about their secret ways. He was sure of his love for only one woman, Eleanor, and that had obviously been puppy love of some sort. He had never got married, or even near it. He was sufficiently attractive so that a fair number of women had gone to bed with him, yet enough of the feeling of sacredness clung to love so that on the one hand he had always felt more or less affection for each of those women and on the other distrusted her for being in bed with him at all.

50

"I'm getting cold," said Jackie, pulling her jacket back up over her shoulders.

"No wonder, baby. You're sitting up there without any protection from the air." She had arranged herself with her back against the steering wheel. "Come on, I'll make a pillow for your head on the seat and you'll be warmer if you lie down."

"Too cramped, Hazie. You'd have to be a contortionist to drape yourself around the wheel and the gearshift and still get at me. I've been through all this before."

"At least you can twist around so you're leaning back against me."

"OK. It's restful." She moved. "You're comfortable, Hazie. —Get out of there."

"Why?"

"Next time we go out, let's go in your convert."

"Why?"

"Because it's so wide, stupid. It's a real rapemobile.—Can't you stay out of there?" She was cross.

"What's the difference?"

"Nothing goes below the belt."

"Little Miss Morality."

"It isn't a question of morality. It's just that I don't like hands in my pants."

"Take your pants off then."

He half expected her to blow up, jab him with her elbow, or even sit apart from him. But all she did was say "Nope" in a calm voice, the voice of one who will listen you out, all night if you insist, and repeat the Nope in exactly the same tone.

For awhile they sat without moving, watching the lights over the misty Bay. Hazen was at peace in a strange way: tired, but soon to be refreshed; drowsy, but conscious; enjoying everything his senses gave him, even the faint odor of gasoline and the slight backache from the awkward position he was in; neither in love nor not in love, just necking with the girl next door on a Sunday night. He wondered dimly that a mature man not used to such prolonged frustration as necking involved should all the same be enjoying himself without any feeling of frustration. The important thing was to keep it up as long as it would last.

He heard her laugh softly and voluptuously. "What is it?" he asked her.

"I was just thinking," she said, her voice a little rough, deeper than usual, a woman's, "the way Mother would jump if she knew what we're doing."

"Doesn't she like you to go out with boys?"

"Sure."

"Well," he said, and began gently to fondle her again, "what does she expect to happen?"

"You're not a boy," she said, and her fingers ran over the stubble of his beard. "Besides, you're different."

"From what?"

"Other people. At least she thinks so."

"Don't you?" She wriggled a little against him. "She's very special too," he said. He brushed his face lightly in her hair. "Sometimes I think of Eleanor as a cactus."

"What?" she said.

"Sure, a cactus. A saguaro cactus."

She twisted around indignantly. "My mother is not in any way like a cactus."

"She is, the way I think of her. Saguaros are solitary and stand out splendidly from everything else, and they're thorny, but if you're perishing of thirst you can get water from them. Birds nest in them sometimes. They endure through the worst difficulties. They are the most striking things I ever saw in the desert."

"Well," said Jacqueline, and settled down again, "so long as you like them."

She guided his hand to her belly and put her head back so that they might begin kissing again.

"Furthermore," he said, his lips at the lobe of her ear, "a saguaro doesn't bloom for long but when it does you never saw anything more beautiful in your life."

"Don't you go getting ideas about her," she said.

"Getting ideas?"

"You know what I mean. Don't play dumb."

"What made you think such a thing?" He tried to kiss her again.

"Just don't," she said, eluding his lips. "I think I'd die if you did." She was serious.

"Baby, what kind of a guy do you think I am?"

"I don't know," she said, head bent from him. Suddenly she put her hands over his so that they pressed her body hard.

"Why would it be *that* important anyway?" he asked.

Instead of answering she turned, facing him, and kissed him with more than sensual pleasure, pressing her bosom against his, rocking his head between her hands. She held him off a little and searched his face intently. Then she smiled. "Dope," she said. "Come on, it's time to go home." She arranged her clothes and snuggled, a girl by a guy, in her riding position beside him. "Don't always bring Mother into the conversation."

He had forgotten, in his blur of feeling, that it was she who had introduced the subject. "OK, I won't," he said. And they shook hands on it.

They spoke only once on the way home. At a stop sign they heard from a car crossing their way a pure whore-cry, a cry of false ecstasy, as indecent and chilling as the nudity of a beautiful corpse. Jacqueline rolled her window down and returned the cry.

"My God!" said Hazen shocked. "What did you do that for?"

"That's one of the girls," she answered. "It just means we've been having some fun."

"But that's a terrible noise for a girl to make."

"Is it?" she said. "So they say."

Yet when he let her out in front of Tower #6, for she wanted to go up separately in case one of her parents should see her, she kissed the tip of one of his fingers and looked at him oddly and ran off without a word, as though she were shy.

As he lay in bed reflecting a little on the evening before going to sleep, he decided that he would doubtless dream during the night, since dreams fulfill wishes, of lying with Jacqueline or perhaps with some other woman who would be a dream disguise for her—surely love-making would fulfill his most immediate and powerful wish. He recognized that he did not *feel* this wish, but he knew by biological inference that he must wish it. Frustration is frustration.

Yet in fact he dreamt about his Major in the Engineer Corps, an unhappy, taciturn, inflexible man who had shamed his men to their dangerous task. For if dangerous acts steadfastly performed was the shell of a part of the truth about Hazen, in it, still alive, was the shame of seeming a coward. That shame was why there had been no boasting in his voice when he had told Jacqueline of his dangerous acts; it was also why he had neither fled from John Henry's bullying nor accepted his challenge. It was also why he hoped he would never have to run a chicken, for he might not be able to turn his car aside at the last moment, even against a John Henry.

In the morning, thinking of the confused dream he had had and the simple one he had failed to have, he did not suspect that he had not dreamt of taking Jacqueline to bed for the good reason that in some profound way he did not want to. Instead, remembering her charm and her sensuousness, he set to imagining the first time he would bed her naked and hot in his arms; but he got no farther than the cataloguing, as though he were doing research.

Eight

Eleanor was never more happy than when she had a necessary task to accomplish that would occupy all her time. The efficiency of Parktilden had given her, for over a year, swatches of free time with which to do what she would. This freedom had put a great strain on her, for though she had formerly found it bad enough to be reading a novel when she ought to be waxing the floors or pruning the roses, she now found it worse on her spirits to be reading a novel when there was nothing around the house to do at all.

She wished she could work with the Friends, whose dogged

charity saw always the hungry man inside the skin, the person beneath the coat of many slogans; but her scruples forbade her working as a Friend because she did not believe in the uniqueness of Christ. Both Jefferson and her mother were unabashed in cultivating their leisure as they wished, and in point of fact she did much the same sort of thing as they; but her mother was old, having raised five children in strait circumstances, and Jefferson did his work in the world day by day, whereas she did not do much and could have done more. She worked very efficiently when the task was clear before her; it was only in gaps of frantic sloth that she could spend a morning from breakfast till lunch washing the dishes or stand for two hours reading old newspapers, ads and all. This leisure, this measurable gift of freedom, this Parktilden time of her own, had not been good for her, for the self which she knew how to esteem never ached more for the harmonies of art than when she was addressing the thousandth envelope for some worthy appeal, and the beat majority of mankind held out their hands to her never more gauntly than the night she had drunk French wine for dinner and gone to an opera.

"Mama, what are you knitting?"

"Some woolen stockings for Jackie, love."

"Why don't you make her a muffler instead, Mama? The girls just wear nylons nowadays."

"You mean feet don't get cold in New York in the winters? Ellie, what are you trying to tell me?"

"Sure it gets cold, but you practically never see girls in wool stockings."

"Really? Land's sakes, I can't just throw all this work away. What shall I do?"

"A muffler, Mama, she needs a muffler."

The old woman took off her spectacles and held her head in her hands. "So much work too. And I asked her, Ellie, I asked her first and she said they'd be fine."

"Did she honestly say so?"

"Why would I lie to you? But maybe she was just talking nice to me and she'd never have worn them after I'd gone to so much trouble and work. Do you think so, Ellie?"

"No, Mama, I believe her. She's a sensible girl."

"And honest. She never lies to me."

"I was just afraid she'd be too modern to wear them."

Mama put her glasses back on. "I read in a magazine that the winters are supposed to be getting warmer than they used to be. Foolishness. Ask Jefferson about it. As though the winters could ever be anything but cold in Pennsylvania. It's just this blessed California climate. People try to forget the cold. But you need wool on your feet in the winters. I remember."

"She hasn't come out yet this morning, has she?"

"No, she's still asleep, I guess. She comes in so late at night. It troubles me. Still, she doesn't look peaked. Maybe they'll make her go to bed earlier at that music school in New York. Ellie, be sure to get her a good safe place to live."

"I will, Mama, I will, don't worry."

"She means the world and all to me, love."

"To me too, you may be sure."

"She's so happy these days, Ellie. Last night when she came in I was awake and she made me some coffee and sat on my bed beside me talking for half an hour. We haven't talked so for months."

Eleanor kissed her and hugged her, then knocked at the bedroom door (Mama slept in the living room). There was for answer the click of the lock's being unsnibbed. "You're awake, Jackie?"

Jacqueline in a short nightgown was sprawled on her stomach across the bed, a pen in hand and a writing pad open before her. "Hi, Mom."

"Writing a letter?"

"Yeh, to Floyd."

"How thoughtful, dear."

"I got to find out what to do with the Ford." She started to get up but flopped back down with a groan.

"What's the matter?" asked Eleanor anxiously. "Where do you have a pain?"

"I guess I wrenched my back yesterday. It's just stiff, that's all."

"I'll rub it for you."

"Golly, thanks."

"You'd better get up pretty soon. You have a dental appointment at 1:30, and I thought we could go on over to San Francisco afterwards and shop for luggage."

"Hazie said I could borrow his suitcases. If I go, Mom."

"That's awfully nice of him. Are you sure it's all right with him?"

"Positive. *If* I go."

"Of course, dear, if you go. Don't you hope it works out?"

"Sure. But sometimes I get the feeling you're giving me the bum's rush."

"What?"

"Ever since you got this idea last weekend you've been bulldozing everything through in the worst way." She glanced back at Eleanor, who was half kneeling beside her on the bed, and patted her. "It's nice of you to care so much." She shoved her writing pad aside and gave herself over to the pleasure of being rubbed. "Even Hazie can't massage as good as you can," she murmured. After that she only sighed and squirmed gratefully from time to time.

Eleanor was pleased by the compliment and yet felt a little uneasy at the thought that Jacqueline had allowed Hazen to massage her like this. She did not know what such familiarity implied, and felt vaguely deficient as a mother that she lacked the authority to inquire further and give stern counsel. She knew as well as common sense and Jefferson's words could tell her that Jacqueline was old enough to be nearly independent of her now, but she did not in the least feel it, for if they her parents had given her (as they ought to have done) everything she wanted and needed, what use would she have had for independence? The notion was silly, of course. She knew her silliness. It had been to combat just such silliness that she was now insisting on Jacqueline's going away to school. Very well.

Her eye was caught by a page of the letter Jacqueline had been writing; it had fluttered out of the pad onto the counterpane; by craning her neck she could read it. "I oughtn't," she told herself, "but after all, Floyd's in the family."

". . . hard to figure out. For instance he didn't know the first thing about intake rocker arms but he talked about clutches as if he had been a mechanic; of course I never saw him dissemble a clutch. Anyhow when I explained about them he got a set of barker hi lifts for Henry. He's *loaded*. He decided he wanted a motorbike so I told him about Jack and Jill's Harley-Davison. Jill's going to have her baby at Christmas and it's high time they grew up and got a family car. As they know too. But they *love* that Harley, especially Jill. Well, he looks at it and takes it around the block doing all right in the saddle. Then he offers $475, which is not a bad estimate either. I already tipped them off so they worked him up to $500, but he got them to throw in Jack's steel shoes since they just fit him. What I'm getting at is this—if I go to New York the way Mother wants me to and that ghoul of Pearl's says I should and I'd just as soon, he will want me to sell Henry to him. *Should I?* I don't want to *take* him, but do you need the dough? I don't."

Eleanor glowed with pleasure after she had read this page; her suspicions were confirmed that the car, the Countess, Hazen, and Floyd were threats of one kind or another to Jacqueline, yet none of them grave threats; furthermore, happily all this would be cleared up by Jacqueline's going away and developing her finest talent, music; best of all, Jacqueline wanted to.

"Come on, darling," she said cheerily, standing up. "I've got some waffle batter waiting and I'll slice some strawberry peaches and make fresh coffee. You've got to get to the dentist and we must talk over what else you can accomplish this afternoon."

"Mom," she said, rolling languidly onto her right side, "I'm not going to do one other thing this afternoon except go to the dentist. You act like we haven't got a minute to lose."

"How's your back now, dear?"

"Swell. Thanks a lot."

"Well, you can practice."

"All right, I'll practice, but leave me alone."

"Tonight there's—"

"Mom!"

"I was just saying, dear, Daddy's getting tickets to the Pro Musica Antiqua concert tonight if it's not too late. Wouldn't you like to go? You enjoyed them so much last time."

Jacqueline seemed to debate something with herself, but presently she stood up and said quite gaily, "Sure, Mom, I'd love to. Slice those peaches fast."

Eleanor closed the door behind her and went over to her mother before she left. "Do you want a waffle, Mama?"

"What, dear?" said the old woman, ready to be alarmed. She nearly always started when her mind was returned abruptly from those peopled lanes where it wandered in peace, in a twilight Pennsylvania where a village was a church and some houses, whose inhabitants rode (when they rode) on horseback and cooked on wood stoves. "What did you say?"

"A waffle, Mama?"

She smiled, easily and completely. "No, thanks, Ellie. Not now. Later maybe? A quarter waffle? Even a half? You're so thoughtful of me, love. But later."

Eleanor hummed as she worked. She put on water for the coffee, she plugged in the waffle iron to heat up, she peeled and sliced the peaches, sprinkled sugar over them, and set them out with a pitcher of cream, she laid the table with yellow napkins, and she couldn't have been happier. She was doing what she ought to be doing, she had no doubt it was the right thing to be doing, and she performed better than her best, like a runner with the weights taken off his feet.

Jacqueline came in soon enough, hungry. She was wearing only shorts and a white tee-shirt.

"My dear," said Eleanor without reflecting whether she should say anything about it, "you aren't properly dressed."

"Why not? It's hot."

"Go put your clothes on, Jacqueline."

"Oh my gosh, here we are living on a desert island practically. We don't even have any delivery men come and nobody ever just drops by. Anyway no man."

"You go through the hall. That's public."

"You mean I might shock Mr. Erskine?"

"And there's Peter Hazen."

"Oh Hazie," said Jacqueline in the adolescent tones of exasperation. She flung herself out of the room.

"She's just a girl," thought Eleanor; "all the same, if she's going to be alone in a big city she must realize the effect she might have on some men." The waffle was ready; she opened the door to call Jacqueline, but there she was coming out of Hazen's doorway leading him by the hand and laughing. She had, manifestly, put on under the thin shirt a black nylon brassière, low and lace. "Only a girl; she hasn't any idea how provocative she has made herself look."

Hazen was expansive and, as always, good-humored. She had never seen him much out of temper, rather quiet sometimes but never fogging others up with his gloom if he felt it. He was amusing them—doodling as he talked—with stories of how some graduate students at Columbia had gone about their research work: one of them spoke of the people he interviewed as though they were stocked with many cans, to get into which he used straightforward can-opener questions like "What pet names do you have for your wife?" or "Would you divorce your wife if she went insane?"; another was nicknamed Mousetrap because his questions couldn't catch anything bigger than mice but were all traps, so that he'd ask you to talk about why you preferred baseball to basketball when what he really was after was how you gestured with your hands. He himself, Hazen said with a certain air, putting a flourish on his doodle figure, tried to use less crude methods—empathy, identification, something subtle.

"For example," he went on, abandoning the doodle, "in matters of taste, it's not just what the subject says that counts, it's the way he says it. You simply cannot quantify qualitative responses in the usual way. So look what Sandy worked out—the professor I worked under." He fetched a sheet of music paper from the next room. "Suppose I ask an East Side kid whether he likes *Blondie*. He says, 'Oh, it's all right.' See what I record?" He entered four quarter notes in a straight descent from F to B. "So I ask him about *Little Lulu*. 'She's OK.'" He entered two eighth notes slurring from G up to A, and two quarter notes on G. "Then I get to *Lil Abner*. 'I *like* him.'" He entered a quarter note on higher C, a half note on the top line of the staff, and a quarter on D. "You get it? The duration of the note is the duration of the word, more or less, but the musical pitch is replaced by emphasis. The top is favorable, the bottom unfavorable. It's just like musical notation really: the quantification of quality. We can turn these notes into numbers and enter them on a graph easy as pie. It's smooth, it's technique, it's beautiful."

Eleanor saw reflected in the glass of the table top a smile on Jacqueline's lips, and she herself had to transform the smile she could not repress into a part of a question.

"How is your research in hot rods coming?"

"Slowly," he said. "I'll know more tonight."

"They don't believe," said Jacqueline to her indignantly, "he made up Stoodley."

"Oh?"

"They don't," she repeated. "So last week they made him tell what was going to happen to Stoodley next, and if it happened in the funny papers this week, then they'd believe him."

"Who are *they?*" asked Eleanor.

"The gang."

"What difference does Stoodley make to the hot rods?" She caught a smile on Hazen's face and a quick frown of reproof on Jacqueline's, and felt a pang of distress to think they were more intimate with each other than either was with her.

"Oh, Mother."

"They'll be more likely," said Hazen, looking at Jacqueline, "to treat me like an equal if they think I'm not a highbrow."

"That red car of yours," said Eleanor, wondering uneasily what was going on between them, "is pretty toney, isn't it?"

"Yes," he said warmly and leaned forward to explain to her. "If they'll OK me I'll buy a motorcycle I've found out about and then it'll be easier for me to sort of merge with the others and see what's what empathically so to speak."

She burst out laughing and he looked bewildered. "You're so silly," she said and patted his hand affectionately. She puffed her cheeks out. "You pretend—pff, pff—you want to study these things —musical notation, pff, pff—quantification, when what you really want is to ride around fast like anybody else."

He stammered and blushed, and Jacqueline joined her in

laughing at him. Eleanor decided it had been only a hot-rod gang secret they had glanced at each other about. She was very fond of him. She was glad that Jacqueline and he were good pals, positively glad of it. He would be a steadying influence. And then Jacqueline, with an impulse of tenderness which Eleanor loved to see in her, controlled her laughter and said to Hazen in a consoling voice, in which all the same a trace of humor loitered, "Don't take it to heart, Hazie."

"Oh sure," he said and smiled a bit painfully.

Jacqueline twisted his paper around so that she and Eleanor could see it. He had drawn a sort of huge praying mantis of a creature cocking his head down at a rodent with human eyes.

"Hazie!" she cried. "Whatever are you going to do with Stoodley now? Send him to Mars or something?"

"Oh, no," he said deprecatingly.

"Come on," said Jacqueline quite warmly. She punched him gently in the ribs. "Open up. We're sorry."

"Open up?" he said, it seemed to Eleanor disingenuously. "What are you talking about?"

"Tell us what you're drawing this for. Be friends."

"Oh, I've been playing around to see if I could do something for the cover of a science-fiction mag. I met an editor the other day. He said they could use humorous, imaginative stuff."

"Well, all right. Just so long as Stoodley doesn't suffer. You know, Hazie, you know."

They laughed and Eleanor joined them, forgiven by Jacqueline's intercession.

"Good luck tonight," she said to him sincerely. Jacqueline stood up to go. "We'll have an early dinner, dear. The concert is at 8:15."

"You can't come with me?" he said to Jacqueline plaintively.

"No. Sorry."

"What time's the concert over?"

"About half past ten, I suppose."

"That's not too late," he said. "I'll meet you at Sather Gate."

"OK," she answered happily, "if you want to. I'll get my jeans and sweater out for you to bring along."

"Where will you change?" asked Eleanor.

"Oh, in the back seat. He can put the top up."

They were so open. They held nothing back just because she was there. She was old-fashioned, which was why they seemed too free and easy to her. But Jacqueline was safe with him; not once, during breakfast, had she seen his eyes drop to Jacqueline's bosom. She told herself again that this was a friendship she liked to see.

"Peter!" she called, bursting into his apartment. "They've accepted her! It's all settled!"

"Fine," he said. "I'm glad it's worked out the way you wanted." He was stretched out on the floor. "Did the mail come so late?"

"Special delivery airmail. See?" She knelt down beside him to show him the letter from Juilliard; he half reared and looked at it. "Isn't it splendid?" She put her arm across his shoulder in her excitement and only then realized he had nothing on but swimming trunks. "What are you doing on the floor?" she said.

"Writing outlines for lectures. It's cooler here."

"Well," she said standing up, "we must have a party." She was flustered when he rolled over on his back spread-eagle and stared up at her; his body was strong and angular as a man's should be and his glistening yellow trunks pronounced his virility like a jeweled codpiece, yet his posture and expression struck her as curiously feminine. "A farewell party the night before she leaves."

"When will she leave?"

"I haven't decided yet. We must find a place for her to stay. Peter, don't tell Pearl about this yet, if you see her. She'll want to take over."

"You are very excited, aren't you?"

This small thrust of intimacy—the tone of his voice, the personal directness of his question, his hand firmly squeezing her ankle for a moment—pleased her, yet startled her a little so that she stepped back. "Yes, yes, of course I am. Aren't you?" She went to the telephone and began dialing.

"How could I be?"

"Are you sorry Jackie is going away?" she said. She continued intently dialing, for she had not meant to ask this question, certainly not so bluntly.

"Of course," he said, and she felt relieved, for she would not have credited any magnanimous statement of how glad he was for this opportunity and so on. "I've got to make the most of the time before she leaves," he added, "so that she'll give me all the help she can in my work."

Eleanor asked for Jefferson. While she was waiting she heard Hazen say, half to himself, "I may be able to get Dr. Edwards to put her up in exchange for child-care," and she shivered a little with joy: these were the sentiments and tones of a mature man, one of her own generation, concerned for a child he was fond of; she could rely on him.

She told Jefferson the news and he told her he had news of his own. "Peter!" she cried when she heard it. "Oh Peter! He has to be back in New York the day after Labor Day, at a conference. He can take her there, Peter, and get her all settled. Darling," she said to the phone, "I am so happy that things are working out. Aren't you?" Hazen was still lying stretched out, one arm in the sunlight, his head turned toward her; the tendon on the upper side of his neck seemed to her strong and perfectly proportioned. "Come home early for dinner. Jackie doesn't know anything yet. She'll be all set up. Good-bye."

"Is Jefferson elated?"

"Oh, I wouldn't say elated exactly. You know." But then she realized he was not being serious. She chewed at a hangnail for a moment. "Who're you making fun of?"

"*You* are pretty elated for a mother whose only child is about to move away from home."

But she looked beneath this question before trying to surround herself with her usual defense of splutters. "Don't look at me so coldly."

"I'm being judgmental," he said.

"Judgmental? That's cant. I thought you were dropping cant."

"No, I've set Thursday afternoons aside for an orgy of jargon. I'm looking at all three of you Devereux coolly and judgmentally."

"Well, don't." She was annoyed by his banter, and if he meant any of what he was saying she would be offended. But she was

64

determined to be happy this day. "The most we can have to the party is fifteen people or so."

"Room?" he asked in a serious voice; he made a little beckoning gesture with his hand.

She nodded and went over to stand beside him. "Do I have to have Pearl?" she asked herself and then answered, "Yes."

"She won't do anything terrible."

"How do you know?"

"I've known her for years."

"Where *did* you meet her?"

"In Paris. I chauffeured her one summer. Who else is coming?"

"Well, there are the Ramseys. We really ought to have them; they're her godparents, in a way."

His hand was idly caressing her calf. "Am I invited?"

"Don't be absurd. Of course. I'm just trying to think of the people we *have* to have."

"Why don't you let Jackie decide?" he asked very mildly. She glanced at his eyes to see if he were reproving her or laughing at her, but his face was bland. Yet his eyes looked into hers intensely. Then, as he spoke again, his hand sensually but not quite lasciviously slid up her leg and pressed the back of her knee warmly. "After all, you're separate women by now, aren't you?"

She felt a very strong emotion of some sort; she knew she was enormously grateful to him for having said this; it seemed to her a revelation. "Of course," she said, "you're right, of course we are separate women. Thank you. Yes. I will." His arm fell back onto the rug in the sunlight.

She went to the door. "I must start dinner." When she opened it, she found Mr. Erskine passing down the hall. "Mr. Erskine!" she said impetuously, "Jacqueline is going to Juilliard School of Music. Isn't that fine?"

"Admirable," he replied, raising his hat. "Mrs. Devereux, you are fortunate in your daughter." She saw the puzzle in his eyes when he glanced at Hazen sprawled undressed on the floor behind her; he decided not to salute him. "Give her my congratulations until I can give them to her myself. Until then."

The touch of Hazen's hand on her leg persisted strongly in her memory, almost tangibly. If he had tried to kiss her, she would have been offended, or if he had been lascivious or crude. But his caress had been not at all surreptitious, but sensual, affectionate, forthright, yet less than an overture to love-making. She had thought she'd left sensuality behind her like a taste for Tchaikovsky and hot fudge sundaes, but she could not get his touch out of her mind. It was only her legs of her person that she had any vanity about; they were still womanly attractive, as she thought nothing else about her was; she was most vulnerable through her legs, and of course the back of the leg is delicate to the touch. All the same, if she had been lying in a sunsuit out on the lawn and he had come up and touched her so, it would have been only a friendly gesture. It was because she had been wearing a skirt and he had been naked that the sudden thrust meant more than it ought to have meant to her. He had done nothing else, said nothing. She was being silly.

She glared at the collie on the wall above the sink-board—a frequent butt of her ire—shook her head sternly, and locked her attention like a searchlight on her *real* cause of worry, Jacqueline.

Nine

When Jefferson came out of the concert hall with Eleanor and Jacqueline and stood on the steps a moment enjoying the full moon and the warm evening, united with them still by the music they had been hearing, he was prepared against Jacqueline's running off from them shouting "Good-bye folks!" and not coming home till goodness knows when. But no—impulsively Jacqueline reached her hands out to them and tugged them to come with her. "Walk over to Sather Gate with me," she said sweetly, "it's not very far." The red Buick was waiting, under one of the trees by Strawberry Creek. She skipped ahead, opened the door crying "Hi Hazie!" and dove into the back. Hazen got out and talked with them, and two minutes later Jacqueline came out again in her old clothes. "Here, Mom, would you take these home for me?" she asked, handing over the others. "Well, let's go, Hazie. Gosh, it's a lovely night out." While they were saying good night, she stood rolling her arms over and over inside the new turtle-neck jersey pullover she was wearing, so as to stretch it loose and baggy as was fashionable at that time. She jumped back into the car and made the white top fold back so they could ride out in the open. "Good-bye, Mom. Good-bye, Dad. Do you know what, Hazie?" she was saying as they drove off. "Dad said the tenor was as good as Gigli, in his way.—So long!" she cried and stood up on her knees to wave. "So long!" Jefferson squeezed Eleanor's arm with his as they walked over to the parking lot. "Dad said." He was her oracle still. And she was leaving.

He started the motor, and then sat back in his seat for a moment.

"She is so happy," said Eleanor. "I am so happy for her." She took his hand; he was staring straight ahead, at the Life Sciences Building. "Did you ever see her gayer or sweeter?"

"No," he said brusquely, a word of agreement in the tone of disagreement.

"Oh, honey," she said, "she enjoyed the concert so much, and she enjoys riding around with Peter Hazen, and wasn't it sweet the way she waved good-bye to us?"

"Sure." He was not speaking at all like himself, judicious and reserved; for him to agree with a "sure" like this was, he knew, more disquieting to her than for him to disagree in his usual manner.

"What's the matter, honey?"

"Nothing."

"Don't you like Peter?"

"Oh for heaven's sake," he said, betrayed into exasperation.

67

The thinness of his voice made him sound petulant, which added to his rage. He turned and glared at her. "You like him, don't you?"

"Yes."

"And obviously Jacqueline likes him?" She did not respond to this rhetorical question. But he repeated insistently, "Doesn't she?"

"Obviously."

He started driving home.

"Tell me," he said, no longer aggressive so much as curious, "are you conscious of any misbehavior on his part?"

"Peter's? Since he has moved in?"

"Yes. I'm not referring to the time in Nebraska when he was fatuous over you."

"Oh, Jefferson, he *never* misbehaved."

"I dare say not."

"He never said a word, and of course I didn't."

"To be sure."

And that was the first time they had ever spoken of Hazen's infatuation for her, and, he realized, probably the last time as well, unless Eleanor provoked the subject again sometime. He wondered why he had mentioned it at all; he must be even more upset than he was aware of feeling.

"No," she said slowly, "I am not conscious of any misbehavior on his part. Should I be?"

He made an impatient gesture. "Nor of any threat?"

"On Jacqueline?" she said instantly.

"Or on you or me or anybody."

"Jefferson, *what* are you driving at?"

"You asked me whether I liked Peter Hazen. I'm trying to make it clear to you that there isn't any good reason why I shouldn't."

His logic was so feeble that even she was not deceived by it. "And?"

"And anyway, as I have told you a thousand times, suppose I didn't like him, why should that affect *your* liking him? Have I tried to prevent your liking him?"

"Oh, Jefferson," she said with melancholy, "you never try to prevent me from doing anything."

"Then what made you ask me that question?"

"I don't know," she answered.

She sounded regretful that she had spoken, and surprised that he had taken her up on the matter. Yet he would not quit pestering her—indeed, got a certain perverse satisfaction in it.

"Are you sure you don't want me to dislike him?"

"Oh Jefferson, don't be so subtle. You're getting fantastic again. It's just that you haven't seemed very cordial with him."

"I've hardly had the opportunity to be cordial. He's so buried in his scholarly researches.—That's unjust of me. Actually, I learned something the other day that sent him up in my opinion."

"What's that?"

"He's sending an Italian boy who was crippled in the war to school, to study literature. Paying his way for him."

"Jefferson." She did not speak for a moment. "How did you discover this?"

"That Countess of Pearl's."

"How would she know?"

"She went to see the boy when she was in Florence last winter."

"My God. How splendid. How did he happen to choose one special boy?"

"You'll have to ask the Countess."

"Well, darling, you *do* like him then?"

After his moment of generosity, he was irritable again. "Jacqueline's going away from us, that's what matters, and I don't like it." He drew up at a traffic light.

"But Jefferson," she began.

He did not start, though the light turned green. "And the sweeter she is, like tonight, the less I want her to go. Don't you understand that?"

"Of course, darling," she said, in a voice that sounded almost relieved.

He tried to analyze his disturbance. He knew perfectly well that he did not much like Peter Hazen, but he certainly did not find him upsetting. It was Jacqueline's leaving, that was all there was to it. Not that he did not think she was right in going. She was free to make her own life; she should leave home; she was no longer a child. He was just being sentimental. Very well.

Eleanor rode beside him in silence, and took his arm in silence when they got out of the car. "Perhaps I shouldn't have encouraged her to go to Juilliard," she said. "Do you think I was wrong, dear?"

But it was as though the silent, windowless, gun-grey, metal elevator in which they were ascending the building should have stopped and opened its doors between floors onto the blank shaft wall: Jefferson did not believe in futile regret, or in the yet more futile talking over actions which one ought perhaps to regret.

"But she's going, that's the main thing," said Eleanor, making up. The elevator opened at their floor. "She will learn so much in New York."

"Of course she will," he said. He opened their door for her. "It's good for her to be getting away, it's good for her to be going to a good school, it's good for us to be getting along without her. Good, good, good. But I don't like it."

"Of course you don't, darling," she said in a warm, indulgent voice. "You go on to bed while I straighten up the kitchen. I won't be five minutes."

Well, he said to himself, when she thought about what she was doing she was a good old wife.

He lay with his hands under his head watching her prepare for bed.

"I know how you feel," she was saying, "but I can't help thinking of all the wealth of experience and training it will mean for Jackie."

"Sure," he said miserably. "Do you know what the Countess told me? That you want Jacqueline to go away." He had not intended to say that.

She was in her nightgown by the closet, stretching to hang up her slip. For a moment, arm extended, she froze. He watched her to see if she was going to plunge into consternation. Had he not accused her in the name of the Countess but directly, he would have hastened to repair the damage, or else to analyze for her in detail how she was doing what she was doing for reasons she did not suspect; and her hidden motives, what Jefferson thought them to be and she usually agreed to, rarely pleased her to look at, even when he exposed them to her dispassionately or regretfully. But the Countess turned over every log she saw, voracious for the grubs to be found under it; she was disgusting and malicious; he did not think Eleanor would be too upset. He did not say anything more.

"Of course I do," she said. "For Jackie's sake I do."

"No, for your own sake."

She turned on him, angry both at his repeating the Countess and also, as he recognized from long experience, at being asked to doubt her motives. "Jefferson, do you believe that?"

"Oh, I don't know."

"Do you believe that I do not love Jacqueline? That's what it would mean, you know."

"No, my dear, I don't believe that."

"That Countess is a vile creature. I regret that we ever came to know her. Why were you talking to her anyhow?"

"Why," he said, not fighting well, "you wanted me to get Pearl out of the arrangements for Jacqueline."

"Oh." She slowed down. "Thanks, darling. It was stupid of me to involve Pearl in Jackie's affairs."

"No harm done. But the Countess is shrewd."

"How does she earn her living?"

"Off the superstitions of the rich, I suppose. She used to have a radio program in New York."

"How can you put up with all that claptrap about the zodiac and palmistry and so on? I thought you were a rational man."

"I try to be." He felt curiously subdued. "Reason doesn't work all the time. I don't think she's a total fraud."

"Peter Hazen goes to see them. Jacqueline goes to see them. You go."

"And it was you, Eleanor, that got them in the whole New York business."

"So it was." She stopped this time. "Why?"

"She talks about important things."

"Do you believe the stars have anything to do with how people get along?"

"About as much as tables of statistics. But something does."

"Oh, Jefferson."

"Well, I suppose you believe in statistics?"

"I don't understand them."

"Nor do you understand astrology."

"You're just trying to confuse me. You told me yourself no one could describe electrons without statistics."

"What matters, my dear—electrons or Jacqueline?"

His voice was controlled; it was only after a moment, seeing her delve into this statement, that he contemplated this odd alternative he had posed her and perceived the appalling doubt concealed in his question. He closed his eyes. He felt Eleanor sit on the bed beside him. He hoped she would not touch him, but when she held his hand on her lap, he was grateful to her.

"They're both important, dear, in different ways."

"Oh yes," he said, "oh yes, very different ways."

She ignored his irony. "Everything is part of the plan."

"The plan?" he asked, befuddled from inattention.

"God's plan."

"There are no electrons in heaven."

"Look," she said sternly, "here we are alive, that's the main thing. There are plenty of electrons around here and let's drop the subject."

He obeyed her. She raised the blind so that they might be lying in the full moonlight.

"Don't," he said. "It's too bright."

"It'll be just for half an hour or so," she answered and got into bed. "It won't be long till the shadow moves down." She took his hand; they lay watching the moon for a while. "Do you think," she went on in her most loving voice, "that Jackie will ever be really first-rate as a musician?"

"No," he said with an upsurge of unhappiness, "and good lord, what fun will the Friday night sessions be without her?" He meant much more than he was saying now; he hoped she could guess how much more. By her silence he guessed she did.

When the moon-shadow had slid down to their waists, they kissed good night and settled down to sleep.

"I only pray," she said, "that this experience may be good for her."

It was a long time till he spoke. "Do you really pray?" he asked sincerely, quietly.

"Sometimes." She looked over her shoulder at him.

"You believe in the sort of God one can pray to?"

"Yes. Don't you?" He rolled his head slowly on the pillow. "I'm sorry," she whispered. He sighed.

This evening reminded him of two other occasions in their life together, occasions when they had lain awake and talked, as close as they could be. One had been a night a month after the death by meningitis of their first child, a son of four. The other had been the evening of the day in 1945 on which Hiroshima had been destroyed by the atomic bomb. On those occasions he had tried to talk to her about chance and will, not about chance as formulas and graphs can deal with it or about the will of a solitary mortal's moral choosing, but about what chance itself was, whether it could be seen as anything other than chance, and about what will itself was, whether it meant anything to say we could choose. Eleanor had treated him as though he were suffering from the chills and fever of doubt, reassured him as she could, and told him she trusted him. He, who knew so much, quailed when he was caught by blasts from the unknown, as she never did, and doubt which she bore like a stiffness in the joints laid him low when it hit. Of course, they were not really losing Jacqueline, and even if she should, as she well might, be going off and marrying someone so far away they would hardly ever see her, still they would not properly have lost anything, for she was no longer, as he himself had said, theirs; and besides, unless she should (most improbably) move out of the country, they would not really lose her even when she married. At the moment he could think of only one good element in her having to leave—she wouldn't be around Hazen any longer. With this spurt of pleasing malice, he turned over and started toward sleep.

Ten

Hazen was relieved when the Devereux took Mama and Jackie
up to Echo Lake for a three-week vacation in August, and though
they invited him to come visit them for a couple of days—there
were plenty of beds in the cabin they were renting—he did not go.
He finished outlining the lectures for one course and got the other
in order, he became proficient at riding the motorcycle he'd bought,
through the Countess he made the acquaintance of a beautiful
dancer whom he took out to dinner for future reference, he consulted with the head of his department about matters of procedure,
he read as he had resolved to do every month a book of poetry. It
was a time of emotional calm for which he was grateful. The first
thing he became sure of, and he was glad of it, was that he was not
in love with Jacqueline: he supported her absence with equanimity,
and when he thought of the running around together they had
done, he looked forward to her return as fun; he thought of her
going to New York, because Eleanor talked of it so, as a fine opportunity. He was pleased that he had such attitudes about her,
for they corresponded to obvious common sense; he had no business getting involved with a girl so young, and he had no business
allowing her to be in doubt about his intentions. Jefferson he was
never comfortable with, as he had never been able to feel comfortable, though they tried to help him to it, with former professors
whom he respected. But with Eleanor he was wholly comfortable;
she was like a dear relative who had always been around, whose
scoldings and anger he ducked from but whose steadfastness he
never doubted. She was not beautiful, certainly not—big nose,
bumpy complexion, too thick in the waist, though she moved
gracefully and her legs were good—but he thought of her with that

warmth which does not so much try to turn imperfections like hers into beauties as to make them unnoticeable, like the worn rugs of home, things one is not grateful to be reminded of.

The most important thing he did during their absence was to drop by Iggy's Igloo every two or three days and hang around for a few hours. He did not try to obtrude himself into any group that came in, but was always ready to talk with anyone who wanted to. They did not invite him to come with them on their excursions: Jackie had not offered her car to him, and his Buick was not with it. John Henry would see him at his table drawing, and say, "How's tricks, Prof? Heh heh." Three or four of them would watch him make Stoodley strips with a sort of hang-jaw incredulity; he always turned aside their questions and comments with good-natured wisecracks, and when he was ready to talk, he put his papers and pencils into a folder. He knew, and resented, that it was Stoodley that made them tolerate him at all, so he resolved not to let them have anything to do with it whatever. Instead, he introduced Stoodley into a group of whacky motorcyclists, and caricatured some of John Henry's gang in the strips. Since the strips wouldn't be out for another six weeks, he would not much care if the gang took offense at his caricatures, for he would have already got from them most of what he wanted. In Stoodley's world, everyone had big noses, pot bellies, and bristly hair, there was no sex, no aging, and no death, the damage done by violence was not permanent, and Stoodley himself was well-intentioned, full of curiosity, and always misunderstanding what people meant. Jackie had once called him a deaf anthropologist with a defective hearing aid. Hazen felt rather like that himself sometimes, listening in to conversations in the Igloo. He understood Iggy, a sad little refugee of fifty or more, better than these Americans only five or ten years younger than himself.

They returned a week before Labor Day, full of arrangements to make. During that week Jefferson scarcely left the apartment, the workroom indeed, but wandered from his loom to the desk (where he was writing a paper on Wittgenstein to be read in New York at the annual meeting of international mathematicians), occasionally pausing to play part of a Handel sonata or a folksong on his oboe. He suggested to Hazen one afternoon, when Eleanor was darting in and out of the workroom to sew for Jacqueline, that they play a game of chess in Hazen's apartment where life was peaceful, and Hazen observed, with a certain admiration, that during the hour they were playing Eleanor called three times on Jefferson to make decisions—a hem length, whether to pack tennis shoes, how they should send the portable typewriter—and that each time he unfolded his opinion immediately and paid no attention to the objections of Eleanor's which clung to it like lint. For that matter, neither did she. Eleanor was in so energetic a state that Hazen and Jacqueline, partly to avoid running her errands and speculating endlessly with her about whatever, went out every evening but Friday. Hazen let Jacqueline take his motorcycle over the handicap run which motorcyclists had informally made for themselves in the hills back of Oakland, but it was too heavy a machine for her to do her best on. She let him double the measured mile that Saturday night in Richmond, but he was not quite sure enough of Floyd's hot rod to make it do its best; also, though he had been accepted by John Henry on suspicion and hence wanted to do as well as he could, he was scared. Doubling the measured mile was a race up that road in the Richmond outskirts, around a flare set exactly one mile from the starting line, and back; however, ten yards beyond the start-finish line were six iron posts marking a dead-end street, beyond them a deep ditch and field of weeds. One of the posts had been knocked loose, leaning from the socket of cement in which it had been sunk in the ground, and another was bent. Try as he might, Hazen did not dare approach the finish line at a high speed, though he was not quite last of the four in his heat, but came to a stop a disgraceful three full yards from the posts. Jacqueline did not reprove him for this performance; she said very little that evening. From what he could gather she had decided during the two-week vacation, as he had, that they were not going to do more than have fun together; she was aloof in a way he could not put his finger on, perhaps bantered him more than formerly, perhaps did not volunteer so much information about her world as she had used to, yet she necked as readily as ever, indeed he thought even more than before, one time so avidly that he was all but put off. The Friday night of the quintet's playing, she disappeared into her music completely as she always had done; watching her, knowing that she would want only to crawl off to sleep when the playing was done, seeing her exchange with the others and especially with Jefferson such glances of intimacy as she had (for the best of reasons) never exchanged with him, he admired her fatuously. There was a genuine tie holding them to one another, not as strong as some ties, not strong enough to hold them very long; but sensibly they were loosening this tie against the time she should have to leave. He was content, though in all truth he would have preferred to have been the one to commence this loosening. He looked forward to the farewell party Sunday night with pleasure: the Countess was bringing her beautiful dancer, and at last he would meet Floyd, whose place by Jackie he had taken so often in the Ford. Jacqueline and Jefferson were to fly to New York Monday morning. It promised to be a friendly ending to a summer's fun, with leads into the future.

The evening began with a scattering for meals. The Devereux were having a dinner for family in Mama's apartment so that the larger one could be readied in the afternoon and left undisturbed for the party; "family" were the four of them, Floyd, and Pearl, six in all, the maximum for a Parktilden table. To avoid the awkwardness of eating alone next door or of being seventh at a table for six, Hazen took the Countess and her friend out to dinner. The dancer had studied ballet, preferred modern dance, and made her living, from time to time when she ran out of money, by dancing in the chorus of one of the night clubs in San Francisco; she was impetuous, her eyes slanted and her cheekbones were broad and flat, her long hair glistened, she sat like a cat relaxed yet alert, and she liked nothing so much as to be looked at; one man, the Countess told him, had threatened to kill himself for love of her and another had run off to Mexico City to forget her in tequila; she could be charming with sweat pouring off her limbs and elusive in a leotard under harsh lights, and, the Countess added, she was easily bored; her name was Flossie. Hazen was, of course, fascinated in a sort of pure way, as by a fine gem, but he did what he could to make himself agreeable and yet not show too much zeal for her. Fortunately for him, she was impressed by science, by the social sciences as much as by any of the others, and looked at every scientist as a guardian of the treasure of knowledge; it was so rarely that he thought of himself, even in a fantasy of democracy, as one of the company of Einstein and Planck, that he had no trouble expanding in Flossie's company, dazzling her judiciously with glimpses of his stores of gold; he would rather have been a scientist than anything else in the world, but failing that—and scientists and philosophers agreed that sociologists were something of both and not much of either—he would settle for being looked up to as a scientist by a girl as brainless and beautiful as a bird of paradise. The dinner was a great success, for the Countess, who had hoped for some such result of putting them together, delighted in nothing more than the pompous cavortings of a man in the spell of a woman who is scarcely trying. At 8:30 they were last to arrive at the party.

A scream from Pearl reached them down the hall. "Lisa!" she yelled when she saw them come in. She embraced them all, but before Eleanor could introduce those who needed to be introduced, Pearl arrested everyone. "What would you do with an Aries baby of Taurus and Libra?"

"Sex?"

"Girl."

"What time of day was it born?"

"Three in the morning, dearheart, and the moon was off-phase."

"Drown it," said the Countess smiling and starting towards the table where Jefferson was offering glasses of champagne. There was a gasp of shock from a man and an ejaculation of real hatred from a woman. She glanced at them, pierced them, a second. "Since that is impossible," she said winningly, "I would love it all I could. It needs love."

"Get it?" yelled Pearl, tossing down a whole glass of champagne. "I was right."

Hazen did not see Jacqueline. Jefferson introduced him to five or six people, but he paid as little attention to them as decency allowed. Through the half-opened door he caught a glimpse of Jacqueline in profile against the window in the unlighted workroom; there was a young man talking with her, no doubt Floyd.

Hazen was irked, for though he had barely met Floyd that after-noon he had been struck by his strange inward force, and he was exactly Jacqueline's age. Eleanor should have fetched them out, so that Jacqueline could greet her guests. He went into the workroom and snapped on the light; they did not start apart in embarrass-ment but looked over at him questioningly. He saw their fingers interlacing, and the sight of that easy familiarity, which he had of course known about in a general way, reminded him with a flurry of all this girl's delightfulness which he was about to lose. He had boasted that he had never been really jealous; but he was jealous now. He had not seen Jacqueline dressed so charmingly, in a blue dress with a scarlet sash, and she was all keyed up.

"Hi, Hazie," she said, and held out her left hand to him. "We've been talking over your offer on the Ford."

"What do you think?" Hazen asked.

Floyd, mumblingly and roundaboutly, thanked him for the offer but said he wanted to take the car down to the base with him; if he got transferred out of California, he would sell it then. The only thing about Floyd in the least objectionable was that Jacqueline was holding his hand; but Hazen could not abide him.

"OK," he shrugged and walked off. "By God," he said to him-self, "she plays the field like any other woman."

Three men were looking toward the hallway; Hazen glanced over and saw Flossie; Eleanor was still engaged in hostessly con-versation with the Countess and her. He joined them, and pres-ently carried Flossie off to introduce her to four of his dear scien-tist-friends (all of them with wives in the room). Everybody was impressed, though a couple of the wives were audibly not de-lighted. As soon as he could, he confronted the two wives with Flossie. But if they did not care for her, she acted as though they were salamanders, odd, cold-blooded, and mildly interesting; they tried to begin a vicious little game of social tennis, giving her every slice and spin and lob at which they were genteelly expert, but she, after she had swung futilely at two or three of these, just walked away, a simplicity which they had no recourse from but to con-gratulate one another on her bad manners. Jefferson offered her a glass of champagne, and in no time at all he was talking with her with more animation than Hazen had ever seen in him. Hazen withdrew into a corner and watched aloof and cynical. And when he saw Jacqueline, alone, come out of the workroom, he gleefully looked forward to the sparks that the friction of the two girls would generate. The girls did not size each other up, but began talking at a great rate, he could not imagine about what, and Jefferson kept looking from one to the other with blatant delight. Jacqueline said something with a little nod of emphasis; Flossie put her hand on Jacqueline's arm and leaned forward, obviously saying no, and Jacqueline and Jefferson both assured her yes; Flossie crossed her hands over her bosom in a rather theatrical gesture of admiring incredulity; and Jefferson embraced them both and kissed their cheeks and they kissed his.

"Jefferson, you old beard you, you billy goat," Pearl bellowed and stalked him. "I love that champagne of yours. Give me some more. So you've got a corner on the beauties." But the girls were looking down. "What're you looking at?"

Flossie was doing something with her feet, Hazen could not see what; then she shook her head vigorously at Jacqueline and pulled up her skirt; she raised her left leg so that her left foot rested on her right calf, and traced the muscle down the inside of her thigh, overdeveloped from dancing; every eye in the room was on that long leg in its mesh stocking, perfect of its kind; when she had made her point, she dropped her skirt and turned back to listen to Jefferson.

"Hazen!" cried Pearl, and looked wildly around. She half-staggered over to him in his corner. "Did you see that?" she said. "Tell me about her, baby, tell me all you know."

Pearl was about as dangerous as a three-legged bull; if she gored him, he'd have himself to blame. Meanwhile, he might tease her a little, the more because of those girls who had no right to like each other so well and who had forgotten that he existed.

"All I know about Flossie is what Lisa tells me."

"The hell you say," Pearl answered and tapped him on the chest. "What's she like?"

"She's devoted to her art."

"I bet she is." Pearl was finding that one of the buttons on his shirt was open.

"She's very sincere and high-spirited."

"Hazen," said Pearl sentimentally, "Paris was a damned nice place." She was fondling the muscles on the left side of his chest. "Why did we ever leave there anyway?" He pulled her hand out. She turned. "Look at her, Hazen. You going to take her home tonight?" He nodded. "Give her a kiss for me." She kissed him lubriciously. "Give her a big one for me." She left him.

But Jacqueline had been watching him. When he caught her eye she looked back at Flossie. He could not tell what she had been thinking. He was afraid she would misconstrue Pearl's kiss. He ached with the desire to talk to her.

Floyd sidled out of the workroom and towards the hall door, but Jacqueline cried "Floy! Floy!" and ran over to stop him. "Aw, J.D.," he said, and ducked his head. Eleanor joined her, but Floyd led them out. It seemed to Hazen that she liked everybody better than him: if *he* had been trying to escape like that she would not have stopped him so warmly; she was not even jealous of Flossie; she scorned him for being on terms of intimacy with Pearl. When he saw one of those scientist-friends, whose name he had already forgotten, showing signs of coming over to talk, he bolted. He made towards the outer door, and it was as though walking generated anger, for as he walked those few steps he prickled with anger; he would catch Jacqueline and give her what-for.

But Eleanor was coming in the door, and held him. "Floyd wants to go visit some old friends," she said. "He'll be back later."

"Oh," he said, "good." He hoped the mask of affability which he put on for a party as automatically as a clean shirt was not betraying him.

"Jackie's going down with him, but she promised not to be long." Eleanor peered at his face, searching for emotions as for blackheads. He knew this abrupt habit of hers, and was thankful he had been at that moment looking at Jefferson, who was still talking with Flossie. "She's charming, isn't she?" said Eleanor. "Jefferson seems very taken with her."

Was he the only one in this place who knew what jealousy meant? He looked down at her, genuinely bewildered. It was the first time he had looked at Eleanor all evening, really looked. She

81

wore a handsome black dress with an old-fashioned brooch, earrings, lipstick and rouge; but more than these, her excitement, her open intention to enjoy herself fully, gave her a radiance which affected him much more strongly than Flossie's gemlike beauty. Flossie's leg, for instance: she wanted you to admire it, as you did, and she herself admired it as well, rather like a mother exposing her baby for everyone to appreciate; every part of her person or all of it together, he like everyone else admired; but he had no clear notion who Flossie herself was. Eleanor, though, was so intensely herself that she illuminated all those parts inferior to Flossie's, one by one, in a way that quite took his breath. Flossie's beauty was so much a matter of youth and plenty of good food and luck that it was only incidentally human; it was animal and ideal; she seemed to Hazen to have more in common with a fine horse or a Greek statue of a goddess than with Eleanor, whose was the beauty of intelligence and strength of character. Flossie's beauty was the diving nude into a clear stream, all ravishing gracefulness; Eleanor's was the smile forgiving the drunk who's just knocked you down, wholly moral, wholly your own doing. Eleanor's beauty seemed to him at that moment the only sort that mattered. No, she was not jealous. What was there about Flossie for her to be jealous of?

"You are . . ." he hesitated, looking for the right word. "I don't know exactly. You're strange tonight." She beamed, but it was a back-scratching sort of smile, the beaming of one who thinks herself flattered. "No," he said, annoyed by her expression, "I mean it. You're not like yourself . . . But that's wrong too. You're *more* like yourself. You're nice."

His ineptness and stumbling about convinced her he meant something. She put her hands on his arm, cocked her head a little to one side, and said, "Thanks." At that moment Jacqueline came back in.

She looked at them, told her mother Floyd would be back at about 11:30, when the party was supposed to break up, and went on into the living room. She gave Hazen only a glance, but it was baleful enough to make up for its brevity.

He felt his luck was against him, that first Pearl and now Eleanor had compromised him somehow in Jacqueline's eyes.

"Very well," he thought, "I'll get even with her." He sought out Flossie, who was drawing out a sand-haired little physicist on the subject of molecules, and he joined them, turning his back on Jacqueline, who was with her father. He could hardly stand still; he thought the physicist was being fatuous, trying to explain the experiments he was working on to one incompetent to understand; he could scarcely listen politely. "*You* understand me, I can see that," said the physicist to him suddenly. Like a sunburned man congratulated with a slap on the back, Hazen hopped, grinned, and swallowed. After a bit, he manoeuvred himself around so that he could see Jacqueline, but she was leaning on her father's shoulder listening to an old friend of the family, her back to him, oblivious of him. He became conscious that the Countess' eyes were on him and had been on him all evening. He abominated her. Apropos of nothing, he butted into the conversation, "Lord, I wish they'd put on some dance music. Wouldn't you like to dance a while?" But the physicist only smiled half-comprehendingly, not easily disentangling himself from Flossie and the molecules, and Flossie herself said no reprovingly. "You dance for us then," he urged her. "Jefferson and Jackie could play something for you." This time her no was fierce. Shrugging, he sought his corner: he would be aloof and cynical again, Byronesque over these creatures.

"I, who have removed myself from all of you for the moment," (his nostrils were slightly pinched) "I, who look at you with amused pity and whom you glance at uneasily from time to time," (he tapped the edge of his glass casually with a fingernail) "I, who hide my contempt behind the mask of indulgence, I understand you." A persistent little tremor in his right knee refused to support the Byronesque stance and when he shifted his weight to his left leg that knee began its own sabotaging tremble. He leaned against the china closet. But Jefferson didn't notice: he had collected the two girls again (surely it was indecent the way he was hugging his daughter so familiarly, and another girl as well, in front of everyone, even his wife), and catching Hazen's eye once when they were both laughing at something he had said, he winked at Hazen and smiled gloatingly at these bare-shouldered creatures in his arms. Neither did Mama: on one of her periodic little trips over from her apartment to see how the party was getting along, she shuffled up to Hazen in his corner by the window and took him by the hand. "Isn't it a picture, Mr. Hazen, isn't it the prettiest picture you ever saw? And those two girls with such lovely brown hair, one of them's prettier than the other, and how Jefferson loves them. He always had a weakness for pretty girls, it's so nice Jackie was pretty for him, but he married Ellie. My Ellie." Nor Eleanor: she pounced on his empty glass and brought it back full of champagne, and when he drained it (bitterly behind the lip-smacking mask of geniality) she fetched him another saying how happy it made her to see him enjoying himself. Jacqueline began making the polite rounds of her guests; her voice was light and a little mannered; "false" he told himself, but he did not believe it, for when she told departing guests she was glad they had come she sounded as though she meant it. And after the censorious biddies and their husbands had left so that the atmosphere was cleared a little, Jacqueline pulled Flossie into the workroom to show her around, with a gaiety he knew to be the efflorescence of simple liking, for he had seen her before with a girl she liked. Jefferson followed them in and presently there was a run on the oboe and a trill of laughter, and they came out again. He smiled disdainfully, shifting to the other leg.

"She is a virgin." The Countess had startled up to him when he wasn't looking.

"What?"

"She is a virgin," she hissed again.

"A minor affliction, easily remedied."

"You are being faux naïf."

"Really, Lisa." He smiled affably and put his hand on her arm.

But she shook it off. "Your charm is inappropriate, mon brave." She was dead serious. "Remember that there is something holy about a virgin."

"What?" he asked, raising his eyebrows. "Her maidenhead?"

"Sht," she said venomously.

"Look." He was annoyed. "How would *you* know she's a virgin anyhow?"

"Is she not?"

"I asked you."

She fixed him with her eyes. "Do you know what a virgin is?"

84

"Of course," he said disgustedly. "Go peddle your tea leaves somewhere else. You're crude."

"Yes. I am crude. Facts are crude."

"We've got out of the nineteenth century. People know about sex nowadays. She knows the score."

"Ah yes. The undertaker lays out 500 dead. He buries them. He knows about death. He knows the score. When the heart stops you're dead. That's all there is to it. Easy score. One to one."

He felt that a smile would be enough refutation for her.

"Are you such a liar, Peter Hazen?"

"Do you mean I should marry her first? Surely that is her father's worry."

"Scheiss," she said. "That she should be entrusted to a fool of fools." Her teeth chittered with rage at him. "American."

"What the hell?" he said. "American? What do you think *she* is?"

"Innocent." Suddenly she turned on a malicious smile. "What do you think the opposite of innocence is?"

"Experience, obviously."

"Ah. You have experience to train her in. Even that takes a certain courage. At least it's 100 percent healthy exercise. You Americans like to be 100 percent something, don't you? Go ahead. Exercise is good. But there is wisdom too," she said gleefully. She jabbed him with her finger in the belly. "And guilt. And sin." She turned, chiming laughter. "What do you know about her?"

She went over to Flossie, and he shook his head at his own stupidity. "She was talking about Flossie all the time," he told himself. "Obviously." And he put them both out of his mind.

There was, therefore, nothing left in his mind but Jacqueline, whom however he could think of only as the Countess had directed him. For Flossie's innocence, if there was any of it left, he cared nothing, but for Jacqueline's, though he was scarcely at ease with the idea of innocence, he felt a strange tenderness. He could not help wondering what she was like and what he meant to her, what he knew of her and what she knew of him. The more he thought and watched her, and the nearer 11:30 approached, the more he had to talk to her. As though to thwart him, she was always busy. He did not trust himself to go interrupt her, ask to speak to her aside for a moment; he was afraid he would act as abrupt and crude as a lovesick boy. He must know her better. She was about to elude him. He concentrated on that—he must know her—and he turned his desire full towards the sweetness of what he wanted (knowing her) and dead away from the consequences (what it might mean to her to be known).

During the general leave-taking, while Pearl was telling the whole tenth floor she'd had to make herself drunk to force herself to get back into the damned elevator, he clutched Jacqueline aside and told her in a desperate undertone that he had to talk to her. She said that Floyd would be coming shortly to take her for a ride. He insisted. She pointed out to him, coolly, that he was driving Flossie home. As soon as he returned then. He could drive them out to the airport in the morning, she told him. Flossie came over and pulled him away—she was sleepy—and kept telling him as they went down the hallway how grateful to him she was for having brought her; he must take her to more parties. He looked over his shoulder. Jacqueline was watching them go.

At that instant she was alone in the hall, uncircumstanced like a vision: her left hand was on the back of her neck, her head bent a little to the left, her face was slightly sullen in a way he recognized, the thumb of the other hand was unconsciously hooked into the sash as though it were a belt, she was slouching a little. He experienced that falling away in the guts which was the sign that the beauty he desired was greater than the beauty he should ever possess, and he wished he had never seen Flossie in his life.

The elevator took them down to the second basement where his car was garaged. He spiraled up and out, and found that the fog had settled. He had not looked out of the window all evening, and in these towers it was permanent summer so long as the thermostats were on and the windows shut. Flossie snuggled against him at sight of the fog. It was still. He drove slowly. At the intersection with Grizzly Peak Boulevard he stopped. A radiance of headlights increased, blazed, and faded past them. This was a high fog, for he could hear none of the foghorns down on the Bay or over on the Golden Gate Bridge, but as he sat he could hear water dripping from the eucalyptus leaves and once in a while a rustle of wind. "It's mysterious," said Flossie. He pulled into a parking space and turned off the car lights. The fog was faintly luminous with moonlight and city lights, but he could not distinguish Flossie's features. All cats are grey in the dark. He kissed her. She returned his kiss with the expertise of indifference: kissing after parties is one of the predicates of a Buick convertible. He snuffled in her hair a couple of times; her perfume was nice. Grateful at his not pressing on, she curled up on the seat with her head against his leg and sighed; it was cozy. The sumptuous sound of the motor when he started it was nice, and it was cozy idling along stroking Flossie's arm, and the fog was cozy if you weren't in a hurry. He had no place to hurry to. Flossie fell asleep: he could feel little twitchings in her body. She was a nice kid. It was all nice and cozy.

Headlights came rushing up from behind and suddenly went out; he heard the roar of the Ford with the cutout open; Floyd bumped bumpers with him and then roared by, turning on his lights only after he'd passed. Hazen could see Jacqueline's head profiled in the windows, in exactly the position that meant she had hooked her right foot up under the dashboard and was resting her left arm lightly along Floyd's thigh, elbow in his groin, hand on his knee. Hazen breathed unsteadily, he shivered a little in the chest, he felt like crying; unconsciously his right hand curled around Flossie's throat and squeezed; she woke up enough to remove his hand and nip it lightly before returning it to its place on her arm; he scarcely noticed. With all his heart he was trying to accuse Jacqueline of malice.

For she was inscrutable to him. The better he came to know her, the more inscrutable she seemed, just as the better he knew her, the less he could tell whether she was beautiful as Flossie was beautiful. For this gem, this bird of high sheen, this Persian cat beside him asleep, was inscrutable only as all beautiful things are inscrutable, beyond science to be sure but this side theology, and not at all as those are inscrutable who can, when they will, do evil. Jacqueline was hurting him and surely she knew that she was hurting him, surely she knew how he was feeling. But it is evil to hurt someone if you don't have to, and he could think of no psychosociological rationale for her doing it. It was a moral matter, concerned with will, with that gratuity of motive which Hazen avoided considering whenever he could. This time he couldn't. He set himself the task—he never thought more steadily, more clearly, than while driving quietly—of understanding why Jacqueline was tormenting him. By the time he had deposited Flossie and returned across the Bay Bridge, he was quite clear about Jacqueline's culpability and his own right to tell her about it; their intimacy had given him certain privileges. He resolved that he would catch her when she came in tonight, though he had to sit up till dawn doing it.

He drove back up into the high fog, into Parktilden Village and his own tower. He was positive Jacqueline would not have returned yet. He put on his pajamas and coat, and installed himself to wait for her. He sat with the lights in his apartment out, facing the hallway, the door to which he had left open. The sound of the elevator door would reach him, even though her footsteps on these carpets might be wholly muffled. He was in no danger of falling asleep: he smoked too much, and sometimes he felt as though he were about to have a chill. There were a hundred occupied apartments in this building, but it was still as a columbarium; all in their sound-proofed pigeonholes slept but him, whose dry eyes watched for the other living being that he might catch her and accuse her. He could not bear the not knowing her.

A door opened, but from the wrong direction. He sat up. There were shuffling noises. Mama peered into his doorway. "Mr. Hazen," she said, delighted. "It's so foggy out, I'm worried. Jackie stays up too late. Well, she's young. This morning she's got to go on an air trip, she needs her sleep. Well, well, I'll just go down to the elevator and take a look out for her." Mama had on many robes and shawls and socks and slippers. After awhile she came back. "If you should see her, Mr. Hazen, just let me know she's home. It'll set my mind to rest. God bless you." He went back to her door with her. While they stood at her door for a moment, Eleanor poked her head out of their apartment door. Hazen shrugged at her; she disappeared.

Suppose Jacqueline should come up the fire escape? There could be no sensible reason why she should, but suppose she did, hoping to get in undetected maybe. How would he catch her then?

A light was on in the Devereux' apartment; Eleanor might be making some hot chocolate for Jefferson and herself; one does not sleep well the night before a great departure. Or suppose Floyd should come up with Jacqueline? Floyd was spending the night in the boarding house he had stayed in when he had attended the University, but he might squire Jacqueline to her door. It was a relic of horse-and-buggy etiquette, seeing a young woman to her door, this young woman to this door, but Floyd, it was obvious, had not been citied out of that shy, antique, country gallantry requiring a guy to bow his girl to her door.

He moved his chair so that when he leaned back in it he could see either way down the hall, and if Floyd showed up, he was prepared to begin talking again about buying the Ford. He was prepared to outstay Floyd at Jackie's door, even if Eleanor, even if Jefferson himself, should join them. He imagined that consternated leave-taking; he grimaced the smiles till his cheeks hurt. He was no longer interested in how absurd he appeared to others; Mama's treating him as though sitting in a dark room in a topcoat at 2:30 in the morning with his door open was a rational way to behave, and Eleanor's rueful response to his shrug as though they understood one another perfectly, both encouraged him to this further absurdity. He ground his teeth once in exasperation that he had not behaved lovesick at the party and pulled Jackie outside and told her he had to talk to her.

He knew what it was like waiting to waylay a woman—in a car outside a dark house, in a bedroom down the hall, in a restaurant at seven in the morning—but desire was only a part of what he now was feeling. He was possessed by a rage that became almost religious: it was herself he desired to know. He had not spent four such miserable hours even in the Army, and he resented Jacqueline for making him feel so bad. Yet, to his own confusion, he would not have had her otherwise, for if she had not done this to him he might always have feared she was, like Flossie, not fully human. He bit his knuckles white.

Eleven

Jefferson found himself drowsily awake for no external reason that he was aware of. He felt that Eleanor was not in the bed, but neither could he hear her rustling around. Without his glasses he could not see the time by the alarm clock on the dresser; he could detect no tinge of dawn in the sky yet. Obviously there was no point in rousing himself enough to reach out for his glasses. After everyone had left the party, he had piled all the left-over pâté de foie onto two crackers, one for Eleanor, one for himself; she had not wanted hers, so he had eaten them both; he could taste the pâté yet; he smacked his lips. With a grunt he turned over to sink back into sleep. He felt neither good nor bad, just sleepy. He was not thinking. He scratched his beard and sighed.

But then an image clanged into his consciousness and would not be ignored; he could not help feeling about it, he had to think about it. The image was of Hazen's face as he had stood in the corner by the china cupboard watching the others. At first Jefferson could not understand why there should be such hostile intensity on Hazen's face; he could not remember hearing any dispute during the party, nor had Eleanor mentioned one to him. He tried to remember what he himself had been doing at the time he had noticed Hazen's expression, but apparently he had not been struck by it at the time for he could not place the moment at all. Oddly, it was not exactly at him that the hostility had been directed, though the image in his mind certainly was glowering in his direction. Why had Hazen been alone? Where had Flossie been, that charming girl? Her perfume returned to his nostrils, and the feel of her admirable flesh returned to his hands. What a creature. Then he remembered himself in the middle of the room, champagne high, with Jacqueline and Flossie one in each of his arms, laughing with a pleasure all the greater because of the not exactly enthusiastic wives of his old friends observing him with the girls; he had caught Hazen's eye and winked at him as his only comrade in mock-lechery in the room; it was the image of Hazen's response to his wink that had bonged back to bother him now. At the time, he had been high above it.

The hostility as such did not perplex him; he had too often watched Hazen's skittering uncomfortably from subject to subject for that, been too conscious of Hazen's forced affability with him, and he presumed that Hazen was not easy in his status as Eleanor's younger former admirer, Jacqueline's older pseudo-pal, and Jefferson's jittery avoider. Even so, Jefferson did not, remembering, think that the hostility and brooding resentment in Hazen's eyes had been for him. What had given the image potency to awaken him was this perplexity about what *had* been on Hazen's mind.

He heard the rustle of paper in the living room. What could Eleanor be up to? Jacqueline was all packed for the morning, and his things were ready. Presently there was a slam, a snort, muted sound of feet walking, clinks in the kitchen. What *was* she doing? She had insisted on staying up after the party was over and washing all the dishes and glasses, and she had insisted, over his hypocritical protests, that he go to bed and rest for the trip tomorrow. He had gone off to sleep immediately, and hadn't even awakened when she'd come to bed. Now what? He heard a door open for a few moments, then carefully close. Then silence.

It was inconceivable that Hazen could have been jealous of him. It had been so obvious that he had been only horsing around with the sumptuous Flossie, in high spirits like everyone else, and that she was flirting only in the most innocuous way imaginable, no more than Jacqueline indeed. And as for Hazen's being jealous of Jacqueline, after all he was her father, she was with Floyd, and Hazen himself was with Flossie—not that Hazen hadn't made a pass at Jacqueline, in all probability, but Jefferson had seen no signs of special tension between them. Yet there was that hostility to be accounted for. Jefferson spent a few minutes enquiring of himself whether this impression of his, gotten from an image which had emerged spontaneously from sleep, should be taken seriously. He decided that it should, if only because the emotions it had dredged up with it were serious.

Rustle of papers in the living room irked him again. Maybe Eleanor had not come to bed yet at all. He knew he would not get back to sleep so long as she was stirring about, restlessly, aimlessly, like a worry nagging at the back of the mind.

"Jefferson!" She started guiltily when he appeared. "I tried to be quiet, darling, so as not to disturb your rest."

"I know," he said, "but your movements have not been silent; they have been loud whispers. My curiosity is aroused. What on earth are you doing here at three o'clock in the morning?"

She was wearing the dress she had worn at the party, but her shoes were lying on their sides under the table. She had guiltily pushed a book behind her when he came in. Her eyes were haggard; she smiled in appeal to him; she looked older and more lined than usual. He was too annoyed at having been routed out of bed to tarry now for useless indulgences. He went over and fished the book from behind her on the chair: the Montgomery Ward catalogue.

"Good lord, Eleanor," he said, "can't you come to bed instead of wasting your eyes on this?"

"I'm sorry, darling. I've been waiting up for Jackie. You know?"

"She's old enough to look after herself."

"I know, but this is her last night."

"She hasn't had much time with Floyd."

"He drives so dangerously!"

Jefferson shrugged. "What can you do?"

"Nothing." She smiled again, hopefully, irritatingly. "I know one thing I *can't* do—sleep."

"You're sure she hasn't come in?"

"Oh yes."

"How do you know?"

"I haven't heard her. I think she would look in to see if one of us were up."

"Nonsense. She's probably in bed asleep right now."

"Not ten minutes ago, darling, I heard noises and looked out.

Peter was talking to Mama in the hallway, and he shrugged in a way that meant Jacqueline wasn't in."

"One shrug and he said all that? A good shrugger."

"Do you want me to go see?"

"Anything that will get you to come to bed."

"I'll go." But she did not go.

"Well, go ahead," he urged her. "I'll put on milk for some hot chocolate."

She went out the door huddled over into herself, as though furtively.

What had Hazen been doing out in the hall with Eleanor's mother? Jefferson saw it would be a good while before he got to sleep even if Jacqueline had actually come in.

Eleanor closed the door behind her with elaborate care.

"Well, is she in her bed?" he asked, with more energy than he had intended.

"No," said Eleanor. She was thinking of something else. She took out the cans and utensils for making the hot chocolate, but then did not use them, stared at them, frowned. "The oddest thing, Jefferson. I went down the hall very quietly. You know how the rug is, and I was tiptoeing as well." She looked down at her stockinged feet as though to verify something. "No shoes. No. As I was going past Peter's door, I couldn't help noticing that it was open. So of course I thought I would just close it. And there in the doorway, just inside, out of the hall light, was his easy chair, and he was in it."

He did not believe her; he thought, not that she was lying, but that what she took to be true was not true. He just looked at her. She had to go on.

"Really, Jefferson, he was in it, asleep. His back was toward the door, the back of the chair. He was quite asleep. So I went into Mama's as silently as I could, without even waking her up, and looked in Jacqueline's bed and came back again. What do you make of it, darling?"

"Well," he said, "I think we need some hot chocolate to soothe our nerves."

She started guiltily and began mixing powdered chocolate,

sugar, and vanilla with hot milk. As she was stirring the paste free of lumps, she gradually slowed down. "What on earth is he doing?"

"You actually saw him in the chair?"

"Of course," she said. "I peeked over. His head was on the back of the chair but his jaw hadn't dropped open. He couldn't have been very sound asleep. His legs were stretched out and crossed. He was in his overcoat."

These details pretty well convinced him of her story, but he puttered with toast and cinnamon to forestall any thinking about what Hazen was up to.

"I know!" she exclaimed. She was convincing herself as she spoke. "He wants to talk to Floyd about the car. Of course. I heard him say something to Jackie about it. Floyd left so early from the party he didn't have a chance to talk the thing over. He's just waiting there for them to come home. Now isn't it silly of him?" She sounded relieved and indulgent. "He could just as well have tacked a note to Jackie's door. Maybe he thought Floyd would be embarrassed to wake him up so late at night. You know, Jefferson, Peter *is* so young at heart."

He recognized from the tone of her voice and the speed of her chatter that she was vigorously putting her mind at rest with a soothing flurry of rationalizations. Not that her rationalizations were necessarily untrue, just that their function was to pacify her.

When they finished the chocolate, Eleanor stretched and yawned. "I'm so sleepy. It was good of you, darling, to get up with me. I'm ready for bed now. You've helped me set my mind at rest."

He did not want to go back to bed; he was keyed up; he would have liked to weave for forty-five minutes or so, thinking. But since he had been badgering her to come to bed, he had to go back to it himself now that she was ready.

He lay flat on his back, his arms outside the blanket, his hands on his chest, his left ankle crossed on his right—the position he found most relaxing. When he should begin to feel drowsy he would turn onto his left side, faced away from Eleanor, his left hand under the pillow and his right arm under the covers, his knees somewhat bent. Meanwhile, however, he lay on his back, thinking.

He gauged the plausibility of Eleanor's comforting hypothesis, that Hazen was waylaying Floyd in order to buy his car. But Hazen had had plenty of time to dicker over the price, and anyway Floyd would not be leaving first thing in the morning. Furthermore, Eleanor had good reasons to divert her suspicions toward such an hypothesis: Hazen had been her admirer and she would not want his attentions to be heaped upon Jacqueline, for mother-daughter competition, even in a matter of flirtation, was really not within the competence of Eleanor's conscience; also, of course, as a mother she would not want Jacqueline to get too much involved with a man of Hazen's age and dubious sense of responsibility.

Eleanor beside him began softly to snore (she had only begun snoring in the last few years, often or loud). She was a bit keener on having Hazen around than a husband might like. Well, the old girl had turned forty. She was entitled to one last sentimental fling. He did not think Hazen, with his zeal for Flossie, would give Eleanor more than sentiment.

There was still the problem: why was Hazen sleeping in his easy chair in the open doorway to his apartment? There was only one probable solution: to waylay and possibly to seduce Jacqueline. If he were quite sure that Hazen was going to seduce her, he would act to prevent it. But he could not be positive that this was Hazen's intention; nor had he tried to prevent Hazen from associating with Jacqueline during the summer, when endless opportunities of seduction must have arisen; neither did he think Hazen would be likely to succeed tonight if he should try, because Jacqueline would have been necking with Floyd and would be tired; above all, he left his daughter free, now that she was a woman, to lead her own life, and freedom meant the right to make her own mistakes. He would have interfered had he been sure of Hazen's seducing her, only out of sentimental weakness in himself: he could not bear to see his beloved daughter threatened by an important involvement with a man whom he could not, in the final analysis, take seriously.

He discovered that his tongue was pressing the roof of his

mouth with great force, making his throat tense. He consciously relaxed it.

He thought he heard whispering voices in the hall. Without reflecting, he got out of bed and went to the bedroom door as quietly as he could, not waking Eleanor. The living-room light was still on; he blinked and hurried to the hall door. There, he listened a moment, and was quite sure he heard noises. He opened the door and looked out, seeing nothing. But he had forgotten to put on his glasses. He stepped into the hall barefooted, in his pajamas, and closed the door behind him. He had never done such a thing before in his life, but he tiptoed down the hall to see if Hazen were still asleep in his chair. The door to Hazen's apartment was closed. He heard nothing. He decided not to go into Mama's apartment to see if Jacqueline were back, for fear of waking Mama—and also for fear of being caught doing what he could not justify. When he was halfway back to his own door, he was sure he heard whispers again, from Hazen's place he thought. Well, they were adults, they were free agents. He was making himself ridiculous.

He did not go into his bedroom for his robe and slippers for fear of waking Eleanor, but went directly to the loom and began to work, whistling between his teeth.

Twelve

The click of the elevator door and sibilant whispers jerked Hazen wide awake. He pulled the chair back into the living room, bumping it against another chair on the way, and went back to the doorway to look down the dim hall. He was on tenterhooks for fear Eleanor should come out into the hall again at this moment; even if she did not, she might very well hear Jacqueline go by her door—worse, Jefferson might hear and come out. He would face them down. But if Eleanor should go into Jacqueline's room with her, he did not know what he would do. He leaned out of his doorway. There were two figures standing at the end of the hall; at sight of him—at such a distance they could not tell which doorway he was leaning from or who he was—one of the two disappeared in the direction of the elevator and the other, Jacqueline, approached. He stepped back just out of sight so that when she came abreast, she must see him. She was walking quietly, glancing back at her parents' door, when she caught sight of him. She was startled and half cried out. "Jackie," he whispered. From her face he realized he must look wild.

He took her hand. "You've got to talk to me."

"What's the matter, Hazie?" she said; her antagonism of the evening was startled out of her, but she resisted his tugging.

"I can't stand to see you go away like this."

"Like what?" she whispered.

He looked at her intently. He could not believe that she did not know what he meant. She was afraid to come into his apartment late at night, in a more than neighborly way. That anger he had been dwelling on all night held him tense, but he could not have been openly unkind to her now if he had tried. His whisper had power to alarm her. "You mustn't go away until I've told you what I think." There was the sound of a door opening down the hall. They both looked, then she leaped inside his door. They stood hand in hand until they heard the other door close. Hazen closed his door as silently as he could and they stood for a moment in embarrassment, not touching.

"Turn on the light," she said.

"Look." He directed her, still not touching her, into the living room, and showed her the light on in her parents' apartment.

"I shouldn't be in here," she said.

"You've got to listen to me, Jackie. You've got to." He made a clenched, broken gesture with his hands.

"OK, I'm listening." The hostility was returning to her voice.

He felt shy, not wanting to touch her. He did not want to ease into necking any more than he wanted to blandish her with light

97

speeches. But he was afraid she would want to quarrel; she seemed set for it. He could see her face by the light reflected from the other apartment; she was scowling at him. Her feet were apart, she was standing solidly against him, her hands were on her hips. He did not know what to do. She would have left completely in four or five hours. He could have cried.

"What's the *matter?*" she said.

He threw himself on his knees in front of her, pressed his face sidewise against her belly, and hugged her legs. "I love you," he croaked. "I can't bear to have you go away."

The rigidity of her body, her hands on his shoulders about to push him away, slowly began to relax. For a long time he remained like that and felt her gradually yield. He realized this was the first time he had embraced her when she was wearing a dress instead of some sort of trousers, jeans, or slacks or jodhpurs; the dress was smooth to the touch, and thin so that he could feel her firm bottom through it.

She turned his face up and bent down to study it. "You're getting mushy," she said. He nodded ruefully. "That wasn't part of the bargain." She began to kiss him playfully.

He averted his lips. "No," he said, "I mean it. I really love you. I want you."

She straightened up again. "What about all your other women?"

"What others?"

"Flossie, for instance."

"She's a good egg. That's all."

"Is it?"

"Jackie, believe me. I don't care a thing about her. There isn't another woman in the world that means any more to me than Floyd means to you."

"How do you know what Floyd means to me?" She was belligerent again, stiffening against him.

He held her tighter. "It doesn't matter. The main thing is—"

"It does too matter."

"Look, Jackie," he said; he did not call her by one of the names of endearment; they were as easy as gifts of candy. "Look. I mean it. I really do." He prided himself that he had always scrupled at using the word *love* meretriciously with any woman. "I love you."

"What do you know about Floyd?" she cried, and broke away from him and began running for the door.

She stumbled over the chair he had been waiting in and fell to the floor. Before she could get up, he was kneeling beside her. "Are you hurt?" But he knew she wasn't hurt. He rolled her over onto her back and crouched over her, a hand on either side of her head as though they had been wrestling and he had at last pinned her down. "Are you in love with Floyd?" he asked. If she said yes, he did not know what he would do. A shiver of anxiety ran up his back while she was staring at him motionlessly. Finally she pulled his face down and kissed him passionately. "Jackie," he said in a sort of frenzy of relief and desire, "Jackie, Jackie."

She still wanted to neck as they were used to and began the requisite adjusting of clothes. But he did not feel simply sensual, willing to portion out his desire. "It's cold on the floor," he whispered. "Let's get in bed."

"Hazie," she said, and pulled her dress back up to her throat in the immemorial gesture of reticence. "No."

"It's warmer."

"No." But her voice was not as strong as it could be, had been.

"Jackie," he said, and lay on her, indifferent to her clothes, and kissed her till she yielded. "Jackie, you're leaving in just a few hours."

She was crying a little. He pulled her up from the floor. "Promise?" she said. "Not everything. Promise?"

He did not promise. Once they were naked in bed, she lay passive and unresisting, as much as to say, "I am defenseless, pity me." But he did not pity her.

After they had made love, she turned her back to him and lay without speaking. Till dawn he looked at her, in a daze of happiness and wonder. He thought she was asleep. "My love," he crooned, "my darling, my dear one. Jackie, Jackie." He shook her gently.

She rolled over and looked at him. By her dry eyes and

a strange sadness of her mouth he knew she had not been sleeping. "What?" she said, in a voice of womanly intimacy, one he had never heard before from her. It excited him and pleased him.

"I am so happy," he said.

"Do you still love me?"

"Of course. Do you love me?"

"I don't know," she said gravely. But then her eyes altered in a way he recognized, and her lips drew up for teasing. "Have a good time, Hazie?"

"Marvellous."

"B minus?"

"A minus."

"Not A plus?"

"No."

She wrinkled her nose at him and pinched his arm. "Do I look the same?"

"Only better."

She did not reject the flattery, but just lay looking at him. "I don't feel the same. I wouldn't dare look in a mirror."

"Why not?"

"I don't know. Maybe I'd be ashamed of myself."

"No, darling, no, not ashamed."

"You never were ashamed? But you're a man."

"Men aren't all that different."

She paid no attention to that. Her face slowly resumed its gravity. She seemed to be studying him. "You have changed me. *You* have changed me. And I bet it doesn't even show."

He could not support her gaze, for though there was no reproach in it, he was afraid it would discover some flaw of his behavior, some slickness of calculation, some coolness of insincerity of which he was not aware himself. It wasn't that he didn't love her; he did, but he was not sure his love was worthy of that great trust she had given him. It had something to do with her virginity all right, unreasonably much to do with it. He had no idea what she was thinking as she lay looking straight into his eyes. He was no longer so fierce to know her, or rather he was willing to settle for the love-making approximations to knowledge. He began caressing her again. Her eyes half closed and she looked as though she were in pain.

Suddenly she came to life and embraced him strenuously. They lunged like foes who fight till they fall.

She lay indifferently stretched out, her face at peace. He said nothing because he could not, and did not want to, imagine what she was thinking.

It was nearly 6:30. She got up to dress. "Jackie," he began with nowhere to go but terms of endearment. She put her finger on his lips and shook her head. She was not smiling, yet she did not look unhappy exactly; different, in a way he did not recognize, strange, new. She was not at all modest about their nakedness in the morning light: she dressed her body matter-of-factly; she drew the covers over him, brushing his cheek with the backs of her fingers; and, looking with melancholy into his eyes, she left.

It was not long before he heard Jefferson's morning call on the oboe. He was not able to fall asleep until he heard them all leaving for the airport. Someone, probably Eleanor, rapped on his door, but he did not answer. Their voices from the hallway sounded normal; they did not suspect what had happened. "It's over," he was thinking as he dropped off, "how sad, how wonderful. It's over."

PART II

One

Eleanor was busy during September taking care of her mother, who came down with pneumonia the week after Jacqueline went east; penicillin arrested the disease, but she was left weak from it. Mama was a fretful patient, and she became endlessly greedy for treats: jello, baked pears, ice cream, arrowroot cookies, peppermint candies to suck. She had never been one to rush for her bed jacket and plump up the pillows the moment she felt a fever coming on; rather she had always fought till she or the illness one or the other had decisively won, and when she'd gone down she'd been short-tempered at the indignity of defeat. Old people's pneumonia had been, in her Pennsylvania, a serious matter; that she survived it because of medication left her befuddled and cantankerous, for somehow she felt that the doctors had tricked and cheated her of her grateful awe and her honorable enemy of his due; she would not have wanted to lose, but it had been a low victory. When she was well enough, she took to hiding goodies around her apartment; Eleanor was distressed to come upon them, sometimes stale and forgotten in a bottom drawer; she minded, not that Mama should have become greedy, but that she should be ashamed of her greediness. Slowly Mama regained her strength, but she napped more than before and she remained querulous. She was far from home; there was nothing for her to do; no one needed her.

In October, Eleanor was free to do her precinct work. It was an off-year election, with neither President nor senator to choose, so that most people were not much interested in it. But she worked hard, visiting every registered Democrat in her precinct and any dubious Republican she heard of. The four days before the first Tuesday in November, Hazen worked with her, mostly, she feared, to please her. He didn't seem to share Jefferson's contempt for elections nor yet her sense that they were important—a shameful shilly-shallying for a social scientist, as she kept telling him. Once he got at it, he did his work fast. On election night he sat up with her listening to the broadcast of results, and when Jefferson would sally in from time to time with sardonic inquiries about how far the Democratic candidates were trailing, Hazen only grinned in that boyish, somewhat painful way that pleased her. All their local candidates lost except the state assemblyman, who had about as much power in the world as the engineer on a train, and the county supervisor, who had less than a bus-driver.

Jacqueline was away, Mama was fairly well, the elections were over: by the middle of November she was becoming nervous.

Mama's complaints that Jackie never wrote to her, that no one came to visit her, that her feet hurt, that it was raining, vexed Eleanor beyond all measure. Patience was her duty, sharp words her frequent dereliction. It was, to others, with an ostentation of forbearance that she accompanied Mama to church on Sundays; in fact, she discovered an unexpected tranquillity in the singing, the prayers, the readings from the Bible, even sometimes the sermons. She was a communicant of no church; but, when one day while they were driving home her mother asked her to join this Methodist church, she did not reject the offer irritably as she might have done; rather, she thanked her and said she would have to decide later, and explained how much she was benefited by attending these services. The old woman leaned her head against the door, letting the tears of her gratitude roll unwiped down her face. At this Eleanor was moved to repent of her impatience with her mother, who needed so little for contentment.

It was rather as though she had begun to wear thin, so that things better kept out got in.

One day she opened the morning paper to read while she drank her coffee. She was in robe and slippers, she had slept well, she had nothing to do that day, she was still groggy. Usually for her, reading the paper had this in common with washing her feet with her stockings on: nothing much came of it and the aftermath was dank; but today she was wounded by everything she read.

Through all that miasma of inexact writing, which surrounded with irrelevancies such as ages and addresses everyone it showed, which made the bad so black, the good so white, the radical so red and everyone else so grey that no one was real, she perceived the many-colored people of these stories: the liar in the Senate of whom everyone was afraid, the photograph of a child in an iron lung saved by *your* dime, the note in the purse of the most recent woman to jump off the Golden Gate Bridge: "I am sick. The doctors got no hope. Forgive me."

And there came a time one evening when she had the instant experience of losing control of herself—defined clearly in a second or two, like the moment when one slips from sobriety after a given swallow of liquor, or the moment when one finally buries his head in his hands at the too great complexity of a problem. It was not a madness: she could make her body do anything it usually did; she could follow an argument as far as usual; she always felt normal again next morning. All the same, of something in herself she knew she lost control. Had she been facing a clear danger at those moments, she would have known what to say: that she was losing her nerve. What she had actually been facing had been the Countess during the break of a Friday night music session. The Countess had only been pumping her about how Jacqueline was getting along, yet she had felt a mounting, silly impulse to run out of the room, followed when she repressed it by that loss of nerve which left her smiling mechanically, doing only what was expected, and taking a sleeping pill when she went to bed.

She had used to garden by fits and starts. In this Village, however, all the grass was cut and all the flowers tended by staff employees. She hadn't even a window box. Such refreshment as she found in nature now she got from the sea. Once in a long while, alone like an exile, she drove to the beach and spent hours watching the waves. She felt a certain deep excitement in perceiving the steadfastness of rocks withstanding waves which will wear them away at last; it is as it should be.

By December she was finding it as much as she could do sometimes to keep her worry under.

She was reading a novel by Howells—a gentle, serene world,

evenly lighted throughout. The combination of a gust of rain against the window and Howells' description of a winter hearth reminded her of something that made her laugh. Hazen glanced up from the chessboard questioningly.

"I just happened to think of those false fireplaces they have in the top-floor apartments."

"Oh?"

"You've never been up on the thirteenth floor?"

"I don't think so."

"Hundred and eighty dollars a month up there," said Jefferson, still studying the board. "Not worth it."

"One of the things they get for their money," said Eleanor, "is a false fireplace. You know, glass logs with glass bark and glass coals and a red light underneath it all."

"I knew a fellow," said Hazen, "who was a salesman for a false-firplace manufacturing company."

"Well, one woman, when I was doing precinct work, had hers on, and she said to me, 'It's better than a home because if the fire goes out here, all you have to do is screw in another bulb.' "

But neither of the men seemed to think it funny. They bent back over their board. "Better than a home," Hazen muttered, and Jefferson grunted.

"Chess," she thought to herself, and looked at them affectionately. They played two or three times a week. They seemed to have very little to talk about: they would talk desultorily for five minutes before a game and analyze it after they'd finished, then separate; they paid no attention to her while they played. She herself couldn't imagine playing games so often with anyone but a dear friend; but when she asked him once, Jefferson had insisted that chess was not a game at all, but a form of warfare; and Hazen, when in outrage she'd told him this, had agreed. She couldn't imagine how anyone could enjoy so intellectual a war; besides, even if she didn't hate her enemy to begin with, warring with him would make her hate him. Yet these men she was so close to were as polite when they parted as when they met. She consoled herself that she'd never known a woman who played chess well.

"Damn it," said Hazen.

"Perpetual check," said Jefferson, and leaned back smiling.

"I thought I had you too." Hazen stretched and arose; he stood rubbing his hands in front of him. "Another atavism."

"What?" she asked him.

"Warming my hands in front of the no-fire. If there was one of those false ones here, no doubt I'd be teetering on my heels with my back to it like a country gentleman."

"I rather enjoy vestiges of our past," said Jefferson lighting his pipe.

"Such as?" said Hazen.

"Hair on the head. Hats do a better job of shedding water, but I'm glad we're not all bald."

"Heavens," Eleanor said.

"Imagine the day," said Hazen, "when they discover the gene that controls hair on the head. The question will become: shall we keep our hair for sentimental reasons or get rid of it because it isn't functional?"

"And who," said Jefferson, "will decide?"

"Put it to a vote."

"No!" cried Eleanor. "Democracy isn't like that."

And they had a little three-way argument of an amiable, silly sort to finish off the evening. The trouble was that Eleanor always defended her real belief (this time, that everyone should have the right to keep his hair or go bald just as he pleased) whereas the two men seemed to conduct such arguments as they played chess, for the fun of it. Only Hazen's grin kept her from being upset; Jefferson never cracked a smile but betrayed himself only by the extremity of his argument ("if God had intended us to be bald or haired as we wished, He would have supplied storehouses of wigs in every district, but since He has not done that, we must infer He intended us to be haired"). Tomfoolery, like chess; warfare without cause or enemies or issue; but at least they hadn't verged too close to something important as they sometimes did, and it was getting late.

"Well, good night, Peter," she said.

Jefferson had begun his nightly chore of winding the old clock on the china closet, his grandmother's wedding present to his mother. She was collecting the dishes and emptying the ash trays. Hazen was in the passage by the kitchen.

"By the way," Hazen said in an off-hand voice, "what have you heard from Jacqueline lately?"

"Oh, not much," she answered. "She's working hard."

She thought it odd he had raised the question. She had noticed that ever since Jacqueline had left, Hazen had been only formally polite whenever she mentioned her: "Oh yes, how interesting, fine fine." As a result, she had quit mentioning her entirely, as he seemed to prefer. There had been, apparently, even less going on between them than she had thought at the time; Jacqueline had not mentioned Hazen once in her letters.

"I was just wondering if she still liked living at Dr. Edwards' place."

"So far as I know," Eleanor answered.

He was obviously uncomfortable. It was his own fault for bringing the subject up. There are many subjects better not mentioned, and this was surely one of them.

Jefferson, still turning the key in the clock, spoke. "Professor Jones at Columbia University, an old friend of mine, had Jacqueline to Thanksgiving dinner." His voice was absolutely, fact-reporting colorless; Hazen might not know it, but this was often an ominous sign. "He informed us that she is well and in good spirits. She has gone to a number of exhibitions and plays." All these desiccated little pellets of information signified nothing; only his unexpected telling them mattered. "She is working on harmony chiefly now, and has been encouraged to develop her talent for melodic composition." He got down off the chair he had been standing on, went to the telephone, and dialed a number. He had not once looked at Hazen. "To the best of my knowledge and hope she has not made alliances with New York hot rodders. At least no one has mentioned it if she has." He listened to the telephone a second, and said "Ah." Then he set his wrist watch, climbed back up on the chair, and moved the clock's hand ahead four minutes. "She reports that she went to dinner at the Waldorf-Astoria last week with Pearl and the Countess, and also a cousin of Pearl's named Beesly Pettibone, who swishes when he walks." He stepped down from the chair and turned abruptly towards Hazen. "Is there anything else you want to know?"

Hazen appeared to be only confused, and mumbling "No

thanks," he left. But Eleanor, who knew that the stronger Jefferson's hostility the drier his voice, was perturbed. Hazen had said absolutely nothing to warrant such an attack. Yet Jefferson was eminently a just man; whenever he had unexpectedly attacked her so, she had later found that she'd somehow merited it. It was true, of course, that dryness did not always mean hostility on Jefferson's part; it might have meant no more than his unwillingness to discuss anything of importance with Hazen. Jefferson was a great deal more jealous of Jacqueline than he admitted, she thought, even to himself. That was no doubt the explanation.

She went over to see that Mama was installed in bed for the night.

"Ellie," said her mother in alarm when she entered, "is that you?"

"Of course, Mama," she said patiently. They went through this every night. "Who else would it be?"

"I was just having a little dream about Jackie. Such a nice dream. What did you do tonight, Ellie?"

"I read a story, Mama. Jefferson and Peter played a game of chess."

"Peter? Ah yes, yes, that reminds me. Mr. Hazen called on me this afternoon while you were out shopping. Such a nice young man. He was asking after Jackie. I couldn't help him . . . Ellie love, you're pulling the covers out at the foot. Haven't I told you my feet get cold so easy? Why do you think I wear these big clumsy bedsocks every night?"

"All right, Mama, I'll tuck you in right. What did Peter Hazen want to know?"

"He wanted to know if Jackie is coming home for Christmas. How could I tell him? I don't know myself. Nobody tells me what's going on."

"I don't know myself either, Mama. It costs a lot of money."

"Imagine having Christmas dinner by yourself in a restaurant in a big city. The lonesomest place in the whole world. Could you let her do that?" Tears appeared in the old woman's eyes.

"No, Mama, of course not. First I'd borrow money so she could be with us. Good night now."

"Close all the windows, Ellie. It's cold on my neck."

"They're closed, Mama. There's no draft."

"There's no draft."

"Good night, Mama."

"Good night, dear."

She stood in the hall a moment undecided. That was all Peter had wanted to know, whether Jackie was coming home for Christmas; he wanted to know whether to mail her present back to her or keep it here. How perfectly sensible of him. Jefferson and she would have to make up their minds whether they could afford to have Jacqueline fly out for the vacation; it was time they did it. A perfectly innocent impulse, and Jefferson had attacked him for it. "Is there anything else you want to know?" How insulting that was.

She rapped twice on his door and stepped in. "Peter?" she called, and presently he came out of the bedroom dressed in nothing but trousers. "I'm sorry," she said, "you were already in bed."

"Barely," he answered. "I'm not wearing pajamas."

That fact had nothing to do with anything, but she was reminded that he was naked from the waist up, still tan from the summer, still handsome.

"About Jacqueline," she said.

"I just wanted to know," he answered, "what to get her for Christmas."

But he seemed indifferent to what he was saying; he was looking intently at her mouth. He had not kissed her since the first day he had arrived, and his little overtures of sensuality he had, quite properly, refused to pursue. Once in awhile, when he was just coming or just leaving, he would hug her affectionately, as though to let her know that he remembered she was a woman. Now, however, she knew by his eyes that he was going to embrace her; and, though propriety required her to leave quickly, what she did was to stare at the blond hair on his chest.

"We haven't decided whether to have her come or not."

"Jefferson's a lucky man," he said.

She was moved by this generosity of his; he always spoke well of Jefferson. "What do you mean?"

Instead of answering, he advanced, deliberately embraced her, and kissed her. She put her hands on his chest to push him away, but the touch of his bare flesh weakened her arms. Well, she liked kissing, she'd always like kissing, and he kissed very expertly, none better. And if there were risks in kissing him thus, well, then there were risks. She gave herself over to the kiss.

He leaned back finally and looked at her. "You see what I mean? With such a wife, he still hankers after mathematics."

It was egregious flattery, of course, but pleasant, a kissing sort of flattery, pleasant as a massage and no more enduring.

"And such a daughter?" she responded. She thought it perfectly likely that he had done a little petting with Jacqueline; it didn't mean a thing, of course, the way young people behaved nowadays; she just didn't want him to get out of hand.

But he didn't turn a hair. "Certainly, and such a daughter." He kissed her again.

Well, he had not been really dishonest with her; he had as much as admitted his attraction to Jacqueline; he was hiding nothing. She yielded again to his embrace. But this time she was aroused to a desire kissing would not satisfy.

"No, Peter. Good heavens." They were breathing heavily. He grimaced. She broke from him, and ran out.

She found Jefferson in bed asleep, or pretending to be asleep. He was flat on his back, one hand by his side, the other neatly on his chest. His Vandyke was neat; even the bedclothes were not disarranged. He had not been in the slightest perturbed by his behavior towards Peter. If she challenged him on it, he would coolly and exactly demolish her arguments. Yet she was positive she was right, that Peter's heart was warm and Jefferson's cold. Not altogether cold, perhaps—he loved Jacqueline, or at least he was proud of her. He had said once many years before, "I am proud of everything I love," a sentiment that had pleased her at the time, so that she had remembered it ever since; sometimes however, as now, she reversed it, "I love everything I am proud of." Besides, he almost never made love with her any more; Peter instantly desired her. She wept.

She could not help making comparisons between the two, to Jefferson's chronic disadvantage. He was at the harpsichord; Ted

Burns having moved to Los Angeles, Jefferson seemed to prefer playing the harpsichord these days to the oboe. He sat prissily before the little keyboard plucking the finicky notes out, neither swaying nor visibly beating time; when he would lead off for the other two players, he nodded over at them like a schoolmaster; when a piece ended, he stood up and performed one vitamin pill's worth of a relaxing exercise, a sort of twist-bobble-shudder-bend. Hazen had come in late, just after the coffee break; his hands were grimy from the motorcycle, and he seemed to her hearty and windblown; he had changed into slacks and loafers but still he walked with a suggestion of the motorcyclist's slouch—tail in, shoulders a little rounded, head slightly inclined toward the front. He propped himself against the wall of the living room near the door, stretching his legs out on the floor, perfectly at ease. She noticed a certain stiffness about the mouth which he often brought back with him from cycling; probably he thought he was tough. Well, let him be silly and pompous and fantastic, he was capable of new experience, he was alive, he took a chance; whereas Jefferson knew the limits of his powers and never tried to violate them, indeed seemed content with them, he was reliable, he functioned well. True, he played Haydn trio sonatas skillfully and performed dizzying feats with formulas and graphs: she had had a country cousin who could rend a Sears Roebuck catalogue in two with his bare hands and skip a flat stone on the lake fifteen or twenty or even, once, twenty-two times; he was the wonder of the countryside for miles about, in all matters of catalogue-tearing and rock-skipping.

Hazen was still young, that is, he enjoyed his body: she had seen him stretch like a cat with a luxuriousness she could remember having enjoyed herself, and sometimes when he was walking away from her she had watched him rise on his toes a little or swing his shoulders or roll like a sailor just for the pleasure of it. He was young, that is, he had not divided himself up into parts very well; his emotions transfigured his face, so much that she never believed him when he boasted he was good at poker; it was true that he pretended he was wearing a mask sometimes, but his voice was subtle as any spy to betray him to her. He was still young enough, and sanguine enough, not yet to know how much he could accomplish in the world, whether he would be able to live up to his ambition. He was fluid, so that if he discovered himself stopped in one direction, he turned in another and kept going ahead. Yet he was not callow, not half-baked; he worked hard and steadily; he was confident in his manner. Experience instructed him how to accomplish best that which youth still fired him to attempt. He would make a fine lover. Quite consciously she entertained the thought of him as her lover—until, that is, she found herself staring absurdly at his chest, across which his black, pearl-buttoned shirt was stretched taut. She shook herself; no one seemed to have noticed her staring.

He had not as excellent a mind as Jefferson nor did he know as much; neither did he doubt as much, as devastatingly much; he never refused to discuss a subject only because he was not its master; he was not ironical about matters of importance; he hoped. He was no more a scientist, she felt, than she herself was; she disregarded all his technical talk about time-studies and work-incentives and the mores of part-time leisure in an industrial society, his percentages and equations and fancy words ending in *ational;* what he really wanted was to make the world better. For if she was sure of one thing about him, it was that he shared her faith that the wrongs of the world could be righted and that he should do something about them. Jefferson did not; Jefferson had the true scientist's knowledge—a sort of faith with the heat gone—that the wrongs of the world could be studied, though not, for technical reasons, very well.

When the evening had come to an end, Hazen touched her good-night and slipped out, merely laid his hand for a second on her arm without saying anything, looked at her smilingly and touched her; no more; yet it made her happy. By chance, Jefferson touched her arm in the same place while they were preparing for bed, in order to arrest her a moment while he plucked some lint out of her hair; he was body temperature, he metabolized, he was capable of syllogisms; yet it seemed to her that he no more touched her like a living man than did the rug her feet. He was wholly safe from lightning.

She lay in bed rigid with bitterness that she should be so bound to this less than man. Quite purely, quite consciously, she gave herself over to hating him, and he hadn't done a damned thing to her.

Two

For half an hour Hazen was the only person in the Igloo. In Iggy's place today, Sunday, there was a bartender Hazen did not know, a heavy-browed fellow reading comics.

A belted motorcyclist called Spur—he wore cowboy boots and spurs—came in with an underslung Mexican girl Hazen had not seen in the gang before. They started up the juke box, sprawled at the table furthest from his, and talked in voices too low for him to eavesdrop on. Hazen did not greet Spur, who had never responded to him even with a nod, but studied the girl; about her straight, thin lips she had drawn a voluptuous mouth in luminous pink lipstick; he recognized her as pachuca by her enormous hair-do. On the impulse, he began sketching a gang of pachucos for Stoodley to fall in with, the boys with duck-tail haircuts, the girls with structures of hair lofty above their heads, all of them provided with spring-blade knives and speaking an argot of Hazen's invention. He scarcely glanced at whoever else strayed into the Igloo, but roughed-in a week of strips.

"Hi, Prof. Heh heh."

Hazen looked up in surprise. "Hello, John Henry. How do you do, Fern."

"What are you doing," said Fern and cracked her gum.

"Fixing up some Stoodleys." He started to put them away.

"Mind if we take a look, Prof?"

He disliked having anyone watch him sketching, but John Henry's friendship could be worth something to him. "OK."

"Let's sit down, Bull," said Fern.

"Don't call me Bull," he said without conviction, looking around the room. He ordered beer.

Fern stuck her gum under the table and began thumbing through the sketches, clicking her chief front tooth with her left thumbnail. John Henry scarcely glanced at the papers.

"Look at, Bull, this girl's a pachuc'."

He glanced at the drawing and pointed. "So's he." He looked at Hazen with one eyebrow as high and the other as low as possible. "What you doing, starting a new outfit?"

"New outfit?"

"Sure, mixing pachuc's in with Stoodley's gang?"

"I'm thinking about it."

"They don't mix."

"Spur seems to think they do."

John Henry scowled over at Spur. "He's crazy. You never noticed that? He's crazy."

"Oh, don't be a bull," said Fern. "She looks like a cute kid."

"I got nothing against her. I got nothing against anybody till they do something."

"Do you know why I call him Bull?" she said to Hazen and winked.

"No, Fern," said Hazen. "Why do you call him Bull?"

"Because he's bull-headed. Like this business of that pachuc' girl Spur's got. So she's a pachuc'. So what? But no, old Bull here won't give an inch. Maybe Spur likes her, honey."

He simply ignored her. "Say, Prof, we haven't been seeing so much of you since Jackie took off."

"I've been here at Iggy's a good deal."

"Sure, but I mean out and among."

Hazen suppressed the anger in his voice. "I don't always know what's cooking."

"Yeh, sure, a guy in your position."

Hazen was reminded of the way John Henry had danced his car over beside Floyd's car the first time Hazen and Jackie had gone to the meet in Richmond; he wondered how John Henry was going to glare a spotlight onto him now.

"Do you know what?" said Fern mincing, her little finger

crooked. "I'm glad that little bitch Jackie isn't around here any more."

Hazen creamed his expression free of anything rough. "I know what you mean," he said, leaning toward her a little. Her mouth was slightly ajar. She batted her eyes. "I can see how you feel that way. Me, of course, I'm a man, so I'm prejudiced, and besides I've been a friend of Jackie's ever since she was a kid, but I can see how a woman like you would feel about her the way you do."

John Henry guffawed.

"What's so funny?" she screeched like a cockatoo. "*He* understands me."

"Sure," he said, "sure. So do I. Sure he understands you." He winked at Hazen. "Don't you, Prof old boy?"

She slid over on the seat next to Hazen and held his arm. "*He* wants me."

Hazen did not know which of them he disliked the more, but he knew he could use John Henry. He rather idly patted Fern's leg and said, in a voice for pacifying a baby, that sure he wanted her; but he kept looking at John Henry. She snuggled self-consciously and muttered, "The dirty son of a bitch."

John Henry yelled "Hey!" at the bartender and snapped his fingers without raising his arm from hanging down beside his chair. "Draw me a beer with plenty of head on it."

"You hear that?" said Fern to Hazen, glaring at John Henry. "He don't even like foam either."

He brooded at her till the beer came. He held the glass up, squinted to see how high the foam stood over the top of the glass, lowered it to his lips, and blew foam into Fern's face.

Hazen braced himself for a loud scene. But Fern did not say a word; she mopped herself with a paper napkin, huddled apart from both of them, kicked John Henry once on the shin so that he winced, and stared in the direction of the bartender, a look of some dignity on her face. John Henry made a sort of man-to-man shrug at Hazen. Hazen just stared at him.

John Henry began flipping through the Stoodley sketches. "You know this cyclist chief you've got in the Stoodley nowadays, B. C. Troglodyte? The guy that looks like an ape?"

"Yes," said Hazen, wondering if he had been reading a dictionary.

"Why the B.C.?"

"He's a Texan. They sometimes just use initials in Texas."

"Sure, sure. But B.C., that means before Christ."

"Oh, yeh," said Hazen sweating. "But I got the idea from a guy I knew in Nebraska, named B. C. Johnson." A double lie: he had not known such a person, and even if he had he would not have named his imaginary character B.C. for that reason. "How do you like him?"

"Oh fine, fine, I guess. Heh heh. Say, you going to have any rods in it too?"

"Do you know what he's getting at?" said Fern with tinny malice, staring at John Henry. "I just now figured it out."

"Shut up," he said and made a fist.

"He wants—"

"God damn it, can't you leave a man to talk in peace?"

"He wants you to put *him* in Stoodley, that's what he wants. The big-headed bastard."

He blushed scarlet and gave her a look of real hatred. "You bitch."

In that blush of John Henry's, Hazen saw his advantage. His instant impulse was to attack, to tease, to avenge himself for the uneasinesses which John Henry had been inflicting upon him during several weeks and especially during this past quarter-hour. He wanted to blow John Henry's vanity up with come-on promises, and then to deflate it by saying in his coldest voice, "But I guess I can't put you in twice, old boy. After all, who do you think B. C. Troglodyte is?" But he controlled himself, remembering his own interests.

"I don't put real people in my strip because they could sue me for libel."

"Sure," said John Henry eagerly.

"If I put in a hot rod chief named John Henry, then you could sue me for libel if you got mad at me."

"Oh, naturally," he said. "It's just a crazy idea of Fern's. Think nothing of it."

"On the other hand, I could give him another name and . . ."

"What name?"

"I hadn't really thought. I'm pretty choosy about names."

"Pretty fancy pants," said Fern nastily.

He cocked an eyebrow at her. "It depends on how you look at it. Anyhow I could give this guy another name but make him sort of look like you. You know—Hollywood haircut, sideburns, that way you've got of raising one eyebrow and lowering the other one."

John Henry blushed again. "Yeh?"

"Of course," Hazen said, "maybe I could give him the same initials you got." He paused as though considering; by the way John Henry waited for him to speak again, he felt his power. "The real question is, do you want the rest of the gang to know it's you, or do you just want to have it a secret, sort of?" Fern started to laugh. "Be still," said Hazen and squeezed her hand hard.

"Oh hell," said John Henry, "it's just a stupid idea anyhow."

"Well, which?"

"I guess I'd just as soon the guys knew it, if it comes to that. You know."

"OK, I make you recognizable, which means you could sue me. That means you'd have to sign a waiver, saying you knew all about it and agreed in advance."

"Yeh?"

"It's not friendly but it's business."

"OK."

"Good. There's one thing, though. I'll have to get to know you a lot better than I do now. You'll have to take me around with you a lot."

"Why?"

"I've got to know how you operate. You don't think I just make all these characters up out of nothing, do you?"

"Well, pretty much so, I guess," said John Henry.

"Pfft," said Fern in disgust at his ignorance.

"Whenever I really portray somebody, I've got to know what makes them tick. Like for example, I've got to see how you handle a road meet, stay right with you, watch the others too, be one of them."

"Yeh," said John Henry.

"That's the only way," said Hazen. "I'd sure like to do you up brown, you're one of the most interesting people I ever met, but that's the only way it can be done."

"I'll think it over."

"I don't even know about that," said Hazen coldly, shrugging. "You can see I've started a new episode here this evening, these pachuc's. I'd have to do something else if I put you in instead. You'd better make up your mind now." John Henry glowered. "I don't know how much longer I'm going to keep Stoodley going anyway." He just barely refrained from saying, "So you'd better make it worth my while." But he saw by his eyes that John Henry had got it.

Slim looked in the door and came over to John Henry.

"What's cooking?" said John Henry.

"My rod's stalled. Gimme a shove?"

"Where?"

"Over at Tommy's. Nobody's home."

"What's the trouble?"

"Battery. It's going dead."

"OK." He turned to Hazen after he stood up. "Go ahead with it, Prof. We'll work something out."

"I'll come along now," said Hazen.

Slim looked surprised, John Henry scowled, and Fern grabbed his arm. "Stay with me," she pleaded with him.

"Stay with her," said John Henry, utterly without accommodation in his voice. "You understand her." He left laughing.

Hazen decided to make this day the test. If John Henry did not in fact change his attitude, then Hazen would lampoon him so that everyone got the point—and he'd be covered by a waiver to boot.

"Well, aren't you even a gentleman?" said Fern. "Can't you even order another beer?"

He ordered. There was an unhappy, urgent look in her eyes that he did not understand.

"That John Henry," he said, "he sure has funny ways of showing you how much he loves you."

"Are you so dumb?" she said bleakly. "I'm just a thorn in his flesh." She laid her head on her folded arms, looking up at Hazen sidewise. "I'm dirt under his feet."

"Yeh," said Hazen.

"Do you know where I came from?" she asked.

"No, where do you come from?"

"Phoenix, Arizona. My folks are still there. I was born and raised there. That's my home."

"Is that where John Henry married you?"

"Who said we ever got married?"

"Why, Jackie told me."

"What does *she* know about it?"

"I don't know."

"She's still got her cherry," said Fern with contempt and melancholy. "What does she know about anything?"

He shrugged. He decided to name one of the girls in the comic strip Cherry.

"Well, go ahead, Prof, ask me."

"Whether you and John Henry are married?"

"Sure, ask me. Don't you want to know? I want you to."

"OK, Fern. Are you and John Henry married?"

"No," she said spitefully. "So put that in your pipe and smoke it."

"That's terrible," he said sincerely.

"You don't know a thing about it," she said. "I never told my folks. It'd kill my father. Or else he'd kill me, I don't know which." She cried a little. "He's going to walk out on me. Then what'll I do?"

"Go back home and look for a fellow you can settle down with. You know, a guy who brings home a pay check every Friday night and wants to have some kids."

"And I'm supposed to stay home and rot? A rotten housewife?"

"You got a job?"

"I'm a beautician," she said, sitting up straight again. "I took a beauty culture course." She explained to him for ten minutes about how to give permanents.

John Henry and Slim returned.

"Well, John Henry," said Hazen, "is it a deal?"

By a sort of jerk of his jaw John Henry indicated that he didn't want to talk about it in front of Slim. "Sure, sure, it's a deal."

Hazen wanted one more security. "When's the next road meet?"

"I don't know as we've got one planned especially."

"Sure, J.H.," said Slim. "Next Saturday out at Diablo."

"Oh yeh," said John Henry.

"Oh yeh," Fern mocked.

"I'll be there," said Hazen. "Where'll I meet you?" He jotted the place down on a piece of paper, and added "Flossie," to remind himself to cancel his date with her for that night.

There was the roar of a motorcycle starting up out in back of Iggy's. Fern jerked. "Where's Spur at?" she yelled.

John Henry, without transition, half stood from his chair, crouched over the table, and looked over at Spur. "They're stealing your bike!" yelled Fern. John Henry told her not to come along and blocked her getting up by pulling the table around. He was closer to the door, but he let Spur and his girl run out ahead of him. The motorcycle roared down East Fourteenth Street.

"I'm coming along!" said Hazen, and ran out onto the sidewalk.

"There's just room for three in my heap," said John Henry. "Bring your Buick if you think you've got the drag." He screeched off laughing.

Hazen left Slim watching the car disappear down the street, and went back to collect his things from the table.

"What's the matter, Prof?" said Fern. "He leave you behind too?"

He looked at her with disgust. She laughed at him.

"So that's the kind of a deal he makes," said Hazen. "I'll fix him."

"He'll come through. Give him time to get used to the idea." She laughed at herself. "I've given him two years. I ought to know."

"Yeh?" Hazen decided to postpone his revenge and see if John Henry would really come through next Saturday. "You want a ride home?"

"Who said I was going home?" Her voice was coy but her eyes were full of fear.

"Where else do you want to go?"

"Oh, I don't know," she said.

He took this to be an invitation to him to try to make her, and he took the invitation to be a sort of life-line flung in desperation. He wanted to make her no more than he wanted her in tow.

"Well," he said, "I got to go do some work. I hope Spur gets his motor back OK."

"If they catch the bastard, John Henry'll carve his ear off. That's why we had to get out of Phoenix so fast."

"He cut a man's ear off?"

"I reckon," she said, holding onto her glass with both hands. Her smile to him was shaky. "Thanks for everything."

He winked, squeezed her wrist, and left her there.

Three

Eleanor knew she did not understand properly what delight, what complement of temper and mind, Jefferson found in Brother Quintillian, whose special knowledge was the theology of the Schoolmen. Once every few months Jefferson would invite him to dinner, and they would sit for hours over Napa Valley wine talking about anything at all, books politics music oceanography chromosomes wasps, anything but the intricacies of theology or mathematics. She admired, quite as though it were a machine work-of-art, the working of their intellects in these colloquies, into which she never obtruded herself: a machine because their minds locked gears or slid past one another or made steady driving motions like beautifully tooled and oiled mechanism; a work of art because, to her recurrent distress, nothing came of it all, no change of attitude, no decision, no true judgment, scarcely any heat, but only the beauty of the working itself and of the occasional realigning of parts into something which looked like a new idea but which, in her memory at least, faded fast. Aestheticism of the senses she could understand easily, and of nature, of art, of experience even; but aestheticism of the intellect, like electricity, she was only used to by daily acquaintance; to her it was intolerable to imagine that those minds might be doing no more than functioning well, for their own pleasure, which explained to everyone else the nine tiers of angels, the inward coherence of atoms, the law. She was Christian enough to admire one who worked simply for the greater glory of God, but Protestant enough to feel uneasy when it was God out there the work was dedicated to rather than God in every man. All the same, Brother Quintillian's courteous company pleased her; except for his clerical suit, he was undistinguished in appearance, slightly above average in every way including manliness of carriage, but his manners were antique and subtle like his Thomism; after much debate with herself, she had invited Hazen to join them at dinner the next Sunday to meet him.

"We were discussing performances of Verdi," said Jefferson as soon as Hazen was installed in a chair, a glass of cabernet beside him. "Brother Quintillian was in Vienna last year."

"Oh really?" said Hazen. "I was there for a couple of weeks shortly after the war."

"How interesting," Brother Quintillian said. "I understand there was a splendid 'Otello' in the spring of '47. Did you by any chance happen to see it?"

"No," said Hazen, "I don't much care for operas."

She winced for him when the other two, nodding amiably ("it's perfectly all right to have bad taste so long as you don't insist on it"), turned back to discussing the advantages of symbolic scenery for "Aïda." Hazen did not look annoyed at being so excluded; she did not know whether to admire his fortitude or deplore his obtuseness.

"It seems to me," he said when they asked him what sort of scenery he preferred, "that opera is a hodge-podge art anyway." They were not perturbed by the thought. "What I mean is," and she thought him a bit sophomoric when he ran his hand over his hair nervously, "I don't think it's a valid or logical art form."

They were scrupulous; they did not pay him out rope to hang himself with. "If you will pardon me," said Brother Quintillian, "it seems to me that the only criterion for the success of an art form is the success of examples of that form."

"Exactly," said Jefferson.

"In matters of art, all is contingent, relative, and such logic as is useful must be inductive."

"And some operas," said Jefferson, "are successful."

"At least," said Brother Quintillian with gentleness, apology, precision, "if I assert they are successful and you assert they are not, we make further dispute impossible."

There followed a brief pause (which she knew so well and Hazen, from his somewhat wild glance about, seemed to know so little) marking their total dismissal of a subject adequately dealt with.

She found a certain fascination in watching them at work on him. He seemed to her not youthful so much as callow, against these his superiors: inferior and refusing to admit it. There was no malice in them, only a zeal for functioning which was likely to overlook the feelings of others.

"Jefferson tells me," said Brother Quintillian, "that you are making a sociological study of motorcyclists."

"Yes," said Hazen.

"I have become acquainted with a few boys at St. Anselm's who are devoted to motorcycles and fast automobiles. I should be most interested to hear what results you have come up with."

It was an embossed invitation, which, however, Hazen declined reluctantly. "I haven't fully organized my conclusions yet. I'm going to get a paper written on the subject during Christmas vacation." Brother Quintillian accepted the refusal with a formal nod. Eleanor knew by Hazen's eyes that he had expected to be drawn on, had wanted to be, and she was actively annoyed by his coyness; she wished Brother Quintillian had rebuked him at least by an eyebrow.

"I have found Stoodley amusing," said Brother Quintillian. "Eleanor said you had threatened to discontinue Stoodley?"

"Well," said Hazen in a depressed tone of voice, "to get in with the gang I wanted to study I had to keep doing the comic strip."

"Oh?"

"It was a condition of their accepting me."

"You study them?"

"I try to."

"I would be interested to know," said Brother Quintillian, and hesitated for the delicate way to put it, "the concept of the person which permits you to study these young people as you do. If you don't mind speaking of such a matter, that is."

"My concept of the person?"

"Yes. You see I have a notion it's very unlike my own."

"I don't have one."

"Ah yes."

And the brief, valedictory pause.

But after dinner, after his drinking more of the good wine, Hazen took the offensive, to her disgust.

"Tell me, Brother Quintillian, you are a Thomist?"

"Yes."

"Well, I never read St. Thomas in my life. I suppose I should." Brother Quintillian did not nod or shrug or in any way react to this statement. "Tell me this, what earthly reason would a mid-twentieth-century American have to study St. Thomas? Except an antiquarian or theologian or somebody like that." This with a little wave of the hand.

It was crudely effective. She saw Jefferson shift angrily in his chair, and she recognized in the stricken look on Brother Quintillian's face, in the way he drew in his chin and glanced at Hazen over the top of his glasses, his dismay at such ill-mannerliness.

"Thomism is a possible way of ordering the world of spirit."

"What has it to do with capitalism, total war, or neurosis?"

This thrashing-about, inefficient attack of Hazen's had to recommend it in Eleanor's eyes only its heat. She could not possibly have entered as an equal into the discussion, but as hostess she began to look for an opportunity to put an end to Hazen's poor display.

Brother Quintillian bent his head a moment, and just as Hazen was about to speak, he continued. "Neither do capitalism, total war, or neurosis have anything to do, directly, with understanding God and saving souls."

"Touché!" cried Jefferson. "Do you want some cointreau, Hazen?"

But Hazen ignored him. "Do you suppose, Brother, that if St. Thomas were alive today he would apply his mind to the same problems he did in the thirteenth century?"

And the discussion became a sort of nagging. Eleanor wondered why Hazen had taken such a dislike to Brother Quintillian that he should be arguing thus neither for clarification nor victory, but only, so far as she could see, for aggression's sake. She was afraid that Jefferson would, as she had seen him do, slap the conversation shut with a firm rebuke, or that Brother Quintillian would retire offended; but she did not know how to stop Hazen.

Presently he leaned across the fence of insult. "Fat bishops, hungry peasants, what does studying the nature of God have to do about *them?*"

Jefferson's lips pressed together ominously; Brother Quintillian frowned. But then she saw a sort of concern come into Hazen's expression, bent solely toward Brother Quintillian. She thought it might be a mask for malice. "Peter, you are intolerably rude."

"I'm sorry, Brother." He had not said it because of her reproof but because he meant it, and for that she was glad. She saw that it had been Jefferson he had been really attacking, and that he repented of wounding this adversary unwillingly deputized. "That was unjust of me. Analyzing comic strips hasn't anything to do with it either, or," waving dismissively at Jefferson, "making tables of probability statistics." At any rate, he demolished wholesale.

"You make the error," said Jefferson, still without rancor in his voice, "of holding each member of the Church responsible for the actions of every other member, or at least of the hierarchy."

"I have already apologized," said Hazen loftily.

Within fifteen minutes Brother Quintillian left; it was true he had a sister in Tower 4 whom he always left them to visit before returning to St. Anselm's, but seven o'clock was unusually early for him to go. She assumed that Hazen would withdraw, the fight being over, and correct papers. She did not exactly understand what the fight had been about: bad temper, clash of personalities, it was of little importance. What mattered was the disgraceful way he had conducted himself. He had stood up to Jefferson; that was something; but any satisfaction she might have felt from that, he had spoiled for her. Better he should withdraw.

But he did not withdraw. "How's about a game of chess?" he said and started towards the workroom where the chessmen and board were stowed; it was a movement somewhere between a lurch and a dart, uncharacteristic of him, impulsive in a disconnected sort of way.

"No, thanks," said Jefferson. "I never play well when I've had much of anything to drink."

"Do you always have to play well?" Hazen asked, grinning.

"I don't enjoy the game unless we're up to scratch."

"Haven't you some work to do?" Eleanor said as pleasantly as she could manage.

"I'll go," he said, calmly because he was not really thinking about her. He took a stance of belligerence opposite Jefferson. Eleanor was puzzled by him, for though he hadn't taken much more wine than usual, he acted drunk—odd, at least. "I got a letter from Jackie yesterday. She said Lisa is going to be on a TV show the day after Christmas."

"Really?" Jefferson, she saw, made the same gesture—not so much a gesture as an alerting, a getting-set—which she had caught the week before when Hazen had introduced the subject of Jacqueline.

"She said she's fed up with music work."

"I can well imagine," said Jefferson.

"It's an intensive course," said Eleanor.

"Do you know what she's homesick for?"

"What?" said Jefferson.

"For the gang. She wanted to know how the gang's getting along. She hasn't forgotten a thing. She says she really wants to get my motorcycle between her legs again."

"I had hoped," said Jefferson, enunciating meticulously, "that the excesses of the night before she left would have purged her of such impulses."

"What excesses?" cried Eleanor alarmed.

"She told me that Floyd got up to 100 miles an hour on the highway to Walnut Creek, and received a ticket for speeding."

"Oh dear, oh dear, oh dear heaven." She buried her face in her hands at the thought of that danger. But it was an old danger; she had safely confronted its like before; it was safely past now. In the dark of her hands, in the dead silence between the two men, she remembered their strangeness and heard their last speeches in her ears still. And into her vacuum of consciousness a doubt clouded, that it had been more than driving fast which they had been talking about. She recalled Hazen's flush when Jefferson had spoken of "the excesses of the night before she left"; she remembered how acutely Jefferson had always watched Jacqueline, how jealously; if there had been anything to see, any inference to draw, Jefferson would have done it accurately. The dreadful thought coagulated in her mind that Hazen had gone too far with Jacqueline the last night she was home and that Jefferson knew it.

She could detect no guilt in Hazen's voice. He was speaking less brashly now. She did not listen to his words so much as to his tone of voice. He was justifying himself for his studies because of his scientific approach to human beings; yet, he was saying confusedly, science must transcend itself. Gobbledygook. She raised her head and looked at them. Jefferson was frigid with hostility; Hazen was more skitteringly uneasy than she had ever seen before, skipping hither and thither about on the surface of his subject like a daddy-long-legs. The men were standing, across the glass-top table from each other, Jefferson next the workroom door.

If it was true Hazen had gone too far with Jacqueline, she thought remotely, then he was morally a slush to be making advances to her now. The thought of being in competition with her own daughter for a man who by reason of that very competition had proved himself unworthy of either of them, clogged her throat with a moment's horror.

She looked at Hazen hard. It was antagonism to Jefferson that was motivating him, obviously, that had motivated him all evening. She could scarcely blame him for that; Jefferson had been treating him for weeks like a sort of family retainer, good for chess and an idle chat now and again, for helping the womenfolk with their errands. Why should she seek guilt in his features? At her farewell party Jacqueline had given her attention to Floyd; she had stayed out most of that night with him; they were first cousins, but first cousins have been attracted before; she had shown no concern for Hazen during this whole semester in New York, nor he much for her. After all, what Jefferson had said about Floyd's going 100 miles an hour at night would have been enough to shock even Hazen. Perhaps he had even been made a little jealous of Floyd. That was no more than human. It did not mean he was dishonorable; she had no reason to suspect him of grave duplicity; in fact, his overture to her the week before was a proof that he could never have been seriously involved with Jacqueline. Looking at the two of them in this strange combat—Hazen warm, childish, confused, Jefferson cold, composed, clear—her heart closed toward both of them.

"Science has been without values too long," Hazen was saying. "I don't mean scientific method, I mean the aims and results of science. Society has tried to make science its highest value." Jefferson had been interrupting him from time to time, but she did not remember what he had been saying. "But science has no values. We are adrift. We must make our own values." Jefferson moved irritably; she did remember the quality of his voice, cold and clipped. "That is the urgent need of our time, for society to defend itself against science. Science has demonstrated its power to destroy us. Man can unmake himself." Jefferson's hand was on the knob of the door to his workroom. "Man must make his own values, give himself back the dignity he has lost, reaffirm himself."

Jefferson was not as tall as Hazen by inches and was much slenderer; his voice was light; as he stood with the door half-open behind him, turning a little, his posture was almost frivolous. Yet when he spoke at Hazen she found him fearsome.

"*I do not believe you,*" he said slowly, colorlessly. "*God is very great.*"

He went into the workroom. Hazen, without glancing at her, beat his way out. Presently she heard the oboe playing a tune of which she recognized only the melancholy.

For she did not know how long, she stood where they'd left her; her mind was a kaleidoscope of notions signifying nothing; she was not even feeling. Out of pure habit she washed the dishes and laid the table for breakfast, and went over to adjust Mama for the night. When she came back into her living room, she could hear the steady sound of the shuttle next door. There wasn't the slightest chance she would be able to go to sleep. She had no book she wanted to read. A thunderclap of jet fighter planes flying low overhead shook the room. She turned on the radio.

A local announcer was reading, in a matter-of-fact voice, news bulletins. Railroad strike threatens to tie up nation. Unidentified youth knifed in parked car. 600,000 South Korean orphans without homes. Colder tomorrow with slight precipitation in early evening. Swanson's bread is better seven scientific ways. She felt herself slipping; her breath caught, as from a suppressed sob.

She was about to lose her nerve again and she was filled with dread, for this time she feared that once she failed to resist that turmoil of emotions inside her she would be wrenched by them beyond her strength to endure. They pressed; she held back. She could not remain in this place. For a moment she thought of taking a long walk down the golf course, exhausting herself physically; but she was not sure that that would remedy her trouble. She rapped on the door of the workroom—it was locked—and said she was going to spend the night in Mama's apartment; only the shuttle answered her, not even the whistling between the teeth, only the shuttle. She went down the hall to Hazen's door, rapped gently, and went in.

The door to his bedroom was closed, with a crack of light showing under it. "Peter!" she called quietly. "May I talk to you a moment?" She huddled into herself; her voice sounded timid in her own ears. She heard the thump of his feet on the floor; the door opened. In the obscurity from the reading light on his bed table, she saw him standing inside the room, stark naked, not smiling, looking at her mouth, holding his right hand out to her. "Peter!" she cried and recoiled with shock. He did not move or speak. His presenting himself nude offended her, yet the sight of his nudeness aroused her desire. She wanted to leave the apartment, or else she wanted him to come pull her into his bedroom. But he did not, and she did not leave. He stretched out his other arm towards her. "Come," he said. She went.

But before she would get into bed with him, she asked him if he had ever made love with Jacqueline. "No." He did not protest, just "No." She believed him. At the back of her mind, vaguely, she knew she had waited to ask him the question at a time like this so that he could only say no, whatever the truth, and that, therefore, she wanted the possibly damaging truth less than she wanted the convenience of this answer. That she might stow this article of knowledge far back in her mind where it couldn't be readily found, along with many others, she devoted herself fervently to making love.

Long after he had gone to sleep beside her, she lay awake happy. She had not lost her nerve again but was at peace, she had eluded Jefferson's sterile power, she was desired and her desire was fulfilled. It was as though all the confusions and trouble of the evening had only made stronger the force of their desire. She felt whole, unified in all ways. She was aware of her body as she had not been aware of it for many years. When she wished, she could feel each several toe as a part in her whole delight. She felt absolutely no anxiety, and knew she felt none. His breathing, his body against her arm, his smell, all delighted her. They had not talked; time enough for that. They were lovers. Dear dear Peter—even now he was not Hazen to her. She looked out over past and future, cause and consequence, as from a high hill.

Sunrise awoke her. She kissed his sleeping lips and got up to dress. On his bureau she glimpsed a note in Jacqueline's handwriting. "Hazie," it began. "It looks like I'm going to be home the 20th." She looked guiltily away. "Go ahead," he said. She started and glanced around at him; he was languid on his pillow and smiling. "It's the letter I mentioned. Read it if you want to." She thanked him and read. "I sure miss the gang and I hope nothing worse has happened than John Henry giving Fern the brush-off. I can't blame him, considering. Is there going to be a New Year's Eve party? Let's have one with everybody. Tell them I'm coming. J.D." Her heart filled with relief: this was the letter of friendly adolescence. All her doubts were allayed.

"Why does she sign herself J.D.?" she asked him.

"Her initials."

"Yes, but she never used them that I heard."

"The gang used them sometimes. They mean juvenile delinquent too."

She laughed at the notion of Jacqueline Devereux-juvenile delinquent, and he joined her. It was harmless, harmless. She had never felt better, for not only did she tingle with contentment but also her unhappiness had all vanished. She bent over him and kissed him good-bye, sensually, friendlily, lover-like.

For a week Eleanor luxuriated in all the wifely satisfactions of having a lover, deceiving her husband, making love often, running risks, receiving countless attentions. On Sunday she drove her mother down to church and, though she didn't have to, went in with her to services; she came out an adulteress. Thinking of adultery, she had no intention of ceasing to commit it, but she was no longer able to overlook the damage her action entailed, especially to Jefferson; she did not believe that what you don't know can't hurt you, and anyway she doubted that she could long keep Jefferson in ignorance about a matter of such importance. Lying awake that night beside Jefferson asleep, she was bitter to think of her duty and her loss; it seemed to her that if she and Hazen were alone and very far away from here, they would be altogether happy; she wept.

Their circumstances obliged her, or at least encouraged her, to go to him, her to seek him out: Jefferson had remained cold towards him since the dinner with Brother Quintillian, and besides, he lived alone. Next morning she went to his apartment.

"It's a fine day," she said. "Let's go to the beach."

"Where's Jefferson?"

It was the first day of Christmas vacation. "He's up at the cyclotron today," she answered. "Mama's all right."

"I really ought to work on my paper."

"Of course, darling, but I have something important we must talk over."

"It's overcast."

"Oh, but the beach is wonderful on a grey winter day. It's not cold and there's no wind. For my sake?"

"OK," he said, cheerily giving in. "But I've *really* got to work tonight."

They lounged along in his car looking at whatever came by. They did not talk much; they seemed to talk together, now that they were lovers, less than before. They walked by the breakers hand in hand, and squatted for an hour by tidepools, watching the disguise and busyness of that still world. She was happy again, as though they were only friends on an outing. Indeed, by mid-afternoon when they were obliged to leave for home, she had decided that her concern of the night before had been no more than a brief attack of guilt—that her pleasure in being with Hazen was as great as ever, that all that was actually necessary for her to do was to protect Jefferson from gratuitous pain.

"What was it," he asked her, as they were driving through the Golden Gate Park, "that you wanted to talk over?"

"Nothing very important really. That is, I was disturbed last night, but being with you today has helped clear up my mind."

"Why were you disturbed?" he asked tenderly.

She found his tenderness and thoughtfulness irresistible. It was true that he had never said he loved her, but he had given her a thousand demonstrations, in word and deed, of his affection and desire. Not passion—for neither of them was it a question of passion; there were the others to keep in mind.

"Thinking about Jefferson," she answered. He made no response. "You know your idea that we might take a little trip together?"

"Yes," he said, "later on some time."

"Later?"

"Well, we can't exactly go off while Jackie is home."

"Oh." She hadn't thought of that. She appreciated his considerateness. "That's true."

"Anyhow, we'll have to wait till we have good enough excuses to both be gone at the same time."

"That's what was on my mind," she answered. "I am going to tell Jefferson that we are going off together."

"What!"

"I want him to know."

"My God, why?"

"He has always been open and above board with me. I have no right to lie to him."

"But he'll leave you."

For a considerable time she did not answer. It was a bad sentence, under the circumstances, for him to leave ringing in the ears. If he was made uneasy, he didn't show it.

"No, Peter, I doubt that he will leave me. At least not for that alone."

"One thing is certain, I'll have to move, and it's so convenient now. Damn it," he said, "why can't you at least put it off for a while? Till next semester?"

"No," she said, "I must tell him. I must do it before Jacqueline comes. The truth will hurt him less if I respect him enough to tell it myself." Then she permitted herself her only bitter statement. "After all, as you know, he is not really threatened as husband, and we are discreet." He absorbed this without expression or word. "You're smoking too much these days," she said, touching his leg as a sign of affection.

"That's right."

"Are you upset, darling?"

"No," he said irritably, "it's just that I'll have to move on such short notice. What will Jackie think? There's no earthly reason why I should stay anyplace in the Village except where I am, and I don't know where else I can move to in the next four days."

"I'm sorry," she said. "You don't think I want you to be away from me, do you?"

"I don't know. I honestly don't see why Jefferson has to come in on this at all. He's your husband in name only, isn't he?"

"We do not love each other," she said, "but he is my husband. I do not have the right to hurt him, but I am doing it anyway; even so, there is one thing I refuse to do—betray him."

His voice when he spoke was altered. "You are right." At the next stop sign he turned and looked full at her, and squeezed her hand. His face was serious, it seemed to her, nearly suffering. "Sometimes I forget your fineness." He spoke almost shyly. "That was the old Eleanor speaking, the one I fell for."

His words suffused her with joy, for she realized that she had been feeling a subterranean worry that after the novelty wore off he would tire of her; on the contrary, he liked her still. And though he had been unpleasant, petty even, about her revealing to Jefferson their status, she saw now that it was no more than one ought reasonably to have expected: Jefferson was not, in all truth, his friend; Jacqueline was; and he had shown a keen regard for her welfare, thinking immediately of protecting her. He wasn't perfect but he was sensitive and appreciative and warm-hearted and handsome. All the way home, touching him lightly, she gazed at him with enjoyment and sometimes, thinking of their embraces, shivered with desire to embrace him now. Yet she did not try to draw him into love-making: they had always been pushed together as much as they had been pulled.

Four

When the elevator stopped at the tenth floor, Jefferson deferred to Mr. Erskine, who in turn offered to let him go first, but then, as the elder, accepted Jefferson's courtesy.

"Mr. Hazen," said Mr. Erskine, stopping at the door. "Excuse me, sir."

Hazen, a portable typewriter in one hand and a suitcase in the other, begged their pardon for having started to bumble in. Jefferson thought he acted oddly confused as they came out, an embarrassed smile on his lips, chuckling or seeming to chuckle. Mr. Erskine tactfully resumed their conversation about whether to watch the Rose Bowl game on television, and Jefferson was grateful to him for making this unpleasant encounter as brief as possible.

He felt in bad sorts because he had just come from a Ph.D. oral at which he had been the professor chiefly responsible for failing the candidate. He disliked failing candidates even when they deserved it a dozen times over, as this one did, for it meant a conflict with the professor responsible for him. In this case the sponsor was a chinless positivist from the philosophy department; the effort of concealing his contempt for this man had soured Jefferson's disposition; at the men's faculty club Jefferson had once said to his luncheon companions that he would not have recommended that one to teach bonehead English in a South Dakota teacher's college.

The odor of frying onions assailed him. He stuck his head into the kitchen for a moment. "Liver and onions?"

"Yes, dear," said Eleanor. "I hope you're in the mood for them?" He grunted. "Was the examination as bad as you feared?"

"Worse."

"I'm so sorry."

"There's been one bright spot in the day. As I got out of the elevator, Hazen was getting in with a suitcase in his hand. Maybe he'll be gone for the holidays."

"Oh. I thought you enjoyed playing chess with him."

"Chess," he said.

She said nothing. Mama came in the door. He nodded to her curtly and picked up his briefcase.

"It will be a pleasure to have Jacqueline to ourselves for a change," he said to Eleanor and turned to go into his workroom.

"When is Jackie coming, Jefferson, please?" said Mama.

"Tomorrow," he snapped and went.

He liked Mama better than he had liked his own mother, took pleasure in her enjoyment of little things and in her lack of selfishness. But her querulousness since her illness irked him, her repeating of questions, her diffidence; and just now the slackness of her lower lip was intolerable to him. He stood, till dinner was served, sipping a glass of straight Scotch and gazing out the window at the perfect, dull view, and he wondered what infirmity of his own permitted him to express irritation even for a moment with the simple infirmities of age in this good old woman.

He controlled himself at dinner by not talking. He supposed Eleanor was quiet and even downcast because of his own bad mood, and he was sorry for it. He thought that the aggravated sense of alienation between them would be healed by Jacqueline's presence again, and also by Hazen's absence. That brash troublemaker, that smiling intruder.

After dinner he went into his study. But he had not been weaving for two or three weeks, and when he looked at the empty loom he realized he did not feel like starting a new project now. He turned to the harpsichord, and could not find the Handel sonata he wanted to play nor any substitute that satisfied him. He played "Jesu, Joy of Man's Desiring" once on the oboe, hitting two wrong notes and not satisfying himself with the tempo. He wished there was something around the place that needed fixing, a door that wouldn't catch or a leaky faucet, and wished too he had tools and a workbench to fix things with. He sat in the front room reading a pocket mystery story while Eleanor was finishing the dishes. Mama dozed by the radio, which was blurring Mozart. He wished it had been raining so that he might have had a good excuse for not going out for a walk.

Eleanor took Mama off to bed.

He had not read a country-house weekend murder with butlers and milords for years, for long enough to forget how thin the skin it stretched over boredom: like a rubber glove it did not cure the itch so much as sadden it, and of course it ruined the scratch. Yet he kept on reading.

Eleanor perched on the edge of a straight chair. "Jefferson," she said, and picked meticulously at every tiniest piece of lint on her skirt. "Are you dreadfully busy?" Her voice was quiet and her articulation very clear, as though she were about to break the news to a child that his grandmother had just died.

"Not at all," said Jefferson neutrally and laid the book aside without marking his place. He was not displeased to see these signs in her; whenever she sat on the edge of a chair and spoke to him with this preternatural clarity, he had learned to brace himself; at this moment, he welcomed the thought of combatting her. And the more outrageous the provocation, the better. She had come to him once all determined to send Mama to an old people's home because she was convinced he could not abide the old woman. He'd spent a week of evenings talking her out of that one, persuading her that she had projected onto him some of her own feelings against her mother.

"I was just thinking," she began, "that it does us a world of good to get things out in the open." He did not respond, though she wanted him to; there was nothing but a banality to reply to such an opening. "I've been thinking over what you said about Peter this evening. You know, when you came in?" He nodded once, and waited. "I've been observing, more or less, your attitude towards him. It's changed, Jefferson." She glanced at him with an intent he did not try to decipher. "Of course," she added with an embarrassed laugh, "mine has changed too."

"Go on," he said.

She scrubbed at a spot, then pressed her skirt smooth over her leg. "Oh, Jefferson, you know what I'm getting at. Don't make me say it."

"You are quite mistaken, Eleanor. I do not know what you are getting at." From the strength of the appeal in her eyes he saw that she yearned for forgiveness beforehand—a sentimentality in her with which he had no patience. "What have you done? Or what are you about to do?" She waited for him to continue, but he sat determinedly on his question.

Finally she spoke, her eyes cast down. "Peter is moving downtown."

"So?"

"After Jackie has gone back to school, I am going off with him for a few days."

His head moved from side to side a little; otherwise he did not alter in expression or gesture. "You are lovers?"

"Yes."

"How very . . ." The right word did not present itself.

"Silly?"

"No. If I thought you would believe me, I would tell you why I think you should leave Peter Hazen alone."

"Jefferson, I wanted to tell you myself so as to spare you the pain of discovering you were deceived."

He smiled a little, doubting her. "Do you intend to leave me?"

"No."

"Make up the spare bed in the study for me."

"Oh. Yes. I see."

"Very well." He used the tone and the gesture which he had

137

perfected over the years for making it clear to an interviewer that the interview was over. He stared at his fingernails till she had made up the bed.

"I laid your pajamas out on the bed," she said flatly.

"Thank you." He went to the door of the workroom. "I shall be going to bed by ten or ten-thirty. I would appreciate your not rattling around out here so that I can't sleep."

"Surely, surely, I will be careful. I'm so sorry."

"You haven't kept me awake yet, so don't say you're sorry." He looked at her where she stood alone in the middle of the living room. "No scandal," he said abruptly. "And Jacqueline is not to suspect what you have done."

"Of course not. Heavens, how could you suppose?"

"Not by so much as a smile. Let Hazen know this." He closed the door. He looked about his room; it was rather cluttered; yet there was an order to it, the order of his own personality. He was at home here. He foresaw a great many hours of weaving in the month or two to come; he decided then and there to buy the finest yarn he could find next day and make as handsome a tablecloth as he knew how. He applied himself to chess problems in a book that Brother Quintillian had brought back from Austria for him as a little keepsake.

But when he went to bed, he became no longer able to suppress his bitter thoughts. He realized that Eleanor had not surprised him with her news but that he had not suspected her beforehand. He was humiliated that Hazen had been the man; he riffled through his acquaintance and could think of nearly no one whom he would not have preferred her to be unfaithful with; in fact, he thought, with one or two he would scarcely have been offended at all, would understand the man's bullish attractiveness and the simple nature of the case. He despised Hazen, and he could not imagine what power he could have over women: he was not sexually authoritative, he was no flatterer, no word-magician, no practised gigolo. Jefferson wanted to denounce him, and even fantasied doing it—telling the world that this man had first made love to the daughter and then seduced the mother. He could not be sure, however, that Hazen had actually slept with Jacqueline; but if he were sure, he would have acted. Eleanor could look after herself, but

Jacqueline, now, might be in need of protection. He was confident that Hazen would be too hangdog ashamed to let Jacqueline know how vilely he had behaved and that Eleanor would be restrained by her own sense of decency and by his warning. He had warned her. What more could he do?

It occurred to him that he had not suspected Eleanor of being in love with Hazen because she was not in love with him. Of course. This was the flurry of a woman who is losing her charm and whose husband—this he admitted—was no longer much interested in her. After she had calmed down a bit, in a few days, he would analyze her motives for her, and make it clear to her that what she was doing was essentially frivolous. The satisfaction of revenge without the guilt. He composed himself on the narrow bed to sleep.

Presently he became conscious of stealthy footsteps in the next room, of a dull thud and a suppressed cry. In a sudden upsurge of anger he pounded on the wall. It was only by sitting upright in bed and straining his ears that he could hear her tiptoe back to the bedroom and close the door with the faintest click. He sat, cooling, till he could detect not the slightest rustle. He felt like crying but did not.

Five

Hazen went house-hunting Tuesday afternoon; the mere thought of living next door to Jefferson as coöperating husband swamped him with uneasiness; he decided on the third place he looked at. It was a second-floor rear apartment, in one of the old brown-shingle houses south of the campus; he had a choice of entrances, through the hallway next the landlady's living room or up a rear, exposed staircase over the garbage cans; there was a gas heater; there weren't enough shelves for his books; the landlady showed signs of being a talkative crank; yet, though it was quite inexpensive and though he had more money in the bank now than he'd ever had before, he glanced around these two rooms, gazed out the rear window for a moment, and gave the landlady a check for the month's rent. Dislike of house-hunting helped decide him to settle on this, as well as the large living room with a fireplace, convenience to his place of work, and the smell of redwood paneling; but what he saw out the back window did most of it. He saw hills in the background already turning green from the November rains; saw backs of houses, one with sheets billowing on a line that ran from an upstairs window over to a telephone pole; saw branches of little Japanese flowering trees, bare, waiting for March, and a tall, dark fir with a tool shed under it; saw a garden cottage behind a honeysuckle hedge at the rear of his landlady's lot, with a patch of lawn and a bright red door; and saw, the jewels in this setting, a fair young woman on that lawn, knitting beside her baby in a buggy and glancing up to smile at her little boy playing in a sand pile.

By the next evening he was moved in. Eleanor came up the back steps to visit him. She came to him directly from telling the news to Jefferson; she was distressingly wrought up. Jefferson had heard her out in silence, and said almost nothing; then he had retired to his workroom. The two of them, in this room to which they were unaccustomed, were depressed and jittery. Hazen drank whiskey like a medicine; Eleanor did not stay long. She promised to come by when she could the next day.

Jacqueline was due in the Oakland airport late Friday night.

He was awakened next morning by the roll and rattle of his first earthquake.

At eight o'clock, he read in the paper that the head of his department, a pedant whose administrative abilities he had respected, a decent, dull old man, had died of heart failure at dinner the evening before.

The egg he broke into the frying pan was bloody.

His head ached.

Not aspirin, coffee, nor all his power of will could collect his scattered wits: he could not write a word; he could scarcely bring himself to grade one student paper at a time without interrupting himself. He wished he could play a musical instrument—there would be, he thought, peace in that. He hardly knew what was the matter. He paced, and smoked too many cigarettes.

The sun was not very bright, but there was little breeze and the yard by the garden cottage was sheltered. By ten o'clock the little boy was out banging around and shouting, and by eleven the mother and baby came out as well. For an hour she just sat fondling the baby and talking with the boy, who seemed never to tire of jumping off a stool into the box of sand. Hazen watched them in wonder. Here was innocence, he thought, joined with experience as part of the same whole; in the young woman herself there was no difference between the two; he, however, was decadent and unhealthy and unredeemable. She turned her chair so her back was towards the house, prepared her breast, and sat suckling the baby, rocking a bit, crooning, peacefully moderating the little boy's onslaughts of caresses. This seemed to him as good a thing as life has, and tears came to his eyes and curses to his lips that he was out of it not to get in. He went back to correcting papers and prowling the room.

His throat constricted at the sound of her voice on the telephone: "Hi, Hazie."

"Jac—" he started to say; "Jackie, how was the trip?"

"OK. Mother's coming down shopping this after, and I thought I'd drop by and say hello. OK?"

"Sure. But why can't I come pick you up?"

"Nope. I'll be there about 2:30. Bye."

He had not suspected she could still have such power over his emotions. He had thought himself quite cured of her, and had thought his affair with Eleanor adequate proof of it. Perhaps, he reflected, his excitement at talking to her was partly the pleasure of seeing an old friend after separation and partly anxiousness about what was going to happen next. He forced himself to his desk and the stack of term papers to grade, and only on the hour would he permit himself ten minutes of pacing, from the fireplace to the rear window, window to fireplace, of pacing and resolution-making. His resolutions reduced to two: not to let Jacqueline even suspect his relations with Eleanor, and not to make love with her, not even neck. It was Saturday and mild; the man of the family in the garden cottage was home, carpentering in the yard, whistling and shouting to his wife to come give her opinion, and calling the little boy "Sonny Jim"; he was young and pale and somewhat too fat, an office-worker no doubt. Hazen disliked him; he was so damned pleased with the world and himself, smug, impervious. The front doorbell rang.

Eleanor was with her—why? He did not know how to greet them thus, together; he shook hands with both of them; it seemed to work, for neither looked surprised. Indeed they were both apparently at ease, talking with animation about Jacqueline's flight out with Pearl, who had panicked at lightning over the Rockies, and the Countess, who had mocked. For a moment he was incensed that they should be so composed and he so agitated; but at something Jacqueline said ("Mom, do we *have* to be family all evening? I want to go see the gang with Hazie tonight.") he realized that his agitation resulted from his knowing more than they. Not, of course, that either of them could have known about his connection with the other, not that he would have been less than appalled should they find him out; but he had, until now, avoided anything warmer than a textbook sort of understanding of his situation. In the middle of one of Eleanor's sentences, he recognized a shameful truth.

"You may go out after nine tonight," she was saying to Jacqueline, "but don't stay out too late." Jacqueline made an impatient gesture away from her. "I'm being selfish," Eleanor went on, and looked at Hazen. As she spoke, he realized he had not wanted them to find out because of the shame and inconvenience to himself more than because of the damage to them. "I just don't want to lie abed worrying."

He spoke with excessive fervor. "Don't worry, we won't do anything wild."

"I'll be back in an hour, honey," she said to Jacqueline, and left.

The moment they were alone, Jacqueline wheeled on him. "How long have you been living in this place?"

142

"Just a few days." He was grateful for her belligerence. "How do you like it?"

"All right. What went wrong all of a sudden with your place in the tower?"

"I got tired of so much efficiency. It's not really restful."

"You never talked that way about it before. You used to go on about how the apartments were perfect Americana, and stuff."

"Do I have to *like* all the Americana?"

"Well, what's wrong with living next door to me all of a sudden?"

He was afraid she was going to force him to talk about his feeling toward her already. "I found it a strain," he said jauntily, "being so near yet so far from you."

She gazed at him speculatively for a moment. "O Socrates," she said, punching him in the belly with somewhat more than affection, "you're a liar. Tell me about the gang."

So he told her what had been going on, how the gang had been chased out into the back roads to do their stuff, how Fern had gone back to Phoenix, how he had been too busy working to play around with them as much as he had used to; and she told him about life in Dr. Edwards' house where there were large, ticking clocks in every room and about how hard she had worked at school; she had not made many new friends. It was all very nice. She seemed not to have changed, really, a little thinner, perhaps, and paler; she smoked now. Twice as they were talking she suddenly fell silent, gazing at him, absorbently silent so that he could not think what to say; but these had been quite short silences. On the whole, he was relieved to discover, she was sensible as ever and did not expect him to pick up where they'd left off.

But neither did she deny by avoidance that they had been more than just friends. "Unrelentingly honest," he thought.

"I really appreciated your letters, Hazie. I got pretty lonesome there a couple of times."

"You know what? After that letter where you said you'd give your right arm to be cruising around in a hot rod again, I darned near hopped a plane just to see you. I missed you something fierce."

"I met a guy that used to know you at Columbia."

"Yeh? Who?"

"A girl I got to know took me on a blind date with a friend of her boy friend's. He's a law student. Stuffy. Steve Goldberg."

"Oh yeh," said Hazen without enthusiasm. "How did you get along?"

"As I say, stuffy. But he's a fast worker. In New York they seem to go together. It's *respectable* to try to make a girl the second time a guy takes her out."

"Second time?"

"Oh, sure, he took me to musicals three or four times." She watched him squirm. "What's the matter, Hazie?"

"Well, you know, Steve was not really a friend of mine."

"So I gathered."

He took her teasing straight. "Just an acquaintance. I hope he didn't—"

"Do anything you wouldn't do?" Her laugh was harsh but not cruel. "Hazie, you're blushing!"

"I was going to say—"

"Don't say another word, friend. He didn't."

He watched her walk across the room to the fireplace. She was wearing heels and stockings, a flaring quilted skirt, and a long-sleeved white blouse; there was that same odd stiffness he had first noticed in the way she walked, but also, so he thought, her motions were more feminine, more fluid and less determinate than they had been; and he was delighted that the cigarette she put between her lips to light stuck out awkwardly (a vestige of Nebraska in him said smoking was properly for men) and that when she had taken one drag, puffed out the smoke, and put the cigarette back in her mouth, she made it droop at a cool angle like a child playing hoodlum. She was loveable.

She glanced over at him. "What are you thinking about?" she asked. But she was not aggressive, as he would have expected, not demanding a response; rather, her voice was soft and nearly diffident. He blushed and stammered. "Tell me the truth," she said, "whatever it is."

"I was thinking that you look like a little kid when you smoke." She frowned. "You aren't really sophisticated, Jackie.

The funny thing is, you look younger with heels on and smoking than you do in jeans and sneakers."

"I thought you liked suave women."

He was touched that she had thought of his taste, today. "Yes. But I never loved any of them."

"According to Steve Goldberg you got around."

"I got around. I like you better than all the women shopping on Fifth Avenue between Fifty-ninth and Thirty-fourth right this minute and the Christmas rush is on."

When she looked at him, pleased, dubious, shy yet undisguised, he felt for the first time that he might kiss her, that she might want him to. The feeling made him blush again, and the blush prevented him from trying to kiss her.

"Hazie," she said with intimacy, "oh Hazie."

The way she bent her head from him then, the awkwardness of the angle at which her feet were placed, the grace of her arm at her waist, touched him to tears; and when he compared the harshness with which she would have treated him for such a blush and stutter last summer to the delicacy with which she responded now, he yearned to hold her in his arms and tell her she was dear to him. She shook herself and snorted. They were gratefully released by the honking of Eleanor's car out on the street.

"I've got to say hello to Pearl," he said at the door. "Why don't you come over and meet me at her place tonight when you can get away from your folks?"

"OK," she said, her usual self again, "so long as we don't have to hang around. I've been having a double dose of Vinograd recently."

But he almost did not go to Pearl's that evening, for, as his feelings for both mother and daughter intensified, so did his consciousness of the risks in the game he was playing, the dangers to them as well as to himself. Jacqueline was the most vulnerable, of course, and he was afraid he might not succeed in keeping the proper distance from her. His feelings for Eleanor were strong, handleable, and contained; both of them knew well enough where they were, where they were going, and when to stop; but his feelings for Jacqueline, and hers for him, were too unknown to be safe, threatening when turbulent and unreliably calm. But he went. He persuaded himself that knowledge of the danger would arm him against it and that it would be a poor tactic to arouse her suspicions and unnecessarily hurt her by giving her the go-by. Also, Jefferson telephoned him at seven o'clock and told him in brief, arid words he must bring Jacqueline home no later than midnight; she needed peace and rest. Upon first hearing Jefferson's voice, Hazen was tense and alert, but after that order, which was also a warning, he felt no hesitation about what to do. Hazen had use and need for a clear antagonist against whom his own forces might marshal. He would get her in by midnight, surely, but there could be no question about his taking her out if he pleased.

Pearl was full of her perilous trip. She had not got out of her housecoat all day; there were empty cans and a pile of coffee grounds in the sink; she pressed him with chocolates filled with rum; she kept touching him, not erotically but for some sort of reassurance. "When are you going to get married?" she asked him. He shrugged. "I'm looking for another husband. It gets lonesome." Tears sloshed in her voice; she kept beating her mouth with her left hand; she looked at him.

He had to answer, and not flippantly. "Who do you have in mind?"

"Nobody yet."

"What sort of man?"

"I don't care so long as he's not after my money."

Without reflecting, he said, "Would I do, mama?" For a moment she seemed to teeter between lachrymose sentiment and a bawdy scorn; to help her, he made an indecent gesture; she laughed her old laugh.

"Lover, I want a husband that'll stick for a couple of years anyway. The first year of marriage's a get-acquainted proposition. You and I, we're past that." But she was still gravid with woe. He was glad to hear Jacqueline at the door. "Well, kids," said Pearl with her arms about them, "have a good time, but don't go too fast. As Lisa always says, look before you leap."

"Where's she staying?" Jacqueline asked.

"With some socialite over in the city—met her in New York. Say Hazen, did I tell you, she's going to be on TV the 26th?"

"So I heard."

"Well, you've got to come up and watch her on my set with me. It's a date?"

"Sure," he said.

"You too, sugar," she said, kissing Jacqueline. "Hazen," she said at the door, "why don't you bring that Flossie over with you? She'd cheer me up."

Jacqueline glanced at him sharply; he was angry with Pearl, but she was so bemused and sloppy that she had obviously had no intention of causing trouble. "Flossie's trying Mexico City," he said, "where she thinks they appreciate her talents more. So long."

"I appreciate them," she wailed. "I appreciate every damn one of them." They walked down the path. "Don't do anything I wouldn't do," she called, and leaned in the doorway, waving, till they'd gone.

Jacqueline drove. She parked suddenly on a side road. "All right, let's talk." Her voice was hard.

"About what?"

"What gives between you and Dad?"

"What do you mean?"

"No injured innocence, friend. I mean, why did you move out all of a sudden and why does he not like you any more?"

"Why should there be any connection between them?"

"I'm listening."

"OK," he said angrily, "so he doesn't like me *and* I don't like him. But the reason I moved out was that I couldn't stand to be so near you and him at the same time. It would have been too much of a strain."

"Why?"

"Guess."

"I want to know why. I think Mother went off to cry when I came out tonight."

"What does that have to do with anything?"

"That's what I'd like to know." He did not reply. "What did you and Dad quarrel over?"

"We didn't quarrel."

"Even Pearl noticed it," she said, "and anything Pearl notices is noticeable."

"It's simply a matter of conflicting personalities. We see everything too differently. And good lord, Jackie, I don't want to get into trouble with your father. You're more important to me than anyone else in the world."

"Yeh?" she said scornfully. "So that's why—" Her voice clogged a little. "Your letters didn't exactly . . ." She started the car. He reached out to touch her, but she slid over on the seat away from him. "I want to get going. Where's the gang?"

"Probably at the Igloo. No stuff tonight."

"What a homecoming," she said furiously, and wiped the back of her left hand across her eyes. "Let's get the hell out of here."

Though it was Saturday night, the bar was empty but for two solitary men drinking highballs.

"Jackie," said Iggy in a delighted voice, "it is so nice to see you, my dear."

"Hi, Iggy, long time."

"Yes. And your music in New York, it was good?"

"Fine. Where's the gang?"

"I am so glad, so glad. Professor, it's chilly tonight, a hot buttered rum?"

"OK," said Hazen. "Prof" was his nickname, but Iggy, having been German, could not so dishonor the high title. "Haven't any of the gang been in yet?"

"To be sure. They were asking for you and Jackie. They told me to tell you, if you should come, they are at Palm Garden. And you have come. See?"

They had to stay for a few minutes longer: a professor and one who had studied at Juilliard School of Music—he was so proud to have them talk with him; besides he liked them both.

The Palm Garden was a dance hall downtown in Oakland where hard liquor, jitterbugging, and unescorted women were forbidden. There were potted palms around the huge dance floor, erect palm leaves fringed the orchestra, and palm leaves and artificial bunches of dates disguised the girders of the building. A large, slowly revolving globe of many-colored bits of glass dimly illuminated the place. The tone was hushed, the music sweet. Half a dozen gorgeous cockatoos, chained to spangled perches in aisles and apses of the place, threatened strollers for crackers. The odor was of sweat and too much perfume; there were a great many bare arms and bright eyes.

It was the atmosphere precisely, genteel and aphrodisiac, of the college gymnasium where he had learned to dance. After two numbers he was conscious of nothing but Jacqueline; she, however, took notice of his altering state only by keeping him at a proper remove; she looked out for friends. He had never danced with her before, and, though she was better at it than he, her indifference cancelled the disparity. That indifference galled him; yet because of it he allowed his resolution to wane, and at the bow of the second number did as some others were doing, kissed her throat. She wrenched free.

John Henry, slouching and flashy and huge, found them.

"Congratulations, Prof," he said, a lopsided smile on his face. "You got the chick here after all. Good to see you, babe." He hugged her, and when he was about to kiss her on the cheek, she turned her face so that they kissed mouth to mouth. He stood with one arm about her waist. "Folks, I'd like you to meet Myrtle."

There was as much judo as clinging in the way Myrtle, after the introductions, took Hazen's arm. In that pretty little face, her long dark lashes and brown eyes were irrelevant perfections; it was hard for him to be conscious of the rest of her. She drawled. She liked pressing her violet-lacquered, oval nails into his arm from time to time.

"Jackie," said John Henry, "you're going to be there Thursday, aren't you?"

"What's cooking Thursday?"

The orchestra started up then.

"Grade-A road stuff, babe. Come on, let's go talk it over."

"Wait a minute," said Hazen and held John Henry's arm firmly. John Henry looked down at him questioningly over his shoulder. "I'll get some beers and meet you over there." He pointed toward an alcove. "OK?"

John Henry shrugged and, bending all his attention on Jacqueline, guided her toward the alcove. His gait was shuffling yet graceful; his voice, when he was talking to her, was musical and intimate. She paid attention only to him.

"They're old friends, huh?" Myrtle asked him, batting her eyes at him up from under.

"Dear old friends," he said neutrally. He thought Jacqueline was trying to arouse his jealousy, so he held it down.

"There's no friend like an old friend," Myrtle said. "Is there? You and John Henry good friends?"

"So-so." He was aware of a catlike desire to lick her.

"Him and me too. Are you really a prof?"

"In a way. Let's go for some beer."

But at the beer bar, Myrtle became so entranced with watching a tanned couple with aluminum-dyed hair that it was several minutes before Hazen could tear her away. He had seen them before, that summer on the beach of Lake Temescal: the woman had a diamond in one front tooth and the man had snakes tattooed on his arms. With a supercilious air they were comparing the merits of various drive-in restaurants around Los Angeles; they dropped the names of movie stars.

"Gee," said Myrtle, "do you know them?" Hazen said he did not. "Do you suppose John Henry does?" He said he doubted it. "Gee whiz."

"Let's go with the beer."

"OK," she said, "but, golly, California sure is a romantic place. I've only been here three months, you know?"

Jacqueline and John Henry took their beers with mumbles of thanks, and presently, after Myrtle had gone on and on about the aluminated couple, he bore her off to dance. Hazen took Myrtle out on the floor; she thoroughly melted against him. He noticed—he could notice little else—that Jacqueline permitted John Henry every liberty of the Palm Garden floor.

Jealousy had nearly filled him up; by the time he had suppressed it there was nothing left over for him to operate on but habit. He inserted apt responses to questions in Myrtle's chatter, and he greeted passing acquaintances with the usual words, and he kept a close eye on the clock. But for the rest he moved like a zombi, desire and resolution and resentment in him deadlocked.

At quarter to twelve he said to Jacqueline, "We've got to go."

"It's early," said Myrtle and dug her nails into his forearm. "Come on, Hazie-Wazie, don't you like me any more?"

"You've had too many beers," said John Henry to her harshly.

"Hazens-Wazens doesn't think so," she said, dropping her head and batting her lovely lashes. "Does hims?"

"Sure I don't," said Hazen and patted her on the head; she purred. "But we've really got to shove."

"What's your rush?" said John Henry. "I'll bring her home later on."

"She was up late and I promised her folks to get her home by midnight."

"Get her home to mama safe and sound, Prof boy?"

"Can it," said Hazen. It was a flat insult.

Jacqueline glanced at him in astonishment, and John Henry glowered.

"I'm not anxious to get home," she said, refusing to stand up from the settee by John Henry. "I'll get there on my own. Go on."

But the pleasure of that assertion had been too great for Hazen to deny himself again: he grabbed her arms and jerked her up. John Henry stood up ready to stop him if she wanted; she did not really resist, but strode out beside him in silence.

He let her drive home. Half a block from the entrance to her tower, she suddenly stopped and without a word leaped out of the car and ran up the street.

He slept like a zombi, deadlocked, and awoke from bad dreams numb.

Neither Jacqueline nor Eleanor telephoned him all day Sunday. By noon Monday, acute uneasiness had invaded him—dread that the two of them had, for some reason or other, compared their experiences of him. Yet he knew, textbookishly, that his discomfort could be as nothing beside their hurt.

He had the knowledge of guilt without the feeling of guilt, an ambiguous state. He knew that the damage he might cause, the mess he had caused, was beyond his power to forgive; and yet, as though his conscience were a hand anesthetized for an operation, he felt none of the sadness proper to his wrong. Everything else about him—except his power of concentration—was functioning very well. Yet, every so often there would be a twinge in a finger of this sleeping member (a sudden imagination of, say, the set of

Jacqueline's shoulders if she should discover his betrayal, or the incredulity in Eleanor's eyes), and he would contemplate with dread the awakening of his conscience. He didn't, it is true, know how to keep it under; but even if he had known how, he would not have done so, for he thought that a man who has done as badly as he had done should, as those he admired did, suffer for it. The dread beneath all his other dreads was: I am less than a man.

He telephoned the Devereux' apartment at three o'clock, and no one answered. At four o'clock, at four-thirty, at five.

"Hello," said Eleanor. There were sounds of music in the background.

"Eleanor," he said tensely. "Where have you been?"

"Jackie and I," she said heartily, "have been over in the city Christmas-shopping." A sudden concern entered her voice. "Is there any news?"

"News?" he answered, baffled. "I just want to see you, that's all the news. Good lord."

"How wonderful!" she cried, heartier than ever. "You can't imagine how delighted I am to hear it."

"Look," he said, "I've got to see you."

"Splendid. Oh goodness, the teakettle's whistling. But don't think I won't remember all about it. Have a good Christmas, dear. Good-bye."

He sat with his head in his hands for a moment. He telephoned the other apartment.

"Hello," said Mama.

"Hello, Mrs. Vinograd," he said. "Is Jackie there?"

"Beg pardon?"

"I say, is Jackie there?"

"Who's calling please?"

"Peter Hazen." He felt, uneasily, he ought to extend her his greetings, but he didn't exactly know how to go about it.

"It's very good of you to call, Mr. Hazen. How are you liking your new place?"

"Quite well, thank you. Is Jackie around?" He thought he heard a voice in the background, but he could not be sure.

"Very good of you to call. It's so nice to have Jackie home for

Christmas, isn't it? You must come see us. I shall tell everyone you called me. It is so good of you. So thoughtful." And she hung up.

Once, when about to walk onto a field sowed with mines, he had felt like this: prisoned in a self—not body but self—whose career he hated and could not control; desperate; half-mad; all appeals misunderstood.

At 7:30 there were steps in the hallway and a rap on the door. It was Eleanor. For a moment, even before a word of greeting, they stood with the door open, staring at each other. She was dear and admirable and herself, but he knew what was lighting up behind her eyes at sight of him and he did not like it—pity, a sort of charity towards the suffering because they are suffering.

"Peter," she said, and entered, "you look unwell."

"I'm not unwell; I've just been worrying."

"I'm so sorry."

They embraced. Her arms were comforting, not sensual. It was as though she permitted herself luxury only when nothing else important was up; being unwell was important.

"When you phoned," she said, "the others were nearby. That's why I half pretended you were somebody else."

"I see." "But," he thought wryly, "if you really love a person you *can't* pretend he's somebody else."

"I've just run Jefferson and Jackie down to a movie. Jefferson is paying so much attention to her. He missed her so."

"Sure."

"They've been practicing together for hours and hours these last few days."

"Fine."

"I don't think they've ever been closer."

"Good."

"Now you mustn't worry," she said. She made him lie on the bed with his head in her lap, and she stroked his hair. "We will get through this period, darling, have no fear. Floyd is coming up for four days at New Year's, and Jackie will be going around with him a good deal. We'll have more time together then." She was being practical, practical and controlled; admirable and exasperating. "Then we shall have our trip together. Where shall we go?"

She spoke about the trip as though it were to be the end of their affair. But, he reflected, this anticipatory joy of hers was indelicate, inappropriate; the joy of release when an affair is over is quite another matter; an ending should be looked forward to with a certain melancholy, and enjoyed tenderly; she was being hearty. She was (of course) a good woman, but also thick-skinned, in a way blunt. "I do hope the weather holds fair," she said, "especially if we go to Clear Lake. I love boating."

He sat up in agitation. How could he tell her she was offending every sentiment he had? She meant no harm. He was in up to his chin with her. To cover his annoyance, his unreasonable irritation, he began to make love to her. She tried to convert his overtures into opportunities to soothe him, but, failing, she begged off: she said she did not think the occasion was propitious for making love. Time limped until she left to pick up Jefferson and Jacqueline.

It became quite clear to him, after she had gone, that this embroilment with her had been a mistake, affection and respect and whatever else masquerading as sexual attraction. She was (of course) an admirable woman in nearly all ways, but she was not for him to love. He felt much relieved to have exposed the thought; their trip, their very short trip, would indeed be an end to the affair, no feelings hurt.

But by the next afternoon, Tuesday, the day before Christmas, still not having heard from Jacqueline, he was in a worse state than ever, for if he was disengaging himself from Eleanor, the result was only that all his attention and desire squandered on Jacqueline, who did not call him up nor come to see him. He went to Iggy's, he talked to whomever of the gang he met, he hung around the Village; but he saw nor heard hide nor hair of her. Nearly all his scheming and fantasy dealt with getting her alone to talk to, and very little with what he would do then—lend her the motorcycle perhaps, or take her to a drive-in movie, or even, if necessary, kiss her once or twice. He railed and paced and chewed his nether lip and forgot to shave.

It was from an unexpected quarter that he was helped toward what to do, from a note prefixed to the term paper of one of his students—a gangly, saturnine fellow with a big Adam's apple, who manifestly had no use for the class, the course, the subject, or the teacher. "Sir," it read, "I am supposed to be writing about the funeral customs of some Eskimos in Alaska. I am not an Eskimo. I never saw an Eskimo. I don't care if I never see one. All I know about Eskimos is what I have read by some missionaries and anthropologists. In this essay I have rehashed what they have written the way you want it. Last summer my father died. We had a funeral for him. We did not do it because we have funeral customs. We did it because it was the right thing to do. That's why Eskimos do it. I want you to know that this whole paper is a lie, but please don't grade me accordingly." An attack such as this one, like spray from a wave, had an effect on him cooling, refreshing, astringent. There was a sort of truth to one's own experience, an excess of honesty, a stubbornness, in this statement which pleased him. And in two great strides from there he made up his mind.

1. What did he, in all stubbornness, want most? Jacqueline for his own.

2. What did society, and he also, consider the right thing to do about it? There were plenty of cultural patterns to wander among as he wished, but what was the right thing to do? Marry her. It was as simple as that: marry her. Anything else would be a lie, for which he would be graded accordingly.

It was six o'clock Christmas Eve when he came to his decision. For half an hour, in plenitude of luck and confidence, he sat deciding his immediate course of action. Eleanor, he was sure, would subside into the proper friendship: she knew she was too old for him; he was sure she did not seriously intend to leave Jefferson. It was realistic to assume that Jefferson would never feel warmly toward him; but once he had broken off, after no great time, with Eleanor, and had declared his honorable intentions toward Jacqueline, he was sure Jefferson would at least be coolly polite; that would be enough. It would be wise for Jacqueline and him to wait several months, a year even, before telling the others about their decision; it would probably be judicious for him to get a job in a college at some remove from Berkeley, where they would be relieved of the grossest strains inevitable to their situation. Marriage was what he needed. That Jacqueline would accept him he did not greatly doubt: their interests were similar, they had proved their mutual attraction, their tie was very strong, he loved her; and he was easy in his mind that she loved him in return, else she would not be hating him now. It occurred to him that he did not really know why she had turned against him last Saturday night; something to clear up later. The immediate question was how to go about getting to talk to her. It would be awkward to telephone her this evening, or tomorrow; awkward at any time, for that matter, which was why he had not done it before. Now that the pressure was off him and he was confident what to do, he did not have to call her immediately; yet, because his intentions were honorable, he was free to call her whenever he wished, now if he wished; it was purely a matter of policy. Whoever answered, he would ask to speak to her; that was settled. He decided, all things considered, that it would be best to call her right away. He considered disguising his voice if Jefferson should answer, but decided against it: open and aboveboard from now on.

Eleanor answered.

"Hi, Eleanor," he said. "Could I have a word with Jackie?" His voice was under control.

She paused a second, then a little quizzically answered, "Surely. I'll call her."

He could hear Jacqueline ask, "Is it John Henry?" and Eleanor answered, "No, Peter Hazen," and the silence surrounding her response.

"Hello."

"Jackie, I'd like to talk to you a little while this evening."

"Sorry, I'm busy."

"About nine o'clock, for half an hour?"

"We're opening presents tonight."

"Well," he said on the spur of the moment, "I want to give you my present." He did not fill in the gap with a word of pleading. The simplest decency forbade her to deny such a request. He waited.

"OK," she said finally, in the same flat voice, but she said it. "Half an hour."

"Swell. I'll be waiting in front of the tower at nine."

The receiver when he put it back in its cradle was sticky with sweat.

Towers 4, 5, and 6 were arranged at an elegant distance from one another according to some asymmetric geometry of taste, in the center of them an oval of lawn banded by a broad drive. The towers were off-white, sheer, and stark; there was nothing between them but asphalt, grass, and half a dozen sodium-vapor lights: no abandoned toy wagons, no benches, no bicycles dumped against a hedge, no hedge. It was scarcely a place to lurk, and besides there are few places where a new convertible with a white top can slink about unobtrusively; all the same, as Hazen drove onto this circuit, he felt surreptitious. He parked and stared at the wall, functionally unadorned, opposite him. The green lawn, his red car, his plaid shirt, were dulled and denatured by the yellow light. He had every right to be here, he had announced his coming, he was intending to ask the woman he loved to marry him—yet he felt as bilious as the seat covers looked.

She half sat on the edge of the seat, the door not closed, one foot on the ground. "What's doing?" She was looking not at him but picking at her skirt.

He started the motor. "Get in," he pleaded.

"We can talk here."

"Oh Jacqueline." His voice did not obey him well.

"I told them I'd be back up in a few minutes."

"Look," he said, unexpectedly brusque, "when a man loves a woman he has the right to know what's going on once in a while. Shut the door."

"Oh a man does, does he?" But at least she was smiling. Her lipstick was made a revolting color by the light.

He leaned across and pulled her leg inside; she let him close the door. Touching her did not affect him; touching was not what he wanted.

"Where you going?" she asked when he drove out onto Grizzly Peak Boulevard.

"Down to my place."

"I thought you were delivering a Christmas present."

"It's too big to get in the car."

"I don't want to go to your place."

"Who in the hell," he said violently, "do you think you are that you should get everything you want? At other people's expense?"

He could feel her tense up. "Oh Jackie, damn it all, I have something important to say. All I want is a chance to say it. Nobody could talk about anything important in that yellow light, could they?" There were tears in his eyes, which he dashed out angrily.

"OK," she answered. "But you can't say I didn't warn you."

He parked in front of his house and walked her back to the old garage by the garden cottage. He caught a glimpse, through a little window in the cottage, of the young wife and husband trimming their Christmas tree, which they had no doubt bought at the last minute so as to get it cheap. He trundled the motorcycle out into the driveway and leaned it on its stand.

"It's yours," he said.

"What?" She was startled into looking directly into his eyes for the first time. His heart pounded.

"It's your Chr—" His voice stuck. "Your Christmas present."

"Oh, Hazie, you can't go and do that."

"I'm not going to be riding much more. I'm too busy."

"I know, but . . . It's not right."

"I've kept it in good condition."

"Oh sure, but criminy." She was stroking the fleece-lined saddle.

"Don't you like it?"

"You know I like it. The thing is, when Floyd gave me his rod for awhile, that was different."

He wanted to take her up to his room where they would be alone and private. He could hear the murmur of the young couple's voices. A car was liable to drive up the driveway or someone come out the back door of the big house. But he knew that if he should mention to her going up to his room, she would lapse into resistance again. One hand holding the grip on the right handle bar, the other on hers on the saddle, leaning toward her, forcing her to look at him, he spoke.

"This is different from Floyd all right. You see, Jackie, you know, I love you, and what I want you to know, what I wanted to say to you is, well Jackie, it's just that I can't get along without you, will you marry me?"

She laid her other hand on his. "I didn't know you had anything like this in mind," she said in a very low voice. "I thought from one thing and another you'd just been playing around."

"I thought so too at first. It turned out I was wrong. I've never been more miserable in my life than the past three or four days."

"Do you really mean it?"

"Yes. I want to marry you. This summer maybe, if you'd like to."

"This summer?"

"Yes. And I mean the bike too."

"We ought to talk about it. It sounds crazy to me, but we ought to. I can't come around tomorrow. Family."

"Not even for a little while?"

"Nope."

"Please, Jackie."

"Look, after we go to Pearl's Thursday. Let's go out to the meet together." She kept looking at him as though trying to understand from the expression on his face the intention of his heart. "Hazie, what's ever got into you?"

"You."

"You're not just blowing something little up big?"

He gestured impatiently. "We can't talk here."

"Take me home."

"Do you want to ride the bike?"

"No. I want you to drive me. Nobody ever asked me to marry them before. I'm not the type really."

"Neither am I," he said. "We're even."

"It makes me feel funny."

"Good?"

"Well, funny. What a thing for *me* to have to make up my mind about. Marrying."

"This is a terrible place to talk."

"I don't mind it. You know, Hazie, you're my first, really. That's funny too."

"I want to be your last too. Your only."

She snorted with an instant's displeasure at his banalities. Then she hooked little fingers with him. "I like being proposed to. Yes. I really do. It's womanly. Maybe I ought to get quite a few offers before I decide."

"Now don't tease me. Whatever you do, don't tease me. I mean it."

"I know you do. So do I."

He put the motorcycle away and joined her in the car. She was in the center of the seat ready to snuggle against him. He did not start the motor but held her hand on her lap and looked at her with a falling sensation in his guts.

"We'd better go home," she whispered.

He kissed her only once, vowingly, and drove back up the hills to the Village. All he said, when she was getting out of the car, was "I love you." She said nothing. He thought he saw a glistening of tears in her eyes as she ran off. He rode home with the aching memory of the touch of her body along his right side. He was sure she would not mention his proposal to her parents. He was happy. He truly loved her. He did not mind having Christmas Eve alone, for she would be with him soon. He would not make love to her, as token of his sincerity, unless she wanted to, clearly wanted to. She was beautiful as Flossie, yet wholly herself like Eleanor. She was honest. He loved her. He had never been so happy. He looked forward to Thursday night as though his fate were to be decided then.

The program started at 7:30. By five past seven Hazen was waiting at the curb a few manors up from Pearl's, watching for Jacqueline to come out of her tower. The moon was full; the night sparkled with clear cold. He was grateful for the warmth of the motorcycle engine on his legs. He had come on the motorcycle instead of in the car so that they might go to the road meet, if Jacqueline wished, together on it, less obtrusively than in the Buick; and too, if she still felt shy about necking with him, the motorcycle would free them from any occasion for it. He wanted her to be completely at ease and trusting with him; she had given him, he now realized with a kind of awe, her great trust when she had gone to bed with him; it was for that, and for her purity, and for her love, that he felt now the same way toward her he had felt before their going to bed, the same only far more deeply. He was entrusting his life to her as she had entrusted her innocence to him; mutual trust is that alchemist's elixir which transmutes the lead of lust into the gold of love. He blew into his cupped hands to warm his nose. He felt indomitable. He champed for her to appear. This was the real thing.

He roared up.

"Hazie!" she cried in that fullness of voice which consummates all hope. "Aren't you cold?"

"It's chilly," he answered gruffly. "I thought maybe you'd like for us to ride out on this afterwards."

"Aw," she said and bumped his arm with her hip a couple of times, "I'd rather snuggle along in the rapemobile."

"Swell," he said. They looked into each other's eyes; he shivered. The feeling that flooded him meant that the dyke of his worrying had crumbled: she loved him, he loved her. "Climb on and we'll take a turn before going in."

"Dad's going to be on the program."

"How come?"

"Somebody fell sick and the Countess roped him in on it at the last minute."

"Oh well," he said. He couldn't have cared less.

She sat behind him for windbreak, and put her hands under his leather jacket in front, holding him. He wove to the nearest dark place he knew of, stopped, got off, and awkwardly—gloved, scarfed, helmeted—kissed her with all his heart.

"Will you marry me?" he whispered.

She dropped her eyes. "I've got to *think* about it "

"Don't you want to?"

"I think so."

"Well then?"

"Let's talk later."

They kissed again.

For a moment she held his face in her hands, looking at him with an expression almost sad. "It's different, isn't it?" she said.

He nodded, and up from nowhere in him rose the urge to weep.

They busied themselves wiping lipstick off his mouth and adding lipstick to hers, and returned to Pearl's.

"Is it really mine?" she asked as they got off the motorcycle.

"Yes."

"May I keep the key?"

He gave it to her.

Hand in hand they walked to the door.

Six

Eleanor had been surprised when Jefferson allowed the Countess to talk him into appearing on the television show. However, she imagined that her own scorn at the mere notion had had more than a little to do with pushing him towards his decision. She did not exactly hate television; she thought it trivial, and ignored it. She thought such programs as novelty-loving friends had sat her before were boring when they were not facetious or in very bad taste, and she thought the small, imperfect, unsteady image hard on the eyes and impossible of beauty; she had supposed that Jefferson, who had shown no positive signs of liking television, shared her opinions. Furthermore, she knew that his vanity, if he had any, was not of the sort which is gratified by public notice; not more than a thousand persons in the world, beyond his acquaintance, knew of his ability and accomplishment, but they were the right thousand. Yet here he was gleefully appearing on a program along with the unspeakable Countess and a Jungian psychoanalyst named Klooch, discussing "Techniques of Foresight." It was all set up, obviously, so that the Countess might peddle her wares; but Eleanor could not, her relations with Jefferson being what they were at the moment, talk to him much about it. He was, he told her, not going to appear as himself but as an expert on thinking machines; and that was that. From this she gathered that in his role of expert he would be content to receive, expert-wise, publicity. She disapproved of this fragmenting view of oneself; the self hiding behind the mask had no right to hide as well from blame for the mask's effect and doing. But this program wasn't a very important matter, after all—she could have changed nothing anyway —so she had thanked Pearl and said she would go over with Jacqueline to watch it on Thursday evening.

She had intended to have an early dinner, but though it consisted only of soufflé, salad, and rolls, she was late in serving it. The mere negative presence of Jacqueline over in her room, reading, studying, when she ought to be chatting with her mother and helping in the kitchen, distracted Eleanor; yet she was conscious of a special uneasiness when they were together. They would talk too fast, or not at all, smile too much; sometimes Jacqueline would suddenly, without explanation, leave, retire to her room. Still, Jacqueline tried. Christmas Eve when Hazen had called her out to give her her present (she had not even yet told them what it was), she had been making meringues, her one confection; and—a sort of symptom of how they were getting along together—Eleanor had taken over when she'd gone out, added double the amount of sugar, and spoiled the meringues. Jacqueline seemed to be closer than ever to her father, yet she had showed no eagerness to go to the broadcasting studio with him. To be sure, no audience was permitted in the interview room itself, but she might have ridden over to the city with him and been there to congratulate him afterwards. Maybe she had a date with that boy, John Henry, who had taken her out one evening. Eleanor was sure, from his voice over the telephone, that she would not approve of John Henry; she would have to ask Hazen what he knew about him; she had heard the name before. Well, a lot was going on she didn't know about; signs of independence; the main thing was that Jacqueline showed no more interest in Hazen now than she had showed in her letters that fall; when she had returned Christmas Eve and Eleanor had asked her what Peter had given her, she'd shrugged and looked bored. Of course, he hadn't been able to give *her* a Christmas present, yet, under the circumstances; perhaps tonight, if Jacqueline went out for the evening after they'd been at Pearl's, Eleanor thought, she might phone him to come take her for a ride.

After dinner she took Mama to her room to prepare her for bed. When she'd finished, there were only fifteen minutes left before the program was to begin. She went to put on her coat; she discovered that Jacqueline had cleared the table and gone ahead; she ran to the elevator, and over to Pearl's. But only Pearl was there.

"Where have you been, sugar?" she bellowed. "Where's Jackie? Don't tell me she up and went over to San Francisco with Jefferson?"

"No," said Eleanor. "I thought she'd come here to your place." A small alarm burst in her like a pod scattering its seeds. "Oh dear. Pearl, let me call up our apartment. Maybe she's still there."

"Go ahead, sweetheart, do it if you want to. She's big enough now to know where she is. Me, I'm going to have a drink." She went into the kitchen.

"Mix me one, Pearl." She sat by the telephone.

"That's the spirit, Ellie. Bourbon and soda, that's the old answer."

The telephone was in a sort of alcove under the staircase, half secluded from the room. She was still there, hand on the telephone in its cradle, trying to decide she was right in calling up ("she's big enough now to know where she is"), when the front door opened and Jackie called in. Eleanor bent around to say hello happily, and saw Hazen with her; their hands were just falling apart; without reflecting she acted.

"Jackie!" she cried and started towards them. "I was wondering whatever had happened to you. The program will be on any minute now."

"Hi, Mom." Jackie was perfectly at ease. Her cheeks were glowing from the cold night air. "I'll get the station." She went to the set and began fiddling with the dials.

"Peter," said Eleanor, taking his hands, "I'm overjoyed to see you. I hadn't been expecting you tonight." From his eyes, which shifted from her mouth over to Jacqueline, from her eyes down to her fingernails, she saw he had been as little expecting to see her, and seemed less pleased about it.

"No," he mumbled. "Pearl just told me, you know, about the TV business. I thought I might as well come over."

"Drink, Jackie?" yelled Pearl.

"No thanks," she answered.

"Hazie boy?"

He started to slide past Eleanor, but she blocked his way. "Sure, a bourbon, Pearl," he called.

"Peter." Eleanor dropped her voice. She was still holding his hands; she looked intently into his eyes. "I want very much to talk to you. Soon."

He pulled his hands free. "Later," he said in an irritable tone. Then louder, "The program's starting."

She watched him, affectionately, go sit in the rearmost, straight chair and stare at the advertisement on the screen. He was so sensitive sometimes; apparently he was afraid now that Jacqueline or Pearl would observe their special intimacy—as though it mattered in the least what Pearl noticed, as though after all she had no special rights over him. Jacqueline was lounging around over the back of her chair jabbing his leg with her finger as though he had been her brother—*she* suspected nothing. Why should she? In her world casual touchings signify little or nothing.

"Hazie," she was saying, "what time are they dragging tonight?"

"8:30." He half swallowed the words. Really, his embarrassment was excessive; he needed kidding out of it. "Last I heard anyhow."

"Here you are, folks," cried Pearl, bearing a tray. She had on her tight black spangled dress and a black hat. "This is a real occasion." She pressed a glass of sherry on Jacqueline.

She made them wait ready till the grey, undependable image of the Countess' face appeared on the glass screen, and then toast her; the same for Jefferson. Then Pearl, with a half snort, half sigh of settling down, established herself in the armchair.

Eleanor pulled her chair back so that Pearl was in front of her to the right, Jacqueline half in front of her to the left, and Hazen

165

half behind her closer than Jacqueline. She felt little interest in what was going on in the television show. The announcer, a smiler named Thurman, was asking Klooch if psychoanalysts were ever obliged to predict their patients' behavior; Klooch was qualificatory as a scholar, cautious as a scientist. "Why," Eleanor thought, "can't he just say yes or no?" She caught, out of the corner of her eye, a toss of Jacqueline's head; glancing sidelong, she saw Jacqueline's hand idly, presumingly, tapping Hazen's ankle. She was aware of a stain of ill feeling spreading up through her guts to her chest; when it reached her head, it made her so dizzy she closed her eyes and held her forehead with her right hand for a moment; when the dizziness passed, she was left feeling taut and unsteady. She hunched into herself, leaned forward, and glared at the screen as though she were determined to catch every word Jefferson was uttering, determined to keep from knowing what she was feeling and why.

"Probability statistics," Jefferson was saying, "are good for predicting what people are going to do only when you have a lot of them; it helps the various kinds of social scientists guess what masses of men are likely to do next, but" (and he essayed a joke) "doesn't help you guess what the social scientists are going to do next."

"Hazen!" cried Pearl, wallowing about to laugh at him. "That's for you! What are you going to do next, lover boy?"

Eleanor glanced at him; he was grinning uneasily. Jacqueline, she saw, was smiling with an odd happiness at him. Eleanor herself could not have smiled if she'd tried. For a moment her eyes met Jacqueline's; Jacqueline glanced away.

Jefferson was lively; he seemed to like the lights. "The future," he was saying, "so far as probability is concerned, is only an extension of the past under similar conditions."

"Ah ha," cried the Countess, "of course. According to certain laws?"

"Well," he answered, "certain trends."

"It is the same for me," she said, "when I foresee what will happen to an individual."

"The fewer the data, the less certain one can be."

"But the more excitement, Professor Devereux, no?"

They laughed politely. Klooch looked left out of it. Eleanor felt just barely amused; it was all so trivial. Long ago she had decided against worrying about the future; the forces that will rule our future rule our present and have ruled our past; if we know so poorly why and where we are now, how should we think of guessing about all the tomorrows of quicksand circumstance? For example, how could she have foreseen that Jacqueline's presence would have made Hazen so uncomfortable tonight? And now, knowing it, what should she do? That was a matter of the future: What should she do to put him at his ease? How could she get him to herself so she might reassure him and let him know how dear to her he was? What would he do if she demonstrated, subtly, her affection at this very moment? She thought she caught a small gesture of his right hand, hanging by his side, towards her. Impulsively, suiting her act to her thought, she moved her left hand over and caught his. When Jacqueline stared over, she let go his hand. He seemed to shrink back from them both as though they were about to collide. What was so terrible about touching his hand? She resolved to keep him after the show was over; maybe he had intended to go out hot-rodding with Jacqueline afterwards, but she had far more important things to do; not that she felt in the least amorous, but that child play, their honking around at high speeds, could wait; she had not talked to him alone for days.

"Countess von Placken," the announcer was saying in beautifully tooled, well-oiled tones, "I think we may safely say that your technique of foretelling is more ancient than Professor Devereux' or Dr. Klooch's. Wouldn't you agree?"

"Oh yes. The lore which I have learned goes back into antiquities so far we cannot trace it at all. I believe, Mr. Thurman, I myself, that my lore is as old as man himself."

"Yet you think astrology is a science?"

"Of course." She shrugged. "The father of sciences."

Jefferson, smiling a little ironically, nodded.

"Now, Countess," Thurman said with a touch of that solemn, available excitement which is the making of a commentator, "would you give us a notion of your method?"

"You do not mean, Mr. Thurman," she said, "a demonstration?" Her loud-speaker voice sounded sepulchral, too open and deep. "That I hope to do in programs to come. Tonight," she went on, looking at the camera, flickering a smile, "I want to present you my method to compare against my distinguished colleagues'. I do not think, gentlemen, we are in conflict. No. We are doing different things. For example, two people with the same birthday, in the same family perhaps."

"Jackie and Ellie!" cried Pearl. "That's you."

"Shh!" said Hazen.

"What does this mean to you, Dr. Klooch? Very little. To you, Professor Devereux? Probably nothing—professionally." They smiled at their private joke. "But to me? Ah."

She was little and ugly behind that plain table, before that white wall, under those unshadowing lights; yet when she paused now and glanced straight out of the screen, Eleanor felt looked at. A woman twenty-five miles away had glanced at the lens of a camera, and she watching the ghostly image of that woman felt that she had been looked at. It was like the spectre of the woman she knew, yet she was real enough, there in San Francisco. The image on the screen wavered; it was as though she were a ghost haunting both her own body and this television set at once.

"Of course, it makes a great difference which sign these two are born under. A Libra is very different from a Cancer. I wish I had opportunity now to go into all that. The Cancer personality for example—many interesting things can be said of it."

"Of course, Countess von Placken," said Thurman, "you do not mean the disease cancer, which is being so wonderfully attacked by American scientists."

"Of course I do not." It was a sideswipe with claws out. "But these two whom I imagine born on the same day, let us return to them."

Eleanor, against her will, was excited. Jacqueline, she saw out of the corner of her eye, had settled in a posture of sprawl, her only movement a nibbling at a hangnail. Hazen's feet were hooked inside the chair legs and he was sitting up very straight, ready. "I wonder what she's going to say," said Pearl, waving her hand back at the others. Eleanor was as agitated as though she were expecting to learn something very important and resented the Countess' showmanship for arousing her silly excitement.

"They have so much in common, these two, no matter what their sign is. If you like one, you will probably like the other also." ("Like Hazen," Eleanor thought, "with Jacqueline and me.") "Or, if you don't like the other one, you will not be indifferent to him. No. You will dislike him very much. Or again, both will like the same people, maybe fall in love with the same person? And there, there's the trouble. When two people are so much alike, when their fates are so similar, then they are apt to" (she gestured oddly) "have conflicts, run head-on, I think one says?"

The announcer said something, the other two joined in, first one face then another, then all four appeared on the screen; she lost interest; the program was over.

"Jackie," she said peremptorily, so peremptorily that Jackie frowned at her, "get me another drink, will you, darling?"

Jacqueline, staring at the glass, went to the kitchen.

"We've got to phone them up before they get out of the studio," said Pearl, pushing herself up. "I'll get Lisa and we can all say hello to her and Jefferson. They did a fine job." She was settling in the telephone chair. "This is a real break for Lisa. She deserves it. She made the most of it."

"Peter," said Eleanor, leaning forward. In the flickering light from the television set he looked pale. "Peter, let's go for a ride, right away."

"No," he said shaking his head. He looked miserable, lacking in confidence.

"Why not?" She seized upon his appearance. "Darling, you look as though you weren't feeling well." She felt she should speak rather loud to be heard over Pearl's bellow; of course, she did not want Jacqueline to hear her. "Do you feel bad?"

"Lisa!" Pearl was yelling. "You were marvellous, sweetheart."

"Look, Eleanor, please. I just don't want to."

"I want to talk about *her*," she said jabbing her finger at the television screen. "You know. And other things." She took his hand. "Peter."

Eleanor saw Hazen's eyes fix on the doorway to the kitchen. She glanced over. Jacqueline was there, staring at her with a horrible expression on her face.

"You too." Shuddering, Jacqueline made a grimace, and a

jerked gesture with her right hand that spilled some of the high-ball on the floor.

Eleanor did not respond, but only stared, inexpressively, back. In those words *you too,* she heard her own voice, recognized her own recognition, inflected her own pain. She did not move.

Jacqueline made two hard noises of inhalation, the sobs of shock, and turned back into the kitchen.

"Peter," said Eleanor, and did not let him stand up, "have you done *that?*" In his eyes she saw the unmistakable answer.

"Oh, you came over swell," Pearl was saying. "Let me say hello to Jefferson. He looked real distinguished." She leaned out of the alcove. "Hey folks, Jefferson's coming on."

No one paid any attention to her.

For a moment Eleanor withdrew wholly into herself and her pain, hunched over, smiling, staring at the floor.

"Hey!" yelled Pearl. "Jefferson's here, folks.—Jefferson, you old savant you, you were wonderful, boy."

There was the roar of a motorcycle outside; Hazen leaped up.

"What is it?" said Eleanor.

"Jackie," he said. "She's going off on my bike."

"Didn't you bring your car?"

He shook his head and ran to the door. She went after him. The motorcycle was disappearing down the street to the right. He pushed back in and put on his jacket and gloves, with fumbling care.

"What's going on?" Pearl cried. "Doesn't anybody want to say hello to Jefferson? Where the hell are you going?"

Eleanor did not try to stop him. He had not looked her in the eye. She felt like a leaf in a storm about to pull from its stem. "Where are you going?" she called after him, "Peter, Peter," running after him to the sidewalk.

"To get Jackie if I can," he cried.

Pearl came to the door. "What's going *on?*"

"Jackie ran off," said Eleanor.

"So?" Pearl said.

"Peter is going after her."

Eleanor, from the sidewalk, could hear Pearl's voice at the phone telling Jefferson there was a big mix-up of some sort, and then guffaw with laughter. It made no more difference than the cold on her bare arms. She watched Hazen, the only moving thing on the street, dwindle away in the yellow light, heading, she supposed, for the taxi stand. She did not know what to do. Slowly she went in and got her coat; she was barely able to say good-night. A certain coldness of eye, despite Pearl's protestations of concern, penetrated Eleanor's consciousness, suggesting that Pearl had guessed already the depth of her hurt and hurting.

As she opened the door to her apartment, the telephone rang. It was Jefferson, alarmed. As well as she could, she told him what had happened. He told her to do everything she could to get Jacqueline back home. Mama came in, confused: Jackie had come running in, in tears, got her coat and gloves, asked her something or other, and run out. Eleanor begged her mother to go back to her room and wait; she would explain everything later. Mama left. Eleanor dialed Hazen's number; no answer. She could not decide to dial the police. Presently she dialed Hazen again, letting the phone ring fifteen or twenty times. In five minutes she called again, and he answered.

"Peter," she said, "do you know where she could be?"

He sounded half throttled. "I'm going to try to find her now. She probably went out to the road meet near Mount Diablo. I'll phone as soon as I can."

"Be careful of her, Peter. She might do something rash."

For a moment he did not answer. Then, "My God," he said, "My God," and hung up.

When Jefferson came in, she was still sitting there by the telephone, incapacitated utterly from every act at all, waiting for it to ring.

PART III

One

Hazen drove out to Mount Diablo as fast as the Buick would
go. No one was at the meeting place. A large three was chalked on
a rock by the road. That meant the place had had to be changed
for one not so good, the third-choice spot, twenty-five miles away.
He hoped that Jacqueline had come to this wrong place first as he
had done, for then he might get to the new grounds in time; but
she might have telephoned someone that afternoon and discovered
the change of plan, John Henry perhaps, whom she had expected
to be calling her up on Christmas Eve. (Why?) He was afraid; he
was convicted by the fear that she would do something dangerous.
His motorcycle had been souped up to accelerate faster than anyone
else's in the gang; but there were two or three others, from Stock-
ton, who sometimes came over on motorcycles as good as his. His
worst fear was that one of these might be there to challenge, who
would not dare refuse a girl's taunt.

As he approached number three spot, he passed a pack of rods
roaring away from it. He topped the hill overlooking the valley
where the races should be going on; it stretched bleached by the
moon, no headlight in sight, perhaps the red of a taillight, he was
not sure, disappearing down at the other end. He drove slowly
along the road looking for signs. There were chalk marks on
the pavement where he expected them; gravel was kicked up and
grass still held tire marks. In the center of a dip in the road he saw
a wide line marking the meeting point of a chicken run; the con-
testants were to have met going fast down into a dip, unable to
turn safely at the last minute. He got out and walked around; he
was shivering; his feet felt clogged to the earth as by globs of clay,

his head light. The barbed wire fence had been broken through a few yards down from the dip. He knew the gang always fled when there had been a bad accident. Even John Henry thought running a chicken on a motorcycle to be stupid. He sat down on the side of the ditch, dizzy. Finally he walked about some more. Under a pepper tree he saw a motorcycle. It was his. The front wheel and handle bars were wrecked; the engine was still warm. He saw no blood. Gasoline was still dripping from the tank. He threw a lighted match into it and watched it burn; the tank did not explode as he had hoped it would. There was no sign of Jacqueline anywhere.

He drove home again and called the police and every hospital in the telephone book; none had heard of an injured girl. He called the Devereux' apartment; Eleanor answered instantly. He told her what he had discovered. He said he thought that she could not have been badly hurt in the accident or they would have taken her to a hospital and that there was no reason to notify the police yet that she was missing. He would try the hangouts of the gang.

He heard Eleanor speak aside for a moment.

"Jefferson says he will wait till midnight to phone the police. You must find her, Peter. We have hurt her dreadfully."

"*We* have hurt her." He sat with his head in his hands, cold, bleak, and thought of Eleanor's generosity and courage. She was in the very apartment, very room even, with Jefferson, yet she remained undevastated.

Jefferson emanated cold, a reverse stove. He was scarcely human, defectively human, a heartless head. It had been partly pity for Eleanor, Hazen thought, that had drawn him to her, pity for her trials with such a husband. Jefferson had known well enough what they had all been up to—from such eyes little was hidden—yet he had been too cold and proud to warn his wife, his rival, even his daughter; he could not have done it without loss of dignity. He, who knew more than others and saw more clearly the probable outcome of events, had not deigned to embroil himself in such a mess. And the Countess—if she had only . . .

Alibis! He tossed them ahead like teetering stepping stones into every bog and stream the downward path confronted him with; there were always plenty. He tried to face his own responsibility.

But he was weary; he was worried about Jacqueline; he did not *feel* guilty. He left for Iggy's and anywhere else the gang might be found, but no one was anywhere.

Next afternoon in a muffler shop, Hazen discovered Spur and a Mexican boy he did not know. He put himself rudely between Spur and his motorcycle. "Were you there last night?"

Spur did not pull his hands out of the pockets of his jeans. There was a dead butt of a roll-your-own cigarette stuck to his lower lip; it scarcely moved when he spoke. "Yes."

"OK, tell me what happened."

"There was a guy from Vallejo on a souped-up Harley. He was gone. She run him a chicken."

"And?"

"There was this dip."

"I know it. I went out there."

"Well, she turned. He was real gone."

Spur tried to step aside so that he could watch the work being done on his machine, but Hazen moved so as to stay in front of him. By this manoeuvre he brought the Mexican in his line of vision and glanced at him: his eyes were cast down, his shoulders were hunched over, his mouth looked as though he were about to cry.

"I have to know what happened. Her parents are half crazy."

Spur coughed. "She turned just as they was hitting that dip. She skidded and fell over and went through the fence. She scraped the clothes off her on one side but I don't think she broke much."

"Her fingers," said the other boy in a voice of anguish. The mechanic looked up. "These fingers." He held up the four fingers of his left hand. "I saw bones sticking out."

"Yeh," said Spur, "but she never even whimpered. She's a good sport."

"All bloody too."

"She was grinning, when she went off."

"Who did she go with?" said Hazen.

"John Henry took her off. To a doctor somewheres."

"Mister," said the Mexican boy, "wasn't she a musician?"

"Clarinetist," said Hazen. "Where does John Henry live?"

Spur became himself again. He spat the butt off his lip and shrugged.

"I don't know him, me," said the Mexican.

"Where the hell does he live?" said Hazen trembling.

For the first time Spur looked him in the eyes; Spur's eyes were cold and his face without expression; he did not even shrug.

Three times that day Hazen spoke to friends of John Henry who did not know where he lived. Yet he was positive he had heard one or another of them say, in the past, that they were going to drop by John Henry's place. "Too bad Fern went back to Arizona," said the girl who had been Fern's pal. "She might tell you." Yes, Fern might have told him because she hated John Henry. "But at least," Hazen said to the girl, "you could tell me where Fern lived here in Oakland after she split with John Henry. Someone there might know." "I never went to Fern's place," said the girl, her best friend, looking straight at him. None of the others hated John Henry, at least not enough to have anything to do with getting him into trouble.

Hazen was an outsider, they had never let him in, he was respectable.

Two

For dinner the third day, Jefferson took nothing but a cup of consommé; he had to raise the cup to his lips with both hands; his eyes were full of grit. He allowed Eleanor to give him one of her sleeping pills. Once down, he was out for fourteen hours. When he awoke, his arms were leaden, his lips were gummed together, his brain thumped, and he regretted, muddily, that he had ever been born.

Showered, shaved, breakfasted, his functions and guards partially restored, he spoke to Eleanor for the first time unnecessarily.

"Let's get out of this place."

"What?" she asked surprised. "Right now? We can't."

"You're going to be here all day?"

"Why, of course," she answered and jerked toward the telephone.

"I'll go to my office. Do you want me to do any shopping?"

She thanked him and gave him a little list.

"We should move to a house," he said. "A year and a half of this place is too much. A little house with a yard."

"I thought you wanted to get away from salesmen and street noises."

"I was wrong. Haven't you ever been wrong?"

The dignity with which she gazed at him for this crack made him feel petty.

"What will you do in your office, Jefferson?"

"Work on my Cambridge lectures. Polishing mostly. There's almost no one around to bother me during the holidays."

"You still intend to go to Cambridge?"

"Of course," he said. "Unless Jacqueline should have been permanently injured. I doubt that she has been."

"Why do you doubt it?"

"Because we have not heard from her. This silence I take to be a revenge on you two."

Eleanor said nothing but left the room.

As soon as the mail was delivered, the bills and late Christmas cards and ads, he drove to the campus. He worked at his lectures, all of which had been written out in longhand, until lunch time. After lunch, however, he was incapable of looking at them again, much less improving them in any way. He dipped into a collection of autobiographical essays by various scientists and philosophers and lounged along for a couple of hours; it was not exactly reading that he was doing, but he did not stop doing it to do anything else. Then a phrase, "the work of my life," sidetracked him into reflections on the work of his own life. All he could see that mattered were rows of figures potently arranged and a broken child.

By next morning, having caught up on his sleep, he had regained his control.

On New Year's Eve, Eleanor made him a highball, which he politely thanked her for and did not drink.

Two nights later she awoke him, panicked. "I think I am going out of my mind," she said. "You must sit with me, Jefferson."

He put on his robe and slippers. "What are your symptoms, my dear?"

"I have a roaring, sort of, in my head. That isn't it really. I am afraid, I don't know what to do, I feel as though I am no longer in control of myself."

He scratched his beard a moment and looked at her speculatively. "You are desperate with anxiety and guilt," he said. "That is a long way from insanity." He poured her a stiff drink and insisted she take it straight off.

"I *must* talk with you, Jefferson. I simply can't stand not knowing what you are thinking."

"I am thinking only what any ordinary man would be thinking in my situation."

"Well, what? Well, what? Talk to me, Jefferson."

"I think Jacqueline was headstrong. I think Hazen is contemptible. I think you were deliberately blind. Now have another shot and I can go back to sleep."

"Just talk to me," she said. "Oh please."

"I will not exculpate you as you—"

"Oh no, dear, not that. I mean just let me know you are there."

"There is only one thing on our minds, and that I refuse to go into."

"Have you ever gone into it in your own thoughts, alone?"

"There is not much to go into. Hazen knew what he did. You willfully neglected to know. I do not dwell upon it."

"I see," she said, and caught her lower lip between her teeth.

He thought she seemed to be repressing the urge to say something, from the look in her eye an accusation; he did not know what she would be wanting to accuse him of and did not want to find out. He took her by her arm and helped her to the bedroom— the liquor had made her unstable—and then went to work on the tablecloth for the rest of the night, till dawn when he could sleep.

That morning's mail brought him a single sentence laboriously printed on the picture postcard of a motel in Las Vegas: "My hand is getting better so don't worry. Jackie."

At sight of it, Eleanor gasped brokenly and said "Thank God." She closed her eyes and held her forehead, her lips moving. Jefferson felt as though an enormous shot of adrenalin had just been injected into his blood, and wondered, even as he sat down to look up the telephone number of the travel agency he dealt with, whether in fact adrenalin had been released in him. He tingled with excitement and spoke very fast. He said he wanted a ticket to Las Vegas as soon as possible, an emergency.

"Tickets for two!" cried Eleanor.

But he hung up.

"I must go too!" she cried. "If you will not get a ticket for me, I will go on my own. I *will not* be kept from her."

"She addressed the card to me."

"Jefferson, please."

"It will be difficult for me to find her, unless they are actually staying in that same motel. She will not want to see me. She will hate seeing you."

"If you don't take me," she said, "I will get Peter Hazen to take me. He would do it."

At any other time Jefferson would have supposed that so outrageous a suggestion was only another of her excesses, to be discounted, to be ignored. But by the desperation in her eyes and the tears in her voice he saw that she meant it. She had lost her bearings all right.

"No, my dear," he said almost gently. "You could do nothing but get hurt. It will be a long time before you can ask her to forgive you. This is too soon. She would hate you and you cannot stand that."

"Oh," she said and wilted. "Oh oh. Are you telling me the truth, Jefferson?"

"So far as I know it." He felt his pity for her cool and congeal. "I could not treat such a matter lightly."

"I know that. I was only wondering . . ."

"What?"

"Jefferson, suppose you had to speak with Peter directly. Just suppose. I am sure it will never happen. How would you go about getting even with him?"

"I would not try to get even with him."

"Suppose the opportunity came up for you to analyze for him his darkest motives in doing—what he did. Would you not analyze them?"

"I might," he said curtly.

"Do you think you might just possibly distort things so that he would look even worse in his own eyes than he ought to? Or deserves to?"

"Possibly." He burst out then. "But it would be very hard to make him look worse than he is. He is a mishmash of abominable self-indulgence and criminal indifference to the welfare of others. He is what the word *irresponsible* means."

"And I?"

He dropped his voice. "I've said enough already. My plane leaves in four hours. I must pack. I will call a taxi."

"Jefferson, is it true that she hates me? Tell me. I no longer know anything. Is that true?"

"How can I know?" he said. He felt his hands trembling. "I am sure of this, however: you must not go to her now or else she will certainly hate you."

"You are not just rubbing salt in my wounds?"

"No, my dear."

"Well. Then I will stay. It will be a bitter thing."

"You have earned it."

She stared at her skirt. "That was not generous of you, Jefferson," she said in a dry voice. She got up and went to the hall door. "You are dreadfully proud."

With drawn, unchanging eyes, he stared at the blank door she closed behind her.

Three

Hazen became subject to sudden images. Eleanor's hand clasping his arm. Jefferson stroking his beard over the chessboard. His father, one foot on the running board, chewing tobacco. Jacqueline's eyes when she did not believe him. The toy size of cars on the Village streets seen from the tenth floor of a tower. The ghost of the Countess wavering and hollow-voiced. The weight of Jacqueline's breasts in his hands. Their last, long kiss.

Two images recurred. They did not have, these two or any of the others, power to divert him from his business for long at a time; he studied and taught and wrote his paper and did what he was supposed to do pretty much as usual. Flossie, back from Mexico, telephoned him on New Year's Day; he made a date to take her out to dinner that Saturday. He won at poker with some young faculty men one evening. All the same, two images did not leave him alone.

One was the smile on Eleanor's face after Jacqueline had gone back into Pearl's kitchen. He simply could not understand it, or, if he understood it, he could not believe what he understood. Her expression had been that of concentration, absolute concentration, like that of a man pulling with all his might on a wrench or of a violinist midway through a Bach partita; yet her concentration had been turned wholly within herself. Surely she had been suffering at the discovery of his baseness, yet she had smiled. Usually she was impatient of her own pains and troubles, and resisted illness with fortitude; but this suffering, which must surely have been dreadful, led her to gentleness and a sort of smiling. It had not been the grimace of shock or an ironic disguise for pain; it was a very intense, very gentle smile. He had not seen her in the ten days after that evening, but when he had talked to her over the telephone her voice had sounded gentler than usual, consonant with that smile, somewhat withdrawn, as though a portion of herself was still absorbed inwardly in her suffering. Yet how could a smile signify the quality of that hidden struggle? For his own part, contemplating what he had done, he felt like anything but smiling. Hers had not even been the gesture of giving way to the enjoyment of pain. It had been somewhat submissive perhaps, accompanied by that slight shaking motion of the head of one who marvels at what is beyond expectation and experience and credibility; yet it had seemed to be affirmative as well. That it was which he could not believe—what could there have been for her to affirm of that inner pain? He preferred to think that he misunderstood her smile rather than to think that it signified an acceptance and affirmation wholly beyond reason. Yet the memory of that smile visited him when he least expected it.

The other image, which sometimes awakened him from a dream, was of Jacqueline's broken hand. He would be walking with her, hand in hand, across a lovely meadow. He realized he had forgotten to bring along his mine detector, but there were too many flowers in blossom for him to need worry. Suddenly a booby trap sprang up to their left and exploded. When he collected himself, he discovered Jacqueline lying on her back holding her left hand up: four of her fingers fell over backward, hinged by skin, and white splintered bone stood up from the flesh. She would never be able to play her clarinet again. She stared at them dry-eyed. It had been the fault of his negligence.

The first of these images filled him with wonder and respect, tinted with uneasiness; the other with sweating dread. Some of the images made him shiver; some were only there.

He knew how guilty he was. Yet he continued not to feel guilty.

Occasionally he performed odd actions. Once after stopping for the red light at Shattuck and Bancroft, he started up again and nearly bumped, quite slowly, into a bus. The new chairman of his department had been, as Hazen knew, recently divorced; yet one day in the corridor Hazen asked him, as he'd commonly asked the former chairman, to extend his regards to his wife. He sent his Italian student in Florence an extra $100, without special occasion, suddenly, just as he was in the bank depositing his pay check.

He had thought there was some sentiment peculiar to guilt, like the feelings that go with shame or victory. His continuing ability to work and to enjoy what came past seemed to him proof of deficiency, and his lack of feeling much of anything when he had done what he had done proved him bad.

He spoke to Eleanor once everyday (she seemed to live by the telephone) to see if the police had found anything of Jacqueline. Something Eleanor said to him once suggested that there were other ways to look at the matter of guilt. "I am not sleeping well," she said. "We will never be the same again." He had started to pursue the idea, but she had cut him off somewhat abruptly; her abruptness had increased markedly. Of course he was not the same: what he knew about himself was different, his affliction of images was new, his impulses to sudden odd actions were strange to him. Did he not once wake in a dreamless dark of the night, sobbing wildly? That was a feeling evidence of guilt. Surely it was.

For his date with Flossie, he bought a shirt with gold cuff links and a stickpin for his silk tie, and was tempted to buy a cane the salesman swished for him. For dinner he took her to a French restaurant which she liked because it was laminated without music or floor show; when all the lights went out and a waiter made cherries jubilee, her eyes shone; Hazen ordered them for dessert, and she did what she could to look blasé while the flames illuminated her face so happy to be the center of stare. When he asked her if Mexico City was decadent, she said a lot of the best people took dope, if that was what he had in mind, but the worst of it was that it was so vulgar; she was grateful to be back. Peeking over the edge of her coffee cup, she told him this was the most refined evening she had had in months. As they stood up to leave, Hazen was conscious that they were admired and envied; he told her, just behind her ear, that he hadn't felt so good in a long time; she tossed a smile to him over her shoulder; they looked, he enjoyed thinking, like an advertisement in *Harper's Bazaar*. Yet, when he gave her a choice between a night club for the evening or a department party for instructors and graduate students, she took the party.

The mulled wine had been spiked with brandy, and Hazen was

drunk by midnight. A handsome teaching assistant named Kaufman was showing Flossie a dance he had learned in an anthropological trip to Chile; she was arching back in his arms and shaking her hair. Hazen, when he found the opportunity, dragged Kaufman to an upstairs bedroom to talk about something important.

"Kaufman, you interest me. You know? You're the most interesting grad student around. By far." Egregious flattery, he was gratified to observe, paid off even when alcoholic and patronizing. Kaufman waved his glass with a most studied indifference. "The thing is, you've got some horse sense. At least you strike me that way. You aren't just a technique man." Kaufman made the sneer appropriate to the term *technique man*. "Here, damn it, you need some reward for that workout you were giving Flossie."

"Flossie?" said Kaufman. "I hadn't got her name. Flossie what?"

Hazen looked at him a long time without answering. "And a liar too. Didn't know her name. Crap. Come on, I like you. You remind me of my brother." He pulled a pint half-full of brandy out of his pocket. "Last of the Mohicans. Snitched it from the kitchen. Just in the nick of time." He gave Kaufman a big slug of it in a cheese glass. Kaufman grinned and tossed down the brandy in three gulps, then rolled the glass under the bed. "Decisive, that's the word for Kaufman. Stout fella. Now this brother of mine." Hazen had no idea what he was going to fabricate for Kaufman; his simple purpose was to keep him from Flossie. "The thing is, I've got a problem, I mean my brother's got a problem; but what's his is mine, if you get what I mean, so I've got a problem. I'd like to get your advice. My brother needs it. You see, there's this girl he sort of fell in love with, a lot younger, nice girl really, only sort of wild the way girls go nowadays. He slept with her. Then she went away to school. This is all back in Nebraska where my folks live, you understand. Well, the girl goes away, my brother keeps seeing the mother, they live right next door, and what with one thing and another he winds up in bed with the mother too."

"Why?"

"Why? My God, man, I thought you were a man of the world. *Why?*"

"Sure. Who'd he love?"

183

"Don't worry about love. Just wait till I get there, if I ever do. I don't know, maybe you're not the right guy after all." Kaufman made no response. "So plunk in the middle of all the stuff with the mother, here comes the daughter home for Christmas vacation. Naturally *he's* the only one to know everything. But what happens? Does he enjoy the situation? Hell no. He goes and decides to marry the daughter."

"No father-husband around?"

"Oh sure. That's more like it, Kaufman, horse sense, that's my boy. Sure, he's there, eye on the game and all that. So he proposes to the daughter, who is practically ready to accept, when poof! the whole thing comes out in the open. The daughter runs away, the mother is all broken up, the father is—well, he's there."

"Where'd the daughter run to?"

"Motorcycle. Took off to a road meet."

"Where, though?"

"Nebraska, man. Nebraska's full of country. Broke her hand. So my brother—"

"I get it—hot rods." Kaufman grinned.

"You get what, hot rods?"

"I just get it. I got a brother too. OK?"

"OK. So the problem is, what does my brother do now?"

"Nobody'll marry him?"

"Of course they won't. Would you?"

"Not me. Well, if I was your brother I'd drink a lot and go out with fast women for a while. Nothing like it for drowning an unrequited love."

"Yeh? Unrequited, huh? Maybe you got something."

"Sure, I got something. Come on, man, the party's quieting down without us."

Flossie was hugging her knees on an ottoman and watching an argument about how to suppress race prejudice in the South, as though it were a game staged for her personal pleasure. Hazen sat behind her, fending off Kaufman, and in half an hour took her home.

He woke up on the couch in Flossie's living room, a crick in his neck, with a vile headache. He tried to make enough noise to

awaken her, but by the time he had dressed and drunk some tomato juice with Worcestershire sauce in it, she had still not stirred.
He looked in her bedroom; she was sleeping with her back to him;
he left.

By the time he had got over his headache and was trying to
remember what he had done the night before, it was late afternoon. He decided he had not said anything revealing to Kaufman
and had not offended Flossie. He thought he would drop by the
apartment of the couple who had given the party and say hello.
The wife had liked his stickpin; he would wear it. But it was not
to be found, in his apartment or in his car. He must drive over to
Flossie's and see if he'd lost it there.

Flossie was all dressed up and not glad to see him.

"Was I stinko?"

"You really were." She shrugged. "*I* haven't seen your darned
pin."

"Let's look around."

She obviously had a date and was expecting the man to arrive
at any moment. Hazen enjoyed teasing her by poking around and
chatting, at an amble. He found the pin under her bed.

"How did it ever get here?" he asked.

"Boy," she answered, "it was all I could manage to get *you* out
of here last night. So come on, Haze, I'm busy."

He put on concern. "I hope I didn't misbehave. I'm really sorry
if I was too—"

"Oh, good lord," she said and pushed him toward the door,
"you make me tired. You and your conscience. You talk too much
about it."

"I'll take you to dinner the day after tomorrow, and I promise
to behave decently. OK?"

"OK. Good-bye." She shut the door.

As he stepped out of the elevator he saw Kaufman coming
across the foyer. His impulse was to hide and see if Kaufman was
coming to visit Flossie, but there was neither place nor time for
hiding.

"Why, if it isn't Hazen," said Kaufman, extending his right
hand. Not even Mr. Hazen, just Hazen already. "Is she all dolled

up?" He hefted a beribboned box he was carrying. "Orchids too, and me a lowly graduate student."

Kaufman's insolence aroused Hazen's malice. "She's waiting. I had to drop over to get my stickpin. It'd got lost under the bed."

Kaufman's eyebrow-work gratified Hazen. He wondered for an instant whether he had been in bad taste to mention the stickpin under the bed, but he decided it was no more than Flossie deserved.

"Well," Kaufman said, making a gesture of complicity with his right hand, the thumb and forefinger making an O, "give my regards to your brother."

"I have no brother," said Hazen, cool and aloof. He watched Kaufman disappear grinning.

On the morning of the fifth, he remembered that this was the day he and Eleanor had planned to go for their little trip. He wanted to see her, for she would be able to help him if anyone could. He was, however, afraid to suggest that they should see each other; he was afraid that anything he suggested she would consider to be wrong, but that suggesting nothing would be as bad. At ten o'clock, as he was wondering whether to call her at all today, she telephoned him and said she was coming by his place that afternoon at three. Her voice was different from what he had become accustomed to, unhappy and flat to be sure, but no longer strained with a sickness of anxiety.

He rose from the telephone happy with relief, for he felt it to be a sign of his luck that she had called him just then. Indeed, as he looked forward to her visit, to talking with her, he thought his whole trouble had had luck hidden in it. For it had brought him face to face with a truth his sociology evaded, that the most important fact about a man is his capacity to do evil; this truth must be understood, the evil cannot be; one must learn what to do about it all. As he strode about the room, he glimpsed his face in the mirror over the fireplace, and for a moment he had the odd impression that he was looking at the photograph of a stranger: the features were bland but the eyes seemed troubled, darkened, blankened. He shook himself and went back to thinking of the good luck he was finding in all this disturbance. He decided to phone Flossie and break their date; he was above such frippery today. Had he not

been, luckily, snared by his own devices just when and as he had
been, he might always have evaded the truth of evil which he was
now facing so maturely. Let it come down; he would be ready.

Four

Eleanor's symptoms were loss of sleep, loss of weight, and a
tendency to sigh. The measuring doctor she consulted shrugged
and suggested she see a psychiatrist. But she did not. She thought
psychiatry could give back their sight to those whom dread has
made blind; but she thought that the cause of her ill was obvious
enough, and that for disorder of the soul each is his own best doctor. Prayer was the cure she started.

In the racking days after Jacqueline had disappeared, she had
inquired more and more deeply into her own culpability; she did
not spare the others, but it was herself most of all she blamed, as
having closed her eyes, not in blindness but willfully, to what had
been before her, to all the necessary consequences. Everything Jefferson had said was true, though he had not said the whole truth.
She could not blame him for having scathed Hazen; it was the
scathing of justice; although she would have preferred kindness.
For it seemed to her, when she thought about Hazen, that after
a certain point of damage it is the damage that matters rather than
blame for the damage—unless someone has acted from malice, as
she was sure none in this circumstance had. Each must learn for
himself to pray for forgiveness; what's done is done; remorse, scathing, abasement, all forms of self are irrelevant.

All the same, her vision of people was not as it had been. She
was as one taking an afternoon excursion in a glass-bottomed boat
full of ordinary-looking holiday folk: she inspects with fascination
and revulsion the creatures below her, which she has been told
about but never seen before, some of whom would eat her if the
glass should break; relaxed a little, she settles back on her bench

and watches clouds for a time, then glances back down; there she sees in the glass not only the shreds and stubs and heelprints one expects but dim reflections of passengers' faces sliding through that blue and soft green world; and directly below her she sees, ghostly and vague and unmistakable, an image superimposed upon the white slab of a shark's face, the image, she recognizes after an instant's shock, of herself.

Her thoughts centered on Jacqueline, whom she exculpated in her own mind: the child's wound is the parent's failure. As mothers do when their children, cruelly or not, leave home, she brought out mementos she had kept from the innocent days when Jacqueline could not have left home had she wished, and had not wished: photographs, ash trays and coin purses which she had herself made for birthday and Christmas presents, paintings, poems, letters. "Dear Mother and Father: Auntie Isabell and I made little baskits of cookies all day. She is going to have a party tommorrow I am the Gest of Honor. I turned three cart wheels in a row. She said I am sure you will go on to do many astounding deeds I hope. So do I. In our baskit we put jelly beans, red hots, kisses, and mixed candy harts with sayings on them. Your loving daughter, Jacqueline Devereux" She did not weep much, but sighed heavily, as though grief was a band about her chest.

Sometimes during the clogged nights of insomnia she wished she was dead. She had not known she could do so bad a thing as she had done, not of malice but of love, yet none the less bad for that. She thought that she would never have courage to risk making a decision for action again in a matter of importance and that there were no matters of importance left to her to decide. She felt that she had permanently lost her nerve; had been cut off from God, having known God; had nothing to rely on, who had inexpiably sinned, but God's mercy, of which she was not sure but than which she knew no other hope.

Mama shuffled in. "Ellie, are you sure we have everything? My drops, did you put my drops on the list?"

"Yes, Mama, I packed them already. Besides, anything we forget we can write to Jefferson to send us."

"Well," said Mama, settling in a chair, "I'm sick and tired of this tower. I'm glad I'll never see it again."

"Don't talk that way, Mama. You will see it again, very soon."

"Just pour me a little cup of coffee, Ellie love." She peeked at Eleanor sidewise. "What did Jefferson find out about Jackie? I didn't have time to listen this morning. We're rushing so. Always in a hurry. What was it?"

"I won't know anything till I see him, Mama. We'll have lots of time on the train to talk about it."

"Her hand? Just tell me that, how's her hand?"

"I told you five times already, Mama, it's healing."

"She'll never play again, never. And to think she came to me that night she was going to run away and do such a horrible thing. 'Mama,' she said, 'what shall I do?' What did I say to her? Did I listen to her?"

"You mustn't think about it, Mama," she said patiently, holding her mother's arm. "You'd been asleep. You didn't know what was happening. Forget it."

"How can I forget it? I tell her 'Leave me alone, I'm sleepy,' when she's in her worst trouble."

"What could you have done?"

"God forgive me."

She came up the stairs and into the hall as quietly as she could, so as not to fetch out Hazen's neighbor down the hall: she loathed that slattern's nosiness and force-fed heartiness. In the silence she could hear Hazen speaking on the telephone. She waited outside the door so as not to break in on his conversation; she discovered she was eavesdropping, too soon to knock, too late to tiptoe away; she just stood by the door hunched over a bit, listening without thinking about what she was hearing, in a sort of suspended consciousness.

"That's what I was phoning you about. No, I know you wouldn't guess it, but it was. I'm sorry, darling, but I've got to call it off for tonight." Cheery and open, not the voice with which he had been speaking to her these past days. "Oh, come on, now. Something came up I can't get out of. Well, sort of, yes I guess you could say it had something to do with my conscience." But his voice had more to do with flirting. "Oh no, of course not you. The *party?* My conscience isn't that tender." Then his voice became stuffy in a way she recognized. "I'm afraid I won't go into it. You may think what you wish. No." Then indignant and cajoling at once. "Oh, come off it. I don't like ultimatums. No, I will not take you out today. Oh come on, babe, what's eating you? OK. Bye-bye, blackbird, bye-bye."

At the sound of his hanging up, Eleanor shook herself erect, glanced guiltily around, took two audible strides in place, and rapped at his door.

He was spruced up, fresh shirt, hair brushed, but his eyes seemed to her changed, and when he spoke it was in the strained voice she recognized from the conversations they had been having over the telephone.

"I'm very glad to see you, Eleanor."

His gaucherie pleased her. "Hello, Peter." His face looked uncertain and drawn. They shook hands stiffly. Her fondness for him stirred again.

"Let me warm my hands by the fire. It's chilly out."

"Tea?" he said.

"Please."

As he arranged the teapot, the cups and cream pitcher and sugar and spoons, she noticed that the first two fingers of his left hand were brown from too many cigarettes.

"Have you had news of her?" he asked in a low voice.

"Yes." She took a sip of tea. "Mama and I are leaving on the morning train for Pennsylvania."

"Jackie's there?"

"No." She snorted with laughter. "Mama wants to go home to die."

"Is she sick?" His genuine concern touched her.

"Not exactly. She has decided her time has come. I will stay with her there as long as necessary."

"But," he said hesitantly, "how can she know she is going to die?"

"Some things just aren't worth living about, when you're old." She was grateful to him for not asking her what she meant.

"Where," he asked in a moment, "is Jackie?"

"In Las Vegas. She wrote a card. Jefferson flew down day before yesterday. I spoke to him on the telephone this morning. He has talked with her."

"She is with John Henry?"

"Yes. She refuses to come home or accept any help from us."

"But how do they live?"

"I do not know. She refuses everything."

"But, Eleanor, if you're leaving tomorrow morning, how will I ever find out about her?"

She shrugged impatiently. He began what she feared was going to turn into a barrage of questions. She wanted to tell him that there are occasions, a great many occasions, when scrutinizing questions ought not to be asked, for the only answers one can give them have to be lies. But since she thought he was doing it because of his training, and his loneliness and loss, she repressed her annoyance as well as she could, and laid a hand on his arm. "Please, Peter, not now." His eyes dropped; he leaned back; his lips drew down till his face was a mask of bleakness. And looking at him, she felt quite apart from him, uninvolved with his emotions, herself arid and polite.

"Well," he said in his pinched voice again, "why did you come to see me today? Just to torment me?"

Her eyelids felt heavy; she lowered them a moment, and then looked at him with her head tilted back a little. "I came to say good-bye to you, Peter. We will never talk again, really. I shall avoid you, as I trust you will avoid me. I wanted to tell you what I knew about Jacqueline. I owe you that much. Anything more you must learn, as I must, from Jefferson. If you want to know it badly enough."

"Eh," he said nastily.

She had the impulse to say to him what Jefferson had said to her: *You have earned it.* "But no," she thought, "it would be no less ungenerous for me to do than it was for Jefferson, and besides Peter knows he has earned it." He was sprawled in his chair gazing into the fire, and as she watched him in the lengthening quiet, she began to wonder just how much he did understand of what he had done, how much he admitted to himself. She recalled and was disturbed by what she had just overheard of his telephone conversation.

"Peter, tell me," she said, leaning forward and watching his face intently, "have you confessed your guilt to anyone?"

His mouth twitched and he looked at her sullenly. "No, have you?"

"Yes."

"Why?"

"It makes me see so much more clearly what I am responsible for."

"Oh, I have a pretty good imagination. I have imaginary conversations with myself and find out that way."

"But you have spoken to no one else?"

"I didn't say that."

"Oh?"

"No, as a matter of fact," he said with his eyebrows up, "I got potted at a party Saturday night and told a T A all about it. Disguised names of course. But he got it."

She shook her head slowly.

"No? You're right, it didn't do a damned bit of good."

"Of course not."

"I suppose you've taken up praying." He spoke in a neutral voice, but lingered insultingly on the last word, slurring it, dangling it at arm's length.

"Yes," she said ignoring his tone, suddenly desiring to warn him. "I pray. I have confessed to God."

He chewed a couple of times on the side of his cheek and turned back to the fire.

"You see," she began, "it's not just getting everything out in the clear that matters. It's sharing it."

"OK," he said, "I've heard this sermon all my life, so spare me now. The thing is," and he meant it, "one learns from experience. An adult does anyhow; that's part of being adult. OK, so I behaved badly. I know it, I've learned. So I will use that knowledge to enrich my relationships in the future. OK?" He had himself once said to her that jargon was a cage: she saw him now cowering in the center of his cage. "OK?" he insisted.

"I heard the word conscience as you were speaking on the phone."

"You hear a lot."

"Who were you talking to?"

"I don't know why I should tell you." He was very angry. But then he shrugged. "Flossie."

"Oh yes," said Eleanor, "oh yes. The beautiful dancer at Jackie's going-away party. Was that the evening you seduced Jackie?"

He stood up. "Look, Eleanor, this is indecent. Get out of my soul, will you? If you've got to talk about God and conscience and forgiveness, talk about yourself. I've got enough troubles without having to sort you out of my hair."

"I'm sorry," she said, feeling humble. "I went about it the wrong way. Forgive me."

"Forgive! Hell! Who do you think I am, to even try to forgive anyone? People don't forgive each other. You know that. They forget, if they're lucky. Or else they never blamed in the first place. Forgive! Nobody can forgive but God and there is no God. What a word even. Jesus."

She thought she was speaking to herself when she said, "You are lost."

But he heard her. "So quit looking for me, will you?" Then with malice: "I wonder just where you are."

"Oh," she said, "sometimes I think I am far more culpable than you, far more."

He shrugged. He was still standing. He lit a cigarette. She could think of nothing more to say, nor did he speak. She stood up and moved toward the door.

On the desk by the doorway, she saw the back of a photograph which he had laid face down. It was a picture she did not know, of Jacqueline seated on a motorcycle, wearing kidney belt and jeans and gloves, her goggles necklaced on her chest, waving and laughing at the photographer happily, carefree and young. She set the picture upright in its place.

"You did love her, didn't you, Peter?" It was a dry, abstract question, the question of curiosity only.

He snapped at her. "Yes, very much."

Behind his hostility, he seemed to be wanting some sort of help from her, she did not know what; she saw it in the helpless hang of his hands, in a brief tremor of his lower lip, in his strange eyes; for a moment she considered whether it was her duty to help him if she could. But she had neither strength nor time for it; anyway, she did not really care; pity would do as well.

"I suppose that was good," she said. She patted him on the shoulder, smiling gently, and left him.

As soon as she had tucked her mother in bed, Eleanor took out the ironing board and set to work. She had always done her own ironing, in contempt of luxury. Until Jefferson arrived, she would need something to busy herself over, and though she might have done her packing for the trip, she somehow felt that was a trivial matter and this important; she would have to pack, but just because the ironing was voluntary she felt challenged to finish it. She hoped he would call her from the airport, as he sometimes did, so that she might drive down and meet him at the hotel in Oakland where the airport bus would deposit him; but she did not count on his doing it, for he had been letting her serve him in almost nothing. At ten when he walked in the door, she was half finished ironing the last shirt.

She put the iron on its stand, but she checked her impulse to go to him; nor did he come to her. Yet his look was not withdrawn, impersonal, cool. She waited for him to speak first, expecting him to account for the plane ride, the hotel, the weather conditions, as was his custom when he had returned from a trip.

"Well, my dear," he said in his most careful voice, and her heart sank, "you and your mother are going to leave tomorrow morning?"

She said that they were, and she bent back to ironing. But then, instead of going in to unpack his suitcase, he said, as he was taking off his overcoat and gloves, that he would put on milk to heat for a cup of hot chocolate.

"Let me!" she cried, and he let her. She bustled in the kitchen, and he came to the door, almost shyly. "How was your trip?" she asked.

He shrugged. "A trip."

"Is Las Vegas as artificial as people say?"

"Stucco and clapboard and potted palms."

It took all her strength not to assault him with questions. He began talking about the weather after all, the aërial view of Las Vegas in the bare desert, improbable, pasted on. She went back to ironing handkerchiefs while he had his cinnamon toast and chocolate at the table.

"I took a taxi at the airport, and I suppose it was well after six by the time I got to the motel on her postcard. The swimming pool was dry. There was a man in his undershirt sitting on one of the stoops. There was a little grass and the roadway was asphalted, but everything seemed dusty. Of course I was at a disadvantage because I didn't know John Henry when I saw him. I hardly expected him to register under his real name, so I didn't go to the office right away but had the cab-driver cruise around the horseshoe of bungalows. There were twenty-two living units, and cars in more than half of them. I hoped to spot the hot rod as Peter Hazen had described it. But it wasn't there."

Gradually she stroked the iron slower and slower, listening. He was speaking with little emotion, yet not dryly and factually; there was no bitterness in his voice when he mentioned Peter Hazen; he was mostly speaking to himself, intently, contemplatively. Yet he was not excluding her from this seeking, for when she said, to urge his narrative on, "So you went to the office?" he looked at her for a second, looked right at her.

"Yes, and the old man there did not recognize my description of Jackie or John Henry or the car. I couldn't tell whether he was lying. He refused ten dollars that I offered him." Jefferson stared at his hand palm-up on the table. "I did not know what to do." And his voice was the voice of one who did not know what to do.

She shut off the iron at last, and sat across the table from him. He turned to face her, his forearms on the table, his hands clasped.

"There are dozens of motels and hotels in Las Vegas, and thousands of cars. I could not hope to find them by just poking around on my own. I thought of hiring a private detective. In fact, after I'd checked in at a hotel, I called up three listed in the telephone directory, but of course it was long after hours."

"The police?"

"These mystery stories I have been reading must have affected me. The police seemed—well, it seemed shameful to have to go to them. Do you know what I did? I spent the evening going from one gambling place to another. I kept looking out for Jacqueline, but I gambled too. Craps. I lost sixty or seventy dollars."

He was not apologizing for having lost the money, but was only impressed, as she was, by his own folly. And it struck her that he had not known to the cent the amount he had lost.

"Did you sleep?"

"Awhile. As soon as I had breakfasted, by 8:30, I decided to rent a car and go back to the Snow Flake Motel, on the chance. There was a young woman in charge, not in the office but out cleaning up a recently vacated unit. She was unexceptional enough, and there was a little boy riding a tricycle around in front of the place, ringing the bell. I told her I was looking for my daughter, who had run off with a man I didn't know by sight. Also, that she had injured her left hand, so that it would probably be in a cast. The woman didn't say no right away but just kept making the bed. I told her all I knew about John Henry's appearance and his car. I'm afraid," he said a little apologetically, "that I laid it on pretty thick about how upset you were."

Eleanor did not respond. She became conscious that the table was transmitting a tremor from Jefferson's arms; she could not see his hands shake; the knuckles were white.

"She asked me if they were married. By this I deduced that she knew about them. I said I doubted it. She asked what I intended to do. I said I wanted to help my daughter in any way I could and to see for myself that she was in good health. 'Oh, she's in good health,' the woman said. She was sullen about it. 'But they aren't here any longer.' 'Well,' I said, 'where are they?' She shrugged. 'When did they leave?' 'Three or four days before.' 'What name were they going under?' 'Oh,' she said, 'J.D. and John Henry.' I asked her their last name but she couldn't remember. If I'd had my wits about me, I would have offered her ten dollars to refresh her memory, but I am so awkward at bribery, and so unused to it, that I forgot to do it and just pressed her and pressed her. Finally she said she'd go to the office and look it up. They'd been in number 14, she remembered that. She was very ungracious about it. I don't think she altogether trusted me, but I pressed as hard as I could. You can imagine. The name was Nelson. She said the car was tomato red and had no eyes painted on the hub caps. I asked her if she could give me any lead at all on where they might have gone. She shook her head rather deliberately. Just as I was going out of the office door she said, 'Mister, I think he drove a cab. You might try the cab companies anyway.' I was terribly grateful to her for telling me this, and I couldn't find words for my feelings. I wanted to shake her hand but she would not extend it to me. Then it dawned on me that Las Vegas was a mercenary city. At last it dawned on me. I pulled out my wallet and offered her a bill. And then. Then . . .'"

"She was offended?"

"Exactly. She looked very unpleasant, with a sort of sneer on her lips; she ducked her head in an odd way. I tried to explain that this was only a token of my gratitude, but she refused to be mollified. She left the office without a word. And to think—if I'd thought to be so damned smart a little earlier I would have gotten almost nothing out of her."

"So," said Eleanor, "did you have trouble with the cab companies?"

"Not really. I told them I was his uncle just passing through and wanted to see him to give him the family news. I was afraid they might tell him, over the taxicab radios, I was there, but the office girl of the outfit he works for was decent enough. She gave me his address. I suppose I could have paid her something, she was a pretty brassy gal, but I didn't see any point in it, after that other one. She did say he would be on duty till 5 or 6, and I said I wanted to surprise him at home. I was all elated at the expectation of finding Jackie alone. The address turned out to be the upper right-hand apartment in a four-unit building. No one was home. I sat till noon across the street from the place waiting for her to come home, and then I began worrying whether or not I had been given a false lead. But the women in the other three apartments told me nothing except that a young couple had moved in three days before. So I sat till 5:30, when they drove up in that hot rod." He spoke with contempt. "It was a vile color and a vile shape. Well. I was reluctant to go in then, because it was obvious from the way John Henry walked, from everything I could see about him, that we would dislike one another intensely. But if Jackie came out with him in the morning I would have to go up and speak to her in his presence. I could not imagine where she had been all day. I had some dinner and went back to watching in the hope he would go out for awhile alone. But he didn't."

"It was chilly?"

"It was quite cold. I got stiff. I stayed till their lights went off, and then got a different car, so as not to arouse suspicion among the neighbors. Next morning at 7 I was back again. A little after 8 John Henry came out alone and drove away." His arms were trembling visibly now. "I went up and rang the bell, and Jackie came to the door in a bathrobe. Three fingers were in splits, with the tips showing, and the last joints free in the middle and ring fingers, but otherwise she was just as always. She was startled to see me, of course, and do you know what the first word she said was?" Eleanor shook her head. "Daddy. You know she hasn't called me daddy for years. She was so—like herself when she said it. But I had to ask her if I might come in, and once I was in she was very withdrawn. I'm sure you can imagine. The place was dreadful, dingy-chic, a Sears Roebuck imitation of this—" he broke his hands apart, waved, and looked about the room, "this lifeless imitation of a place to live in. She refused any help of any kind. She said she was in good health. She said she was never coming home again."

"Are they married?"

"I asked her that and she was unpleasant. She said if I bothered her any more about it she would marry the guy. Those are her own words. She said she had to get ready to go to her job. She would not tell me what kind of work she was doing except that she made change, nor would she allow me to drive her to her place of work. She did promise to let me know if she got married, or had a baby, or anything else important, and to let me know where she was so that I might tell her of any important news about us."

"Oh yes," said Eleanor, "I am so glad you did that. In time, in time."

"We can hope so."

"Did she offer you anything to eat?"

"Orange juice. I took it. She smoked. The radio was on all the time I was there, not very loud to be sure. She did not kiss me good-bye. When I looked back up to her windows before I drove off, I saw she had pulled the blinds down."

There was a long pause.

"Jefferson?"

"Yes?"

"Jefferson?"

"Yes, my dear?"

"Jefferson, does she hate me?"

"Oh no." He spoke without hesitating, even warmly. "There was no question of that. I told her that you would be taking your mother back to Pennsylvania as soon as I returned. She even asked how you were."

"Oh. What did you tell her?"

"I told her, I had to tell her, you see . . . I told her I didn't really know."

He looked utterly wretched. But he did not reach across the table for her hand.

She closed her eyes and recited the Lord's Prayer to herself. Then she got up and set about her tasks. She expected him to withdraw to his bed in the workroom; but instead, he stayed near her as she worked, speaking seldom, about fragments of his narrative which he had forgotten, about nothings.

When at 2:30 she said good-night, he asked to come to her bed. There, as though she were a delicate stranger, shyly, courtlily, he offered her overtures of love, which she could not possibly have refused.

The alarm awoke them at six.

"Eleanor," he said before she had got up—she knew by his

voice that he was about to make a great confidence, "Eleanor, she told me I was guilty too. Is that what you think?"

"Why, of course," she said.

"But I loved her, I love her, and I've always tried to do the right thing."

"We all love her and none of us did the right thing."

For a few moments they wept in each other's arms husband and wife.

end